D0115584

BONE
HOLLOW

BONE HOLLOW

BILL BRAINE

A Hudson Heartland Mystery

HUDSON

HEARTLAND

Hudson Heartland Books
Cornwall on Hudson, NY

Library of Congress Cataloging-in-Publication Data

Braine, William, 1969-
Bone Hollow : a Hudson Heartland mystery/ William Braine.
pages cm. -- (A Hudson Heartland mystery)
Includes bibliographical references and index.
ISBN 978-1-59738-101-7 (alk. paper)
1. Married people--Fiction. 2. House buying--Fiction. 3. Land use, Rural--Fiction. 4.
Murder--Fiction 5. Conspiracy--Fiction. 6. Catskill Mountains (N.Y.)--Fiction. I. Title. II.
Title: Hudson Heartland mystery.
PS3602.R344457B66 2015
813'.6--dc23
2015002085

Cover design: Mark Lerner, Rag and Bone Shop Graphics,
  Phoenicia, NY (ragandboneshop.com)
Photo by Emily Waterfield-Buttner, Em Waterfield Photography,
  Cornwall New York (www.emwaterfield.com)
Printed by IBT Hamilton,
  Castleton on Hudson, New York (www.integratedbook.com)

A Hudson Heartland Mystery.
Hudson Heartland Books is an imprint of Sloan Publishing. LLC.

  Sloan Publishing, LLC
  220 Maple Road
  Cornwall-on-Hudson, NY 12520

Copyright © 2014 by Bill Braine

All rights reserved. No portion of this book may be
reproduced, in any form or by any means, without
permission in writing from the Author and the Publisher.

Printed in the United States of America

10 9 8 7 6 5 4 3 2 1

ISBN 13: 978-1-59738-101-7
ISBN 10: 1-59738-101-2

This is a work of fiction. Names, characters, places
and incidents either are products of the author's
imagination or are used fictitiously. Any resemblance
to actual events or locales or persons, living or dead,
is entirely coincidental.

for Claudia

Prologue

It was a small place—a scoop—weedy, cliff-enclosed on one side. On its western edge were the remains of the glacier that had unearthed it, a puddle called Roosa Lake with a stream tripping out of the space between two ridges. The whole thing was a late chapter in a story of erosion; first the erosion of the Everest-high Taconic range, which left the Catskill plateau a pile of sand and mud, which then wore away into terraces and peaks over eons. And when the cold came, it left ice in the summer time and the ice pushed down hard on anything beneath it, and it flowed, and gouged, and bulldozed.

And then it left.

And behind it all was wreckage. Rivers took new paths. Giant stones lay atop mountains dozens of miles from their homes. Scratches marked hard rocks.

And Bone Hollow lay wet under the weak sun. Lichen dared a comeback, then moss, then ferns, and then, fast-forward, hemlocks and trout and otters and deer and finally the larger predators, rousting each other over generations until just the most tenacious and adaptable remained.

ONE

September 2008

He'd had to climb up to get into it, and so assumed it was a truck. It had a truck's throatiness to its engine. There was a driver. Not the guy who'd held the gun on him, tied his hands, then pulled out a greasy bandanna and tied it around his eyes. There'd been no truck, and then a short time after he'd been tied he'd heard its engine, and now he was in it.

The truck was turning a lot. Felt like a winding road. But he had no idea what direction they were heading. It sounded like highway, then it sounded like back road. All he could hear was his heartbeat and voices of regret in his head. Stupid, stupid, stupid, he was thinking, while his stomach grew hollow and fear spread through him from a core he hadn't known he had. His hands were behind him and sweat was running down his forearms making him itch.

His attempts to talk were met with open-palmed slaps to his forehead from the gunman, sitting to his right on a bench seat. The driver didn't say anything.

Even now the words he wanted to say sounded pointless. "Where are you taking me?" He'd tried it, feeling scared, feeling stupid, and choked on the inhale, not even getting to "where," and getting an open-palmed slap on his forehead, not hard, and told to shut up.

Who are you with? I can pay you to let me go. Think about what you're doing.

None of that was going to work.

He'd seen the guy, the one with the gun, and didn't think those things would work. Stringy and hard, with a mircomanaged beard under a feed cap, bloodshot blue eyes and what he figured was an easy way with weapons.

A cell phone went off, to his right, muffled in a pocket. The gunman shifted to pull it out, turned to speak into it with his mouth pointing toward the window, away. He strained to listen, but the guy didn't say anything intelligible.

They were in the car for a long while, maybe an hour, and they never seemed to go slow enough to be in a town where he could maybe struggle and be seen. The guy'd said "we're going to see somebody" early on. If he didn't consider the gun, he could interpret all this as precautions. But there'd been the gun.

Eventually the truck slowed and gave a dip over uneven pavement, angled down, and the temperature dropped inside. They slowed further, turned more sharply, and the wheels touched gravel. It was quiet outside now, no whoosh of other cars. They stopped.

The guy who'd had the gun hustled him out of the truck — big step down — and the door slammed. Silence settled down hard on the echo. The driver hadn't seemed to get out.

A hand in his back, indicating a direction. "Take a walk, buddy," the gunman said.

The hand moved to his elbow as he felt ahead of him on the ground with one foot. He walked, haltingly, really wanting to talk now, really wanting to say something that would unlock his predicament, come up with a key. Words had been his friends, but they wouldn't work against a wall like this guy. He wished, again, that he'd told his three closest associates where he was going. But he hadn't.

He choked again, hating the sound, that sounded like sobbing, like weakness. Absurdly he worried this redneck thug would judge him. And he walked on, soft ground underfoot, descending.

The light hurt for a moment despite the forested shade in which he found himself when the blindfold came off. They stood at the edge of a pond, on a little spit of sandy mud. It was dark water without clear edges, except on the narrow spot where he stood. Elsewhere it merged into shore plants and undergrowth, extending with glimmers and dark patches into the forest. Ahead of him, the far shore rose up, steeper as it went back. He felt the gunman cut the ropes.

He found his voice. "I don't know what you—" but the guy with the gun had started to say something at the same moment, so he stopped.

"We're just gonna wait here now, and you're not gonna fucking move. Got that?"

He nodded, looking at the water. He could see a narrow patch of sky in it, surrounded by black reflections of needled branches. The sky reflection made an irregular spiky hole in the blackness. He breathed. It was cool here under the trees, and so quiet he could hear the guy breathing behind him, hear as his boots turned in the sand and he paced a bit. He heard him take out the cell phone.

There was a moment then, where his fear left him. Maybe, he thought, this was the start of the next phase of the fight. Maybe they really were meeting someone here. Maybe this would launch something new. Tip the balance. He looked into the water, somber, but feeling futures pooling out from this moment.

The first shot surprised him because it was far off, not from behind his ear, and he turned to the gunman, wondering why it had been so far off, only to see him staring back, a black hole opened in his forehead, eyes wide, gun falling, and the guy falling.

He spun, saw a glint of metal high up and far off up in the sun, and bolted, but bolted into the water, away from the guy falling down at the water's edge, and was caught there by the next shot, and fell.

TWO

"The mountains don't seem to be getting any closer," she said.

"No," he said, peering up through the windshield. "Just taller."

The High Peaks of the Catskills loomed above Serena and Jeffrey, almost impossibly close and quite tall at this distance. They weren't the tallest mountains in the world—even the highest of these looked like they had trees all the way to the top—but they'd been approaching for a long time and expected a certain steepness that did not come.

The two were in a rented compact car, picked up at the train station in Poughkeepsie. Now, instead of climbing with it into the mountains, they had entered a broad vale south of the foothills. As they topped occasional rises they could see long distances across farm fields, woodlands, roadways.

Jeffrey thought he was too self-reliant for a GPS unit, and Serena didn't mind him thinking it. They had a map, and they had Serena's memory of coming up to the Trop Rico resort with her family in fourth grade, to guide them through the hills. That last bit, Serena's memory, was not as flawless as it seemed. Untested, her memory trod surefooted through the countryside. It pulled up the display case at the roadside museum featuring the man in buckskins and a coonskin cap holding two otter pelts out to an Indian fellow at the edge of a forested river, a

5

long musket in the crook of his arm. That was around here, someplace, she knew.

For certain, she knew that the you-pick-em orchard she'd gone to that year in the early nineties with her parents and sisters was here somewhere. She knew its southeast-facing slopes, its graveled roads between orderly rows. There'd been a corn maze and a tribe of girls her age. That was here. County Road 2, she thought. There'd be pie.

On the ground, though, confronted with the rising mountains and the occasional farmhouse amid hayfields, her memory had other ideas.

"I don't know," she said. They were miles off the Thruway.

Frankly, Jeffrey thought—looking ahead at the peaks above that seemed to rise like a wall of gold straight out of the rolling land before them—being lost up here was okay. From a distance the Catskills had looked blue, as mountains do, but as they drew closer, bands of color emerged. Fall was in mid-kill up there on the terraced-looking slopes. Rubies, gold. Amethyst, he figured. Or, wait, flames. Yeah, flames done in oak up there, orange and red cascades. Somehow, at this range where colors were distinguishable, and despite the palette, green still predominated. But it was a green set off, a near-black green, with explosions and treasure in it.

"I'd rather be lost with you," he said, "than found with anyone else."

He pretended to lean forward and scan the tops of the peaks through the windshield again as he said it, long enough for her to look at him with half-rolled eyes and a smirk, before he shot his eyes sideways and smiled to show he would never say something that schmaltzy, not in real life, but that here amid their fleece outerwear and in the intimacy of the car, he could come closer than in the half-light din and crowd of a Brooklyn Heights barroom or in their apartment. Here, their glances seemed to suggest, was the kind of place that permitted that sort of thing.

That fit right in with the orchard, in her mind. Her parents wore flannel in the evenings that early fall when she was ten, and flannel wasn't even in vogue for the vilest hipsters anymore. It was of the past, as were sentiments like Jeffrey's, like the Catskills themselves. Even the word. The Catskills were an old Patrick Swayze movie. They were vaudeville—she even thought they might be Woodstock. Yeah, that movie *A Walk on the Moon,* where Diane Lane swam with Viggo Mortensen before he was Aragorn and then they went to Woodstock. Catskills. Wasn't this where Rip van Winkle fell asleep for twenty years?

So, yeah, Jeffrey making quaint love-noises at her was okay, up here, and she loved him so very much that she was full with it. Literally, she felt, laying her hand lightly on her still-flat, still-toned stomach. Thirty-something weeks to go.

Being pregnant again fit right in with the time machine, too. She didn't see it as something of the future, yet, but as something of the past. Her aunt Jill, pregnant that same summer, that Catskill summer. That was pregnancy. Flannel, and her aunt Jill round and pretty, sharing an apple with her boyfriend who proposed on the last night of their long weekend at the resort. Serena's youngest sister Jessica, born four years earlier when Serena was six, her mother's big belly, that same aunt in the kitchen making spaghetti when her parents fled the house for the hospital just before dinner.

She skipped over her own—their own—past in her mind. This time would be different.

In any case, pregnancy happened in the past, and it didn't get more *past* than the Catskills in autumn.

But the future inside her was what had brought them up this way. Since they'd decided to start trying for a baby again—start trying, hah, she was sure she'd gotten pregnant the first time they'd had sex without protection—they had both instantly begun talking about where to live, neither of them hesitant. As if they didn't currently have a place to live. Which they did, in Prospect Heights, with a bedroom for an eventual baby that was now customarily used by a rotating cast of guests. Adequate space in a kid-centric neighborhood that nevertheless somehow suddenly felt like the rehearsal space for real life.

Jeffrey had had no idea where to go, but the idea of leaves and mountains appealed to an idea of himself. Sure, he knew he'd been diverted from the path to pioneerhood from day one, having grown up on a tree-lined street in Bergen County and mistakenly attending Rutgers and after that getting proofreading jobs at pharmaceutical companies, instead of going on a crab boat in the Bering Strait. Still, though. When Serena had suggested the Catskills, after they'd ruled out the Berkshires and Columbia County and Litchfield, it had taken root in his mind. Her face, talking about an orchard she'd gone to, and corn, and how cheap the houses had to be, now.

They passed a sign for a place called Krumville, which they both repeated incredulously, and Jeffrey immediately said, "there's a place." There was a place, a somewhat divey-looking pure-country place with one pickup in the gravel parking lot and a sign that said Country Inn over the door. PBR sign in the window. A house across the road. The road went on, and Jeffrey could see, a little way past the house, the back of another sign that presumably said Krumville on it.

8

"Krumville?" Serena said again as they pulled into the lot and the sound of gravel under the wheels and the angle of the light was 1991 in a bottle. Now even flannel seemed anachronistic; she thought she ought to be wearing gingham, or wool. Didn't matter, though. She needed to pee and they could ask about the orchard inside.

Inside, it became clear that the PBR sign was perhaps a bit of a joke. The place was paneled in dark wood, there was a fire in a gray stone fireplace, heads on the walls, a couple of round wooden tables with chairs loosely assigned to each, and a big slate menu hand-lettered with city food selections—words like coulis and chutney—that immediately made them feel at home. Best of all, Jeffrey thought, there was a long, clean, polished bar with white ceramic taps up top, German and Belgian crests glowing in the artful lighting, and a board with a wall sconce shining on it that listed the names of more beers than he could count.

He handed Serena the keys. "Sorry, hon," he said, "but I just got hungry."

They stayed a while, the dark interior betraying little of the changes in slanting light outside. They had a bean soup with chevre sprinkled on top, and shared a roast quail with roasted blue Adirondack potatoes, and Jeffrey had three ales while Serena toasted him with water. They ate at the bar, and talked to the proprietor about the area. They asked about houses. He suggested renting first. They asked about jobs. He suggested keeping a place in the city. They asked about the orchard and he hadn't heard of it but knew a couple other ones. He didn't make them feel like city folk, and even though they didn't tell him about the baby, the knowledge that they were fleece-clad mammals looking to den someplace before parenthood lay over their talk.

The thing was, they'd been here before. They'd been at this stage of delighted anticipation, of budding fear, of an opening future, of closing options. They'd been okay with it.

Some days, in fact, she'd been absolutely great with it. She'd felt so little morning sickness that time. There had been many days when she'd awoken when she almost forgot, but of course you didn't forget, like you don't forget what you do for a living or who your parents are. She was pregnant, she was five foot eight, and forget was the wrong word. But some days she awoke feeling *fresh* in a way that was new for her.

When she began feeling cramps in waves, she knew right away what was happening. Well, not right away. For a second, she'd thought she was getting her period; forgetting. And then she remembered "pregnant" and knew something was wrong.

She'd been alone. It was March. Jeffrey was at a training conference in Minneapolis, there was sleet, and he couldn't get back. She'd had the sense to call him second, on her way to the doctor. It was all too late, though, and he wasn't home.

He paced outside of a hotel ballroom on the phone, calling the airline, his parents, Serena, trying to talk her through something he couldn't talk her through, and when she got to the doctor she had to hang up and he paced a while longer. Men came out of the ballroom in pairs or threes to go out to a terrace he could see, where they would smoke, clutching themselves against the cold.

A day later, Jeffrey got home.

They talked it to death in the months after, and they healed some. Some things between them were stronger, and some still had some knitting up to do. She went to a shrink. They went together a couple of times.

But now here they were, more than a year later but in the past, taken back before that time, to one earlier, and Serena was feeling it even if Jeffrey wasn't quite there yet. He just looked at her on her barstool at the Country Inn, felt the beer bestowing hope.

They left happy, and optimistic, and with the name of a B&B fifteen minutes away, and directions. Jeffrey was singing songs by Great Big Sea because the beer had made him. He held the map. Serena drove out of Krumville and they talked about the houses they'd seen that day and Jeffrey, seeing a For Sale sign, said "turn here." She made a right off the main asphalt road onto Upper Bone Hollow Road, a good road heavily graveled and Jeffrey said "mwuhahaha" about the name because Halloween was coming. There were a couple of houses back in the trees as they descended into a patch of dark hemlock woods with yellow-leaved birches interspersed and chunks of rock jagging up through the leaf litter and needles. The light down in here was old, and quiet, and somehow pristine.

They could see the house back there through the trees, someone's abandoned country place, the driveway sprouting weeds and another For Sale sign's bright lettering dulled. There was a realty agent's face on it in black and white, a woman with a burst of curly hair over a plump face, and a phone number.

"Check it out?" Jeffrey said, and Serena turned the car up the driveway, the four corners of the car bouncing individually as each wheel encountered potholes. She pulled into the clearing surrounding the modestly sized house, tall board and batten sides, round skylights, one big window, stone chimney, a deck. Raspberry bushes crowded an old woodpile. Some plantings had decayed into deer-pared rhododendrons and scraggly weeds, their plastic-edged borders fading into the needle-covered yard. The light here was precisely the same, just more of it.

When she cut the engine the silence was like a gong. Not a crow, not an engine, not the trickle of water or the sigh of a breeze.

It was probably the light that did it for her, she thought occasionally, later. At the edges of the clearing, everything was a shadow, but none of it darker than anything else. Within, though, the light shaded brighter through infinite soft degrees, a directionless glow that seemed to come from within the house and its immediate surroundings, as though Vermeer had stepped outside to capture a landscape, Serena thought. She looked at the house and her hand went to her belly and something shifted irrevocably inside her. This was it.

"Wow," she said. He nodded.

They walked to the house holding hands, peering in the windows. It was empty in there, the kitchen looked nice, white walls, tile floor in the kitchen and wide planks in the other rooms. The door at the top of the stairs to the deck was painted red and had a window running down the side. There was a button for a bell, the kind that would ordinarily be lit, but it was dark.

Around back they saw an outdoor shower in a little palisade and a small slate-covered terrace at the foot of a staircase that came down from another deck, up where the back door was. Under the stairs a grill with a tarp on it, a couple of propane cans, and more split wood. A clothesline ran on pulleys from the deck down to a shed at the edge of the trees. She led the way. Trim, with board and batten siding like the house, padlocked, a little window showing a small empty room with a concrete slab floor and some cobwebs. A half-started hornets nest was stuck to the tiny eaves over the plank door.

"We could have chickens," said Serena.

Jeffrey said "No, we'd better just have a baby first." He circled the shed and took in the woods at its back. There was a path there. It pushed off from the yard and dropped about ten feet away between two stones. Beyond it, a way off through the trunks, he could see that cool northern shadow-light on water.

"Hey," he said. "Wanna go swimming?"

She looked where he was looking and said no, but started down the path.

At the top of the little drop, she looked back over her shoulder and raised her eyebrows in lascivious invitation, wiggled her hips once, and stepped down. Jeffrey's breath caught. It hadn't been like this—she hadn't been like this—for a year. He came along, his buzz just right, the wife he loved before him, leading him in mystery. He smiled, caught up, and tucked two fingers into the back pocket of her jeans to stay with her.

The path only dropped a few feet, then became nearly flat, a single sinuous curve intersecting the edge of what they could now see was a small pond set against a wooded hill up ahead. As they walked toward it, Jeffrey stepped closer up behind Serena to smell her hair and the autumn and the woods and the past in one luxurious inhalation. The only thing missing was wood smo—

Serena stopped and reversed in one motion. She moaned and gasped at the same time. The force of her reversal was so strong that she stepped backwards into him, onto both feet at once, and as he tried to back away he fell instead, the fingers in her pocket his only grasp on stability but he just pulled her back on top of him and his thought as they fell and she landed on him was "the baby!" but Serena kept moving, backing crablike off him. She leapt back to her feet and turned to him and he saw horror on her face and panic. She reached down and started flailing for his hand, trying to haul him to his feet but he was looking past her saying "What? What? What?" trying to see what it was.

A body was sprawled at the water's edge a few feet away. It almost looked like part of the forest floor, green and brown mottled, except that the forest floor wouldn't wear boots. Its head, pointed away from the water and toward them, was mostly missing. Bone glinted through old blood and spoiled flesh. Another corpse was in the water, ten feet out, bloated and floating, fabric taut and rounded over some unspeakable rot-sourced gas inside it. Arms and legs faded into the green-black pond.

Jeffrey scrambled to his feet, flight response hammering through him, instincts demanding that he gather more information before choosing a direction. He looked left and right—were there more?—before beginning to back slowly away. The motion itself got him going, and he turned to swing into a run.

But he stopped. Serena had covered fifteen feet in a rush and then stood while he had taken in the scene. Her body was tensed, her green eyes so wide there was white all around them, but she wasn't running. She looked at Jeffrey, and mixed with panic there was—embarrassment?—and she muttered "oh fuck" as she threw up into the raspberry bushes.

She wiped her mouth, sobbed once, and then they panic-jogged back up to the clearing, past the shed, around the front of the house back out to the black car, the peppy rental car that smelled like factory and had a heater which was good because their hands had gone cold and Serena was shivering.

Both doors slammed simultaneously and they were embracing each other across the cup holders, catching their breath. He soothed her with his hands running over her fleece and finding her muscles and urging them to relax and saying in a voice that trembled and for which he felt contempt "it's okay, s'okay Serena," although his mind was racing, his Belgian buzz gone, the car's engine restoring sound to the silent woods. It wasn't *quite* okay, he knew.

"What the *fuck*," she said. Another sob. "What the *fuck?*" She drew in a long breath and let it out, and some of the trembling left with it, and his too. The car, being in it, that helped some. He started it up, and drove down the bouncy driveway. His eyes stayed on the rearview, looking at the house, the narrow window beside the red door, the stone chimney. At the corner, they saw the realtor's well-fed, smiling face and her phone number and Jeffrey made a right.

When Serena's cell phone showed a single bar she said stop and he did. She dialed 911 and spoke for a minute, and said "okay, we will" and hung up. Then she turned to Jeffrey and looked at him steadily for a moment, and he didn't know what she meant with it, and he said "What." Instead of answering she closed her eyes for a second and muttered a number under her breath and dialed the phone again.

"Hi," she said brightly, her voice with only a slight sob-thickened edge to it, her drawn face in complete contrast to her tone. "My name's Serena, and my husband and I were wondering—what's the asking price for the house on Bone Hollow Road?"

THREE

The cops were kindly enough; while Ulster County wasn't Vermont, tourists were still its stock in trade, especially in fall, and the troopers knew how to keep witnesses comfortable. They met Serena and Jeffrey at the B&B, a place called the Hollybush Inn in Olivebridge. Amy Berenson, proprietor.

Dusk was hitting now. The police had arrived in the driveway of the place about at the same time as Jeffrey and Serena, and they ended up conducting their first interview standing up outside among a slow-moving squad of chilled mosquitoes. Their stories, told separately, then together, the two deputies taking careful notes and asking questions. That was fifteen minutes. One of the deputies off on a cell phone for a while.

"Can you take us to the site?" he asked when he came back. "We'd like to meet an investigator from the State Police there."

They got into one of the two patrol cars with their overnight bag still sitting on the porch. The other deputy got in the other car, Amy Berenson looking after them in confusion. Serena waved as Amy picked up the bag and brought it into the chintz-covered front parlor.

"I'll call Amy, let her know you'll be back in an hour or so," said the driver. It was hard to hear in the back seat, through the Plexiglas. Jeffrey held Serena's hand and tried the door handle.

It didn't do anything. He hated that. They pulled out of the driveway.

"First time?" he asked Serena, gesturing around the back of the patrol car. She said yeah it was. She was still pale. And against the glow of the computer screen from the front seat, and the sky going pale against the trees outside, against her dark hair and green eyes, against her lips and the shadows of her face, her skin was paler still, and he thought she'd never looked more luminously beautiful. He felt a crushing need to protect her.

The radio squawked, the deputy in the front seat replied, and they arrived at a crossroads where an island of fluorescent lights picked out gas pumps and signs on a brick convenience store advertising milk and coffee. The car continued past.

He knew he didn't need to protect Serena, really. Knew that he wouldn't have found her so intriguing when they'd first met if he'd thought she was helpless or needy or high maintenance. He'd seen her fix things with her hands, in fact—in his mind the ultimate test of competence. Somehow that made the thought of having to protect her a little laughable. The way she'd called the realty office, after they'd found the bodies—pure Serena. She'd made an appointment for the next day, hung up, and turned to him.

"Hey, man," she'd said. "The landscaping could use some work, but I thought the house was okay."

She killed. He'd banged the steering wheel laughing as they passed the Country Inn again on their way to the B&B.

Protect her? Nah, he thought. She does that herself. But still, instincts were instincts, and his were on fire. There was a baby coming.

Serena realized she was possibly actually starving, having *barfed*, she thought, having barfed the quail and potatoes and the soup and the water from the afternoon. She watched the lights of the convenience store fade behind them. Those two bodies in their dark pond seemed far enough off that she could handle some ham and Swiss cheese, but she didn't want to ask.

The distances weren't great. The B&B was up the road a few minutes from the Country Inn, the gas station not too far from the B&B, everything about ten or fifteen minutes from Upper Bone Hollow Road.

This time they came at the site from the other direction and Jeffrey realized he was completely lost again. This was largely farm country, some working, some not, with that farm-country cluster dominating the landscape—a wood frame house with a shed or two, a copse of trees, and across the road a barn. The occasional Napa-looking mansionette couldn't hide the place's past. To the north, the peaks. Rolling fields bordered the road in many places, empty wooded lots or swathes of unoccupied woodlands others. Everywhere were stone walls; not manicured English-style things, but humped caterpillars of rock trailing off into the trees or setting off flattened hayfields or cornfields from the woods beside them. Those walls weren't art, they were work. The road bridged minor streams with freeze warning signs, and dips and curves guided the road, which had clearly been laid down with respect—possibly enforced respect, but still, respect—for the topography.

And there were more roads than he'd realized. In looking out for the turnoff they'd taken previously, he'd started to notice many minor turnings that weren't the road he was looking for. It was a web, out here, lots of roads with conventional or vaguely familiar names like Weber and Vly. The name Kripplebush jumped out at him once or twice. Single-digit county roads crossed each other, sign posts arrowed down nondescript gravel tracks to design shops and gun stores and smokehouses.

He was surprised when the deputy turned onto a road calling itself Lower Bone Hollow, making a left off the road they were on. Even more surprised when, three minutes later, they pulled up in front of the realty sign. The other car was parked there, and a State Police car, and an unmarked police car, all of them on the road. Down here, in the dip the land made off the main roads, it was nearly dark. They could still see the outlines of the house down the driveway picked out against tiny pieces of sky and the birch trunks, but with the cop-car headlights and the hemlocks and the western hills blocking the sky-glow, it was gloomy in there.

They got out. Serena looked around and shuddered.

"Deputy?" she asked. "Is this Upper Bone Hollow Road or Lower Bone Hollow Road?"

He looked at her blankly. "Sorry?"

"Well, we turned onto Upper, you know, before," she said, "and drove down. But this time you turned onto Lower and drove up. I was just wondering which one the house is on."

"Oh. Uhh..." he thought about it, obviously for the first time. "We just call this Bone Hollow Road. Why?"

"Just wondering what the mailing address would be."

The deputy looked at her curiously. "You going to mail them a letter?" he said after a moment, smiling.

She gestured at the realty sign. "I figure this house just became a steal. Wonder how long it's been for sale, anyway."

He looked at the sign and then to Jeffrey, but Jeffrey was turning to greet a tall pale man in a thick canvas work jacket over a shirt, tie and khakis. The guy had gray hair and a limp; he came over quick from where he'd been talking to the other two policemen, stuck out his hand and said "Sorry to get you back out here. You've probably had better road trips, am I right? I'm Senior Investigator Bill Gerow, you can call me Bill, hi," he said, pivoting to Serena. Then he turned to the deputy who'd driven them there and said, "so?"

"So," he said. "Serena and Jeff here called 911 about forty minutes ago to say they'd found two dead bodies in a pond a little way behind this house with the for sale sign. They're visiting the area to look for a summer house. We asked them to come back to show us what they found and to give us any other details we might need. Apparently one of the bodies is gassed up and floating in the water, the other one is missing tissue, and they both agreed that the scene did not look recent. Is that right?" he said.

"Jeffrey," said Jeffrey automatically.

The deputy corrected, unstressed. "Jeffrey, sorry. Those facts right?"

"Yes," said Serena, although she wondered if it was in fact a summer house they were after.

Their party now numbered six, with Senior Investigator Gerow, the other state trooper, who was a thick-set blond woman with a tight braid coiled around at the back of her head and pinned in place, the two deputies, and the couple. No one was walking down that driveway yet; in fact, the police were setting up a couple of lights over it. One of them had a roll of crime scene tape, but the investigator waved it off. He asked a couple of questions: what time had it been? Did they smell anything? Were the bodies clothed? Then he examined the area around the house. A deputy and the trooper accompanied him, murmuring at the traces of the rental car's wheels and older tracks from who knows who.

Gerow stood and turned to the trooper, who was taking notes in a pad. "Get that realtor's number for me, would you Meg?" he said.

Standing, the detective looked again toward the house, gave a quick look at Serena and Jeffrey's shoes—good enough, leather and flat—and said "let's not walk right on the driveway, okay?"

They set off through the trees, reached the clearing, and paused at its edge. Although patient and methodical in the way of detectives, Gerow was also getting eager to start off the meat of his investigation.

"Jeffrey?" he said.

Jeffrey moved next to him. "Yeah?" he said.

"You say the path starts behind that shed back there?"

"Yes."

"Okay, let's not mess with the house, let's go around here," he said to everyone, indicating the borders of the clearing, "and let's not all mess up the trail there too; I'll just go down with Jeffrey and Serena and Deputy Hatch here. Deputy Hatch, do you have that camera?"

"I do," said Deputy Hatch, a heavy man who was probably Serena's age but who stood a six inches taller and had a red face and who had such seriousness of purpose that he could have passed for a grandfather.

Around they went, and back to the head of the little trail. Serena felt Jeffrey squeeze her hand as they reached that little lip where she'd given him that teasing over-shoulder glance... boy, the end of this trail had turned out different than she'd hoped it would.

But this was something. The story of it had been burning in her since they'd gotten out of there and over their original shock. In the ambiguously comforting presence of all this cop-gear, flashlights, and stern competence she—and her husband too, she could tell—was rehearsing wordings, imagining reactions on the faces of co-workers, seeing the play of details between her and Jeffrey as they would spin their tale. They hadn't had a chance to talk about it apart from that first drive up to the B&B, and a lot of that had been repeats of her original "what the fuck" theme. Both had tried their hand at a theory or two, but the best they'd been able to muster was that it was probably not a two-person hunting accident.

Serena's thoughts faded as they drew closer to the pond, which still glimmered in the dusk through the trees. She said "uhh, detective? Bill?" she said.

They all stopped. He looked down at her. "Yeah?"

She said "I don't know if this is important for, you know, evidence, but I... well, I threw up over there," she gestured to the clump of berry bushes alongside the trail.

"Oh, that's all right. Was that after you saw the bodies?" he said.

"Yes, after."

"Gotcha. You weren't drinking or anything beforehand?" he said.

"No."

Jeffrey joined. "I had some beers, at the Country Inn," he said. "Before."

Gerow looked at him for a moment. "Did you throw up too?"

"Oh. Uh, no."

"Okay." He looked at Deputy Hatch. "Deputy Hatch will note that," he said.

They rounded the final stretch of the trail and saw ahead of them the thin band of dark sand and mud. Its grisly cargo was still there, undisturbed, less threatening in the near-darkness, even when picked out spookily by Deputy Hatch's flashlight. The humped body in the water, a round gray rock with arms and legs fading down as though to root in the obscured bottom of the pond, floated as before. The light caught an oily sheen radiating outward from the body. The deputy lowered the beam and swept the narrow beach and they all stood still, Jeffrey and Serena suddenly aware of the evidence beneath them.

Deputy Hatch swept the light back and forth several times. "I don't see any tracks," he said, "but that doesn't mean anything."

"Everything look the same as when you got here?" Gerow said.

It did, they told him.

"You didn't change anything?" he said.

They hadn't and they said so. "Just the puke," said Jeffrey.

The cops paused, then both smiled. "Just the puke," said Gerow. "Okay, Deputy Hatch, can you take a few pictures of the area here and then we'll get these guys back to their road trip, and we'll see about getting a forensic team out here and continue the investigation."

"Detective," said Jeffrey.

"Yeah?"

"We have, uhh, an appointment with the realtor tomorrow..."

"Well, that's okay, if we need you tomorrow we can work around that."

"No, well. It's for this house."

"This house?" said Gerow.

"We love it," said Serena. They were holding hands again.

"Oh." He looked back up the trail toward the house. He couldn't see it back there. "I didn't really notice it. Nice?"

"It's kind of perfect," said Jeffrey.

"Well, we need to get in touch with the realtor and the current owner and take a look around in there. I'm afraid it's going to be off limits tomorrow and maybe Tuesday, too, but I bet you'll be able to get in there after that. Unless we find something related to this," he said, indicating the pond.

He thought of something. "When did you make this appointment?" he said.

"After," Serena said.

She had their attention.

"After? After you found the bodies?"

"Yeah," she said. "We went back up the path and kind of ran to the car—you know, we were scared—but once we got in and we got back out to the road I saw the for sale sign again. I'd been imagining us in that house, you know? And walking down to the pond I was wondering if it'd have a raft or a dock....Just seemed unfair to have to give that up."

"So you called a realtor," he said.

Jeffrey said "oh, well, no, we called 911 first."

"But then," she said.

"But then we called the realtor," Jeffrey said.

"Ah, okay. I hear ya," the detective said.

He'd stood during the exchange. Hatch's light was shining up into the trees, but his eyes were sideways on the detective's face. Hatch never smiled, Gerow knew. But if he was ever going to, this'd be a prime occasion. Gerow didn't look at him. He peered out over the pond, squatted down again to sight along the waterline at the body floating a few feet out. "Must be quite a house," he said.

Was this anything? he was thinking. They'd come up for a little romantic getaway, look at real estate in their rental car, and found their way to what had to be a murder scene or a body dump. House was unoccupied, up for sale a while judging by the overgrown driveway and the sun-faded sign. Sign lured them off the road, right? Or had they found it online first?

"I'm sure you covered this with the deputy, but what exactly brought you down here?"

Serena answered. "Well, once we saw the path, we could see there was a pond, and I thought—"

"No, sorry, I mean down this particular road. Did you know the house was for sale?"

Jeffrey took this one. "Oh, no. I was reading the map, and it's almost Halloween, and, you know, 'Bone Hollow.' We were driving past, and saw the realty sign up at the main road, and just figured we should check it out," he said.

"Bone Hollow, huh? Couple beers, seems fun, I get it." The detective stood up again and faced them. "Guess you got your Halloween right here."

"I guess," said Jeffrey.

"And, Mrs. Gale," he said to Serena, "You say you didn't have anything to drink at the Country Inn?"

"Water," she said. "Somebody had to drive this guy. He was singing."

He reflected on that, and gave it a little smile. Most people who drank would have a little something, he thought. "Well, we're done for now. You two okay?" Gerow said. They said they were, and everyone turned to walk gingerly up alongside the trail, conscious of disturbing old footprints.

The detective and the deputy walked behind Serena and Jeffrey back up to the car, skirting the clearing, murmuring together about whom to call and how to preserve evidence until a forensics team could be assembled and come out from Middletown. They'd have to formally establish jurisdiction, and there were going to be forms. They'd take formal statements from these two. Gerow turned over their presence at the pond a couple more times, didn't have any real problem with it. How old were these bodies?

He was pretty sure he knew the answer to this next one, but had to give it a try. Here, after all, were the two who'd called it in. How many hours could he have saved over his career if he'd just made an arrest on that basis, bypassing a lot of bullshit that so often led right back to that phone call?

He fell in at Jeffrey's side, and dropped the formality from his voice.

"So, this your first time visiting the area?" he said.

No hesitation. "Yeah. We were looking in Great Barrington a couple weeks ago, and Connecticut over the summer," he said. "Pretty expensive."

"And kind of precious," said Serena. Jeffrey nodded in agreement.

All right, file that, the detective thought. If anything looked weird later he could always pull it out. He started turning over missing persons reports instead.

"I guess..." Jeffrey said.

"Yeah?" said the detective.

"That's, like, definitely a murder down there, right?"

"I've learned never to jump to conclusions about these things," Gerow told him.

"But—"

"But yeah. Looks like at least one, maybe two. Still early for theories. We'll have a team out to do the whole CSI thing here, check missing persons, talk to the homeowner and the neighbors. All that cop stuff," he said. "We'll figure it out. This isn't exactly a first out here, but it's never something you get used to." He sighed. That was true, and twenty years in the Bronx—his youth—didn't make it any easier, either.

"And then maybe we'll get you two in that house." He looked at the two of them standing there together, ready to get back in the patrol car. "You don't let anything get in your way, do you?"

FOUR

No, they didn't. The police drove them to the station in Accord. The building was an old one, stone facade, wood frame behind, brick annex, courtroom upstairs, a single holding cell down a hall near the bathrooms.

This time they stopped at the little store at the crossroads on the way. Serena got two sandwiches.

And the next couple of hours were them giving separate accounts of the events. Then follow up questions from Senior Investigator Gerow and the town police chief. They kept offering coffee, but Serena wanted to sleep. There was no decaf at all until someone ran out for Serena and brought back some apple cider donuts that were so good the Gales couldn't believe they were real food.

At the end, Gerow told them solemnly that the house wold be off limits as expected, but they could give him or the realtor a call to find out when it would be available for viewings. Business cards and handshakes all around, apologies and thanks from the police chief and the detectives and Deputy Hatch, who was also on hand to deliver a statement.

It was midnight when the other deputy drove them back to the Hollybush, and Amy Berenson met them at the door, anxious. She had B&B-owner eyes and wore a thick sweater and jeans. Over the creaking floors she took them to a parlor where she had herbal tea up and some pastries and sat them and fussed, but not in a dowdy way.

"It's very nice," said Serena.

"Thank you," Amy said. They would never, ever, outlast her in waiting for a question. Jeffrey realized it.

"Sorry about that, earlier. When we took off."

"Oh, that's no problem at all. The police called and explained a little. Was everything okay?"

"Ahh, not exactly. I mean, we're fine. It's just..."

"Well," Serena broke in. "We found a couple of dead bodies."

"You *did? Here?*"

"Down..." Jeffrey gestured vaguely southwest. Ish. "Outside Krumville?" That sounded right.

"Wow. Where were you?"

"We'd gone to look at a house, on our own" said Serena, and she lay her foot atop Jeffrey's foot and pressed once—the international sign for lying by omission and don't contradict me. "We were driving around and spotted a for sale sign that pointed down a side road. They were in the woods behind a shed out back."

"Oh my god," Amy said. "I'd've died. What did you do?"

"We got out of there and called the cops," Jeffrey told her.

"Well, who was it?"

Serena said "We don't know. They didn't know, or at least they didn't tell us. One of their—well, one of the heads was partly...missing. That's why we got so close." And now she was remembering a bit, that panic. *A fucking dead person. Jesus.* "I thought it was a log or something, but then I saw boots."

"Oh, honey," said Amy. She patted the hand holding a forgotten petit-four, then stood, cleared the table, and brought them up to their room. Their bags were on a folding stand at the foot of the bed. There was an electric kettle and white-painted paneling. A print from a medieval herbal book and a photo of a barn in winter, then in summer. The bed took up everything else.

The bath was an old claw-footed one, and Serena turned it on, and got in when it was full. He washed her; there was a tub and a hand-held sprayer that looked like an old French telephone, and she sat under the warm water and he let it run over her shoulder blades and soaped her back while she sighed at the right moments. He helped her tilt back to get her hair without spraying water in her eyes, and then he worked it around to play the water over her collarbones and run down. She lay back further, stretched out as far as she could so he could look at her, and handed him the soap, and got her grin back that he hadn't seen since the trail.

In bed, afterward, close and nude and sated, beneath strata of duvets and flannel, he said "what are we doing?"

"I don't know. But doesn't this just feel so much like a Sunday night?"

"Fucking Sunday nights," said Jeffrey. "You can take all the Mondays off you want, but there it is."

"Let's go around with that realtor tomorrow and see if there's any other houses like that one," she said.

"I don't know...that one had a water feature."

She laughed. "Water feature. 'But it had a fucking water feature,' he says."

"Let's say we get that house."

"Okay."

"No, I mean, let's suppose we get that house. How often are we there? When are we moving in? Are we working? What are you wearing in this scenario?"

"I can't ride a horse until the baby's born," she said. "So I can't wear those thigh-high riding boots and the little fox-hunting jacket and white pants. Besides, those don't come in maternity sizes."

"Fuck," he said.

"I don't know, honey." She put her hand along his neck and slid it around the back to the short hairs and squeezed. "You can work remotely, I think?"

He nodded. "I'd probably have to go to the city sometimes."

"And I've given this some thought. I could work here. Potholders. I would become the northeast's largest producer of macramé potholders and little dioramas with trout and kids fishing for trout. It's a wholesale outfit," she said.

"Or," he said. "You could actually work in Kingston, maybe. There's a hospital there, they need your kind at hospitals, don't they?"

"I'd need a name for it..." she said. And they fell asleep.

. . .

The next day they went back to Accord. The realtor's office was directly across the street from the police station.

Angela LaPorta was there to meet them, watching them from inside as they crossed in their black fleece and blue jeans, and Serena in a dark green corduroy jacket and Jeffrey in a fleece ski cap. They carried coffees. Glancing at the listings arranged in a grid in the window, they came in. The bell rang over the door and Angela came out from behind a desk at the back, hand out.

"Hi," the realtor said. "I'm Angela."

They introduced themselves. She had that well-fed face; one that looked like nothing could ever happen to it. Curly, almost bushy hair. But she was wire underneath all that, Jeffrey could tell. A couple of lines down her cheeks, a little tightness in the skin of her neck. She wasn't all plump and aunt-like.

"C'mon, sit down, I see you've already got coffee." The office was clean and white, three desks, brochures and mortgage companies and title search companies and listings. CountryHome offered "CountryGold Service," they saw from one of the posters of a young family in front of a McMansion in horse country.

"Now, here's what I like to do, and you tell me if it sounds right," she said. "Before we even go out, I like to get to know you a little, and make sure that we're a good fit. Because that's the most important thing. I've met hundreds and hundreds of people who are looking for a home, and I can usually start to get an idea of their interests right here so we don't waste gas driving around to houses that you don't want."

"Okay," said Serena, "but real quick—what's 'Gold Service?'"

Angela looked over her shoulder at the sign. "That's our full-service package, where we work through an exclusive mortgage broker to get buyers the best deal on a mortgage, plus home warranties, title searches. A lot of people choose it, but you don't have to."

"Oh, okay, thanks."

"There's also some paperwork to fill out, including an agreement that if I take you out looking for houses, that I'm your buyer's agent. That's to protect you from conflicts of interest because I might show you houses that we're also trying to sell for our other customers, and we have to make sure you know when I'm showing you a house that I might have an interest in selling."

"Ah," said Jeffrey, taking a sip of the coffee.

"I think I'll join you with coffee. Can I top you off?" She slid from the desk and walked to her own coffee machine. She poured, watching her hands, and said "So where are you living now?"

"Brooklyn," said Serena. "Near Park Slope."

"Whereabouts, Prospect Heights?"

Jeffrey laughed once. "Is it that obvious?"

"Oh, I just meet so many great people from the city," she said, coming back to sit behind the desk, taking a sip and setting down her cup. "I get to know the neighborhoods. I lived there for a little while myself, but in the Bronx, in Riverdale. That was a long time ago. Are you looking for a seasonal or weekend home?"

"We need to get a sense of the place," said Serena, "but we think if we found the right home, we would move here. We could both work in the area."

"Oh, that's wonderful. What is it you do?"

"I'm a healthcare recruiter," Serena said, and resisted making air quotes around it. "Jeffrey is a technical writer for a pharmaceutical company."

"And you can both do that from home?"

"Well, Jeffrey would need to go to the city a couple of times a month for meetings. My company has clients all over the place, or another one does, so I could probably get work with any hospital in the area. I do a lot of work on the phones. If I had to do any interviews I could make it down to New York, too."

"Do you have an apartment now, or a brownstone?"

"We're renting," Jeffrey said.

"And when would you be looking to decide and move?"

He looked at his wife, said "I think if we were in by Christmas, that could work, but if not we'd go for spring."

"One last winter without having to shovel snow?" She smiled.

She brought them to a computer and called up the CountryHome website, and it was substandard, but she got it going, obligatory comment about being no good with computers but then zeroing in and eliminating houses left and right. She showed them the listing for 64 Bone Hollow Road. It looked different. Thin branches, devoid of leaves. Weak early spring light shining through, the house looking bigger. They wanted three hundred fifty thousand for it.

"How long has it been for sale?" Serena said.

"We first put it up in the fall last year," she said. "But as you might remember, things really fell off around then, and a lot of people couldn't hold on to the house they already had. So the owners decided to wait, and they put it back up in spring with a lower price. I've shown it a few times since then."

Her phone rang. She ignored it.

Serena said "we were driving around yesterday and saw your for sale sign."

"Yes, that's right, you said in your voicemail. Did you take a look at the house?"

The phone rang again.

Jeffrey was looking out the plate glass window, across the lawn to the street and the police station beyond. The front door opened and Bill Gerow stepped out. He looked across at the realty storefront, then looked both ways and started across.

"Yes," Serena said. "We'd love to take a look inside."

"Well, we'll definitely put it on the list," said Angela, hitting an animated print button on the listing, "and that helps a lot in knowing what you're looking for. It has three bedrooms—"

"You see, though," said Jeffrey, watching Gerow reach the sidewalk, "we won't be able to get in there for a few days."

"I thought you wanted to take a drive out there today," she said.

"It's not that," Serena said. "It's the police."

"The police? Oh, yes. I saw you come from there. What were you doing over—"

Gerow entered and set off the bell. "Hi," he said.

FIVE

"Hello," Angela said from behind her desk, and looked at Serena and Jeffrey, back and forth. Gerow was wearing a badge at his belt, and a jacket and tie. He covered the distance from the door quickly.

"Sorry to barge in," he said, and came over to shake Angela's hand. "Senior Investigator Gerow, I'm with the State Police. Not sure if Mr. and Mrs. Gale told you anything about what's going on, but they called us last night because they found an apparent crime scene out at one of the properties you're listing."

"A crime scene?" she said, and now her gaze bounced three ways. "What happened?"

"It's probably better if we speak alone," he said. "Maybe if the Gales want to get some lunch, we can talk for a little while and then let you talk real estate? I don't want to ruin anyone's day, but we're working on this one real hard right now and want to make sure we get off to a good start."

There was a pause. Then he looked at Jeffrey and Serena, an eyebrow up.

"Oh, right," said Jeffrey. He got up and Serena rose too. "We'll be back in...?"

Gerow looked to Angela as though asking her for an estimate. "Let's make it an hour," he said, more to her than to Jeffrey, and

Angela nodded as though in confirmation. The couple moved toward the door.

Serena walked to the printer on her way out. "May I?" she said, slipping her hand under the short stack of listings in the tray.

"Yes, sure," said Angela.

They took the papers with the wheat-harvest CountryHome logo out with them and turned down the street toward a diner they'd seen earlier. The bell dinged behind them.

"What'd'ja think of her?" Serena said.

"I don't think she did it, but she knows something," said Jeffrey.

His wife laughed, grabbed his hand. "You're so cute," she said.

. . .

They had six listings and ate wraps at the diner while they looked through them. Mixed bag. Two were way over their price range, big Napa-style ones, logs, giant windows, high peaked roofs. Another looked like it was shrinking downward into a sea of brambles and shadow, its blurry picture suggesting more decrepitude than seemed likely in a home listing—except that the price, ninety-seven thousand and on seven acres, seemed like it might make sense. Jeffrey held that one out to his wife. "How many floors does this one have?"

"I don't know," she said, looking at it. "Three?"

Then there was one on a tidy village street with a manicured lawn; it looked like it could have been in Bergen or Amityville and it didn't look like anything special. The price was high, just over the price for "the" house, which was now the price they had started to think of as "normal" for a house.

The other one looked okay. They could see hills in the distant background, fields closer in, some trees shading a white house with green shutters and a porch. In the right range.

They shared fries and put the houses in order and gave them names. "The" House, The Farmhouse, Village Living, House of Usher, Napa One and Napa Two. They agreed they were destined to misremember which of these last two was which.

"Angela's not going to let us see all these anyway," said Jeffrey.

"Why not?"

"It's gonna take a while to get around to houses up here, all these roads."

"Let's look at the farmhouse first, then we'll come back up in a week or whatever and we can get a look at the house, the 'the' house. I'm going to get sick of the nicknames quick."

"Yeah, me too."

They finished and paid the bill, then walked back into the crisp sunshine, waiting for their hour to finish.

"So who did it?" Serena said. She stopped outside an antiques store and looked at some stoneware jugs on a child's school desk.

He joined her, hefted one of the jugs. "Hunters?"

"What, by accident? And when's hunting season, anyway?"

"I don't know, I think in fall."

"Well, a double hunting accident?" she said.

"Maybe... maybe the first one was an accident and then the accidental shooter felt so bad he shot himself."

"Murder-suicide," she said.

"Manslaughter-suicide."

"Nice."

Jeffrey said "What were their names?"

"Roy," said Serena. "And Carl."

"That's if they were hunters," he said.

"Also if they were closeted gay lovers," she said.

"Is that your theory?"

"No, no, I'm not ready to commit," she said.

"Okay," he said. "Let's think this through. Let's assume it wasn't a murder-suicide, although it could have been. Let's say there were three people out there."

"Let's not," she said, "and say we did."

"What? Why?"

"Because that means someone killed those people on *our* property and then walked away. I don't like that."

"You like the house, you're saying."

"I'm saying."

"Then it's a good thing you found evidence of the crime," he told her. "So Bill Gerow can catch the perpetrator. Angela's probably spilling the beans about her cousin Earl's boss, named, uhh, also named Carl, who's a little off in the head." He stopped. He didn't like that tack either. A lunatic out there, killing people by the pond back behind that house? Although similar thoughts had occurred to him before, talking it out brought on the gooseflesh.

The price dropped a little in his mind.

"It's more than that," she said.

"What's more than what?"

"Liking the house. It's that I want to have the baby and be in that house. Sometimes I feel like...before...wasn't right. The apartment. Brooklyn."

"This feels right?"

"Nothing else would, is my problem." She had stopped on the sidewalk and was looking at their reflection in a store window, turned a little to the side, unconsciously trying to see if her sweater showed anything beneath. She sighed, took his hand.

Jeffrey resisted being pulled along the sidewalk for a moment longer, looking at where their reflection had been, trying to see it there still, like they could walk on down the sidewalk and know that those two figures remained. He turned with her.

They walked on, past the remaining shops in this short stretch of prosperous-looking commerce, nice places, country places, but the kind of places you'd starve to death or have to live on croissants if they were your only choices. Decorations, antiques, soccer equipment, luxury snacks for the day-trip crowd. Local places.

They reached a crosswalk at one end; the next building on their side was an elementary school, set off by a fence and a driveway; kids were shouting behind it at recess.

Serena took his hand. "I guess I ought to buy one of those books," she said. "You know, *Pregnancy: Taste the Fear,* or whatever."

He looked at her. "Right here with you, honey," he said, and he caught her gaze and squeezed her hand. "We can do that now, if you want." They crossed at the crosswalk; she noticed a sign resting on the double yellow line, warning drivers to yield to pedestrians. State Law.

"Get a load of that," she said. "They ought to put one of those up at Vanderbilt and Park."

"Bad enough crossing Vanderbilt at a light. You could open a law office at the corner," he said.

"Or a blunt-force trauma clinic," she said. Then "What would we do here?"

"For work? We said already."

"For everything else."

"I could chop wood," he said. "And sell it. And we would make friends with my customers. And they would come over for macramé bees, and your line of potholders would be famous, and we would have potlucks."

"No, really," she said.

"Okay, really? Really that guy Peter said he stocks more than five hundred beers at the Country Inn. That would occupy the first couple of years, and by then we would be the toast of the town. Little Sam Elliot Gale would be very popular as well."

"Sam Elliot," she said.

"Okay, fine, not Sam Elliot. Peter Saarsgaard Gale."

"Maggie Gyllenhall Gale."

"In other words, we would do what we do at home," he said. "Go to the bar, eat out. We could visit your old boss in Woodstock, and sometimes drive down to Poughkeepsie and take the train down and stay at my brother's apartment, or James and Emily's, or wherever."

"Drive our car. Shovel our snow."

He pointed at a marquee a few storefronts ahead. It bore a sign reading "Is He Dead?" and underneath "A Play by Mark Twain."

"We would attend community theater," he told her.

She looked at the sign. "To answer their question, yes."

"Yeah, right," he said, looking at it and at her. "Are you okay?"

"I'm pregnant."

"I mean about the bodies," he said.

"Not really," she said.

"Me either. Are we wasting Angela's time, or are we really looking for a place to live?"

"We really are," she said.

They finished their circuit of Accord's main street and crossed at the far crosswalk, then covered the remaining distance back to CountryHome. Gerow was gone, Angela was back at her desk. But she was up before the bell died out, and coming at them.

"You *poor things!*" she put her arms around Serena and squeezed, stepped back with her hands on her shoulders, then let go. She did the edited version on Jeffrey, just the double shoulder squeeze.

"Oh, we're okay," said Serena.

"Scared there for a bit, but we're okay now," Jeffrey said.

"But you called me *right after*," she said. "I would have completely freaked *out*. My god, you know I've showed that house a few times, too! What if they were back there when I showed it?"

"What did Detective Gerow say?" said Serena.

"He asked who I'd showed it to, and when, and how many times I've met the current owner, and if I'd ever seen anything strange there," she said, "but I'm afraid I didn't have anything useful to say."

"Did he have any theories?" Serena said, while Jeffrey said "Who *is* the current owner?"

"You first," he said.

Angela said "If he had any theories he wasn't telling me. My god, you two. *And then you called me.* You must have really liked that house."

"What do they call it," Serena said. "Curb appeal? It has curb appeal."

"I just can't believe it," Angela said.

"So who's the current owner?" said Jeffrey.

"Well, it's an estate. The owner died, and her three children are selling the house. It's been unoccupied for a year. They've dropped the price, but the market is just terrible. And now this," she said.

"The detective said we couldn't get in to look at it till they're done investigating," said Jeffrey. "But we'd still like to see the farmhouse." He handed her the listing. "We looked at the other listings, and this was the one we liked best."

"I'll call them and make sure it's okay for us to come," she said. She sighed, then brightened. She tapped on the keyboard and spoke to the computer. "Wadaya gonna do?" she said.

"Macramé," said Serena to Jeffrey, quietly.

Angela drove. The farmhouse was a really nice place. It was actually perfect. It was perfect, and nice, and the fields were perfect for a little cowboy or cowgirl and nice to look at, and they worked at it, really, they each put themselves into it, Jeffrey seeing how the crown moldings would make him feel about himself, and Serena imagining nursing the baby in front of the fire on a night in autumn, and there was absolutely nothing wrong with the house except that they didn't love it very much. It wasn't "the" house, and the other house just was.

So they thanked Angela, and they said they'd be back and that if she heard the house could be shown again, she would call them first, right? And Angela told them yes, she would, and she put their numbers into her cell while they pestered her to do it. Maybe the coming weekend, they said.

Their peppy car, their rental, pulled out of the lot at the police station, where it had been undisturbed during the afternoon. They hit the concrete apron at the edge of the lot. Jeffrey was driving again. He turned the blinker on to go right. That way was the Thruway and Poughkeepsie and the car drop-off and the train home along the river.

He turned left, shutting down the blinker's clicking sound.

"Yes, let's," Serena said.

It was a copy of the day before, the sun slanting down, the peaks aloof, shadowlight gathering under the stands of hemlocks and birch. Serena's late-summer holiday again.

Vly, Bremer, Van Leer, said the roads, branching off into farmland, rippling over low hills. They passed Kripplebush and found the turnoff to Lower Bone Hollow and dipped off the main road onto the firm-packed gravel.

They pulled up at the house. There were no cars, but there had been activity. Crime scene tape spanned the rutted drive. More had been strung across the stairs leading up to the deck. They could see a couple of small orange flags stuck here and there in the knotty grass of the clearing.

"There's a light on," Serena said.

There was a glow in the bottom corner of the big window, like someone had left on a worklight. Then, curiously, it danced a little.

And very suddenly, it grew and shot up the side of the window frame, inside, and hit the ceiling.

"Oh *shit!*" they both said. Fire. Big and fast.

Jeffrey got out of the car.

"No," Serena said to him, but he got out and walked as far as the tape, looking at the fire down the driveway and across the clearing. Outside the car he could hear it, a flamethrower sound, not crackling like a campfire, but rumbling, and it was clambering through the house fast and angry. It had just looked like a candle flame, but now, the thing was going up in flames.

She got half out of the car. "Jeffrey," she said. "Get back in here."

He stared at it. He just wanted to say "But, but, but," but he couldn't. *What the* fuck *is up with this place?*

And then implications suddenly suggested themselves and he spun around. "Get in," he said to Serena, but she was looking past him, at the fire he thought, until he saw her eyes get wide again that way they had before, and he saw her draw in her breath very suddenly. As he started to turn there was a shadow behind him, a momentary blocking out of the flames, and something hit him very hard between his shoulder blades and he fell forward and hit his chin against the top of the open car door.

The white flash of impact and Serena's scream merged into one thing as Jeffrey's hands tried to break his fall. He toppled forward, half into the open door, feeling blood start from his lips, then tried to roll over, but he was so slow and wasn't sure which way "over" was.

The horn was sounding, but Serena was screaming almost as loudly, as Jeffrey managed to flip himself over. She was above his head leaning across the seats with her hand on the horn and her scream had curses in it now.

Jeffrey opened his eyes and could see two boots, one on the gravel, the other slightly raised and further back. He was starting to squint at it as it began to rush forward toward him, and his slow hands came up to shield his face. The blow hit him in the ribs and all his breath left him. He curled reflexively on the gravel roadbed.

Serena's scream escalated, with his name in it now, and the light from the fire was huge against the sky. Jeffrey could see a towering figure, a man backlit, leaning forward over him, scrabbling to get Serena's hand off the horn. She clawed at his hands, punched.

Nuh-unh, Jeffrey thought, and kicked as hard as he could at the nearest kneecap. His heel hit dead on, a satisfying crack, the impact shivering up his own leg and he knew it was good. The attacker sagged, caught himself on the door, looked down—they both saw a face in the dome light—and ran.

Serena's hand came off the horn, and her scream stopped for a second. But she wasn't done, and after drawing breath she let loose another one, all *Jeffreys* this time, and she crawled across the driver's seat and reached for him.

Over his name and her questions, while he gasped against the pain and the effort to breathe, Jeffrey couldn't hear the rushing whoosh of the flames anymore.

He could see though, and what he saw as he lay there was their house, burning.

SIX

Serena jumped out of the car and squatted down next to Jeffrey, saying his name, stroking his face, asking where he was hurt.

A short distance up the road an engine roared, and a white pickup truck launched itself out of the underbrush, cut a big swath of gravel, and tore away from them up toward Upper Bone Hollow road.

She could feel the heat of the fire on one side of her face and the sound of it was still overwhelming. The light made the fading day darker, and sparks flew up in a molten spray into the hemlocks surrounding the clearing.

Jeffrey was getting his breath back. He sat up and looked at Serena. "You okay?" he said.

"I'm fine. Don't stand up. Are you okay?"

He pulled himself up by the door. "My chin hurts," he said, "and my hand." He showed her where the heel of his hand had hit the ground breaking his fall. "And here," he said, and rubbed at his side.

"That *fucker*," she said. She helped him get up and guided him onto the driver's seat.

New lights flickered through the trees, red, white, and sirens got impossibly loud. Around a bend in the road they could see the rushing presence of a truck, flares of light hitting the treetops, shining out over the slope back up to the main county road, coming this way.

It arrived, big, loud, competing with but losing to the burning house for sheer presence. Men clambered off it, young faces quickly hidden by masks, quick looks at Serena and Jeffrey before turning to the tasks, hoisting hoses. A smaller truck appeared behind the engine, and there were more sirens off in the distance.

The second truck, "Fire Chief" emblazoned on its side, pulled up just behind theirs. Serena remained by the open driver's side door, Jeffrey sitting back in the seat. The door opened and a big guy with a beer gut and real-life soup strainer mustache jumped out and shout-spoke.

"Is there anyone in there?"

Serena turned toward the house. "I don't know," she said. "It's supposed to be empty, but someone was here. He attacked us and drove away."

"Attacked you? Quickly, what happened?"

"We saw the fire start a couple of minutes ago, and then some guy ran out of the woods and shoved my husband, and kicked him," she said. "I leaned on the horn and he heard the sirens and ran away. He just drove away in a white pickup truck before you got here."

"You didn't see anyone inside?"

"No."

He ran quickly back to the main engine and conferred with another fire fighter, gesturing in a semi-circle. They ran hoses out, hustled one down to a tanker as it pulled up.

Two state police cars pulled in, one from each direction, and the fire chief came back. "Is your husband injured?"

They both turned to look at Jeffrey. He had blood on his chin from a badly cut lower lip and had gravel embedded in his hands and an unhappy expression on his face, and he was slumped over his aching ribs a little. He said "I'm okay, I think."

The fire chief leaned in. "We'll call an ambulance just to check you out. Your chin looks pretty bad," he said. He went back to the truck and came back ripping the seal on a gauze pad. "Hold that on," he said, and went back to the fire. A line of men ran into the clearing holding a hose.

Next in line was a state trooper in a tan Stetson. "Hi there, folks. Can you tell me what you're doing here?" He peered down at Jeffrey. "And what happened to you? Do you need medical attention?"

"He said they were calling an ambulance," said Serena.

"I asked him," the cop said.

"What?"

"Let's just let him speak, okay ma'am?"

Jeffrey stood up. "She can speak for me," he said. "The fire chief said they were calling an ambulance. I got knocked down and kicked."

"Who knocked you down and kicked you?" the cop said. The other trooper strode over from where he'd been speaking with the fire chief. Another fire truck arrived. A couple of men were erecting big lights on the road, pointing at the trucks, illuminating the controls on the hoses. The sky still held an oceanic blue up above, but the sun had gone. Generators roared.

"A guy," said Jeffrey. "He ran away from the house right after it went up, attacked me, then drove away. My wife scared him off."

"All right. How'd she do that?"

Jeffrey looked at the guy. About his age and about four inches taller. Fit. Gray uniform, belt with the gun, pepper spray, handcuffs. A flashlight. Boots. Nameplate with "Fine" on it. Unamused, detached expression. A kind of wall there.

"I leaned on the horn," Serena said. "And he heard the sirens."

"You could maybe," Jeffrey said. "Go after him."

They both pointed up the road. "He went thataway," said Jeffrey.

"In a white pickup truck," said Serena.

The other trooper spoke up. "Did you see the license plate? Make and model of the truck?"

"I didn't," said Serena.

"I was on the ground," Jeffrey said.

The second cop trotted back to his car and grabbed the radio, spoke into it.

"What are your names?" the other one said.

"Serena Gale," she said.

"Jeffrey Gale," said Jeffrey.

The ambulance pulled up. More lights, more engines. Their black car was in the middle, now, of a sea of light. A man and a woman in blue coveralls stepped from the ambulance and trotted over.

"Hi there," said the woman. "I'm Nancy and I'm going to take a look at you. First of all, can you tell me what happened?"

They said it again. Nancy looked him over, shined a light in his eyes, inventoried his hurts, had him lift his shirt. There was a big red blotch starting to bruise on his right side. She felt it and rated his pain. She and her partner, Mark, cleaned the gravel from his hand and bandaged his chin.

Meanwhile, Serena looked back and forth from the medical assessment to the house. There was less house in there now. The smoke, fortunately, was rising straight up. The firefighters had hosed down the trees and were working on the structure itself, closing in as their hoses dampened the flames' fury.

"Do you want to go to the hospital?" Nancy asked him when they had finished. "You'll need an x-ray and I think you should get it done quick."

The state trooper who had spoken to them first stepped forward.

"We're going to need some information from you both as well," he said. "If charges are filed, you'll want to have a medical report, too. We can take your reports at the hospital."

"Where *is* the hospital?" Serena said.

"Nearest one is Kingston," Nancy said. "We'll take Jeffrey and you follow."

"And I'll follow you," said the trooper.

A police car arrived. Deputy Hatch got out, towering, and lumbered over to their conclave.

"Deputy Hatch," said Serena.

"Ma'am."

"Looks like someone didn't want you guys poking around in there," she said, gesturing at the house.

"What d'you mean? Arson?"

"We saw the house go up. It was fast," she said.

Hatch looked at Jeffrey. "And what happened to you?" he said.

The trooper broke in. "You know these two?"

Deputy Hatch, young, imperturbable, looked at officer Fine. "They've been helping in an investigation," he said.

Jeffrey said "I got knocked down."

"And he got kicked," said Serena.

Hatch looked at them.

"We wanted to take one last pass at the house," Serena said.

"Hmm," he said, and looked over at the blaze. Part of the roof collapsed, sparks flying, firemen reversing with their hoses still trained.

"Crime scene guys were here all day," he said. "What time did you get here?"

"About fifteen minutes ago," Jeffrey said.

A gray sedan pulled up with red lights flashing inside the grill and across the back windshield, skidded to a stop, and disgorged Bill Gerow in one motion. He hit the gravel and continued the car's motion, entering the circle.

"What the hell's going on here?" he said, but didn't know where to look.

Deputy Hatch said "Hello Detective Gerow." Absolutely deadpan.

Jeffrey's nerves broke. Terror and sudden weariness snapped something in him, and he burst out laughing. Serena looked at him, startled, then saw it too and joined in. She hooked a thumb at her husband.

"The house went up," said Jeffrey. He started laughing more, but starting to shake.

"Then this guy here got kicked," she said, tears starting in her eyes.

"I got knocked down, too," he said.

"He got knocked down!" she said.

Nancy looked at them sideways. She said "we're planning to take him to the hospital."

Officer Fine said "They say they saw the house go up and then someone attacked them and ran off, then drove away in a white pickup truck."

"Thataway," Jeffery and Serena said at the same time, pointing. He gulped back another laugh. She took his hand.

"I called it in," said the second trooper.

"Everyone shut up," Gerow said. They did. He looked at the fire first. The circle was quiet. The house crackled, the generators roared.

"Okay," he said. Took a breath. "Let's have one person tell me—" but the fire chief and his gut edged into the circle.

" 'Lo, Glen," he said to Hatch. "Hi Jim, Devon," to the other troopers. "Nancy. Mark." He turned to Gerow. "Don't believe we've met. I'm Chief Karas, Bill Karas."

Gerow sighed at the interruption. "Bill Gerow, Senior Investigator with the state police. Sorry, one second." Gerow turned to Jeffrey. "You going to the hospital?"

Karas said "we're gonna need to talk to you two."

Mark, the other medic, stepped forward. He was about six or eight inches shorter than most of the men in the circle, just a little taller than Serena, but he had a baritone voice and it was loud. "Listen up," he said. "Let's get Jeffrey to the hospital, and you can ask them questions there."

They paused and looked at him. He clapped his hands, and the circle broke. Nancy wheeled the gurney over. Jeffrey sat on it. They helped him lie back and raised the thing's legs, Serena kissed him, and they slid the gurney in. She got in their car.

Gerow stopped her with a hand on the elbow. "Mrs. Gale," he said. "Why don't I drive you into Kingston? We'll talk on the way."

"My car's here, though," she said.

"We'll want to take a look at it," he said.

"What? Why?"

"Evidence," he said.

"What kind of evidence?"

"Didn't you say you were attacked? Were you in the car at the time?"

"Oh," she said. "Yeah." She looked at the car. "He was trying to get my hands off the wheel..." and she sobbed once, then caught it. Her head turned to the ambulance. Mark, at the wheel, started backing and filling to get out of the morass of hoses, trucks, floodlights, and men. Further back, more cars had arrived and bystanders were clustered behind one of the trucks. The house was blackened, hoses still playing over flames here and there. The chimney stood, and parts of the ground floor.

She turned back to Gerow. "Okay," she said.

He'd followed her gaze to the partial wreck of the house. "Too bad," he said.

"Huh?" She looked again. She sniffed, her nose running a bit. "Oh, yeah. But still. It's gotta be a steal now."

. . .

It was six when they got to the hospital fifteen miles east. A gleaming, sprawling complex, two or three old brick piles with Edwardian smokestacks, now sprouting new steel and glass prostheses that shined with a kind of sterile warmth. What had been buildings were now pavilions—the Weygant Cardiac Care Pavilion, the WestGen Orthopedic Health Pavilion—and what had been wards were now Care Zones. Trademarks and corporate logos abounded.

From the ambulance Jeffrey was wheeled to the Alan and Margaret Payson Emergency Medicine Center (formerly Room), where he awaited examination while Serena handed over an insurance card to a woman in scrubs sitting at a computer. She pinched it together with her own business card, saying "here's the insurance, and here's my card—I do recruiting for health care jobs, and I would love to speak to someone in your HR department. Can you see that they get this?"

The woman looked at it, said sure, wrote something on it and slid it into the corner of a small corkboard next to her computer. Then she gave Serena a clipboard with a few forms on it.

Serena stepped back to where Mark and Nancy were explaining the nature of Jeffrey's injuries. She filled out forms while they sorted out Jeffrey's next stop, which was a curtained alcove a few feet away with its own television, currently playing a professional soccer match. He didn't want to lie down. They said he ought to. He did.

Gerow appeared with two cups of coffee. "You drink coffee?" he asked Serena.

She did, and thanked him. The ER was crowded with equipment, and alcoves like Jeffery's obtruded into aisles where family members, EMTs, the wounded, doctors, nurses, and techs walked or ambled. Though there was a chair next to Jeffrey's bed, the space couldn't have comfortably held all three of them. Serena caressed his face again, kissed him on the forehead and then kissed him again on his injured lip. "Back in a couple," she said.

He gestured her close to whisper. "Trust no one." He grinned. "Okay, trust the detective. And the other cops. And the EMTs. But that's it."

"Trust me," she told him.

Gerow and Serena stepped out to a waiting room, but Serena kept walking, through sliding glass doors to the ER parking lot. Gerow kept pace.

It was cool out here, and full dark. To the west a parking garage, and beyond it mountains, blocked any remaining blue sky-light left over from the sun. Serena leaned against the grill of someone's SUV in a reserved parking space. He took a spot across from her, leaning against the brick wall of the pavilion.

She sipped the hot, burnt coffee.

He took out a notebook, didn't open it, and said "Now—" but she interrupted.

"What I don't see is why they'd try to destroy evidence after you guys had been in there all day."

She'd done it again, tried to grab the initiative. Fine. "I wonder the same thing," he said. "But, listen, you might want to play cops now, and I understand. People do it all the time. Witnesses have theories. Reporters have theories. Family members have theories. But listen," he said. "We're the cops. You're the citizens. We're very good at this."

"You forgot homeowners," she said.

He shook his head, smiled. "I get it, Mrs. Gale. You really, really like the house. Liked."

"Present tense will do. I can still remember what it felt like to walk into that clearing yesterday."

"Okay, then, *like.* So what's the homeowner's theory?"

"Too early for theories," she told him, and smiled at him.

She was pretty, he reflected momentarily, but he didn't think she was using it on him. He'd had that light shone on him from a lot of pretty women over the years, women trying to get something, women trying to get out of something, women attracted to the uniform. He still got it shown on him by his pretty wife of twenty-five years, from time to time. The Gale woman was pretty, and smiling, but she wasn't turning it on, no.

He realized he'd caught her eyes for a second while he ran that through his mind, so he transferred his gaze to the parking garage roof.

"What did the guy look like?" he asked.

"Tall. About as tall as you," she said. "White guy. He had a goatee. Dark hair. Kind of a full face, not a skinny guy."

"What was he wearing?"

She thought a second. "Gray hooded sweatshirt. Jeans, I think."

"Could you see any lettering?" He had opened the notebook, was making a couple notes.

"No. There was a logo on his sweatshirt, you know, the brand, but I don't know what it was."

"Would you recognize it if you saw it?"

"I think so."

"What about him? Would you recognize him in a lineup or on the street?"

"I think so. I only saw him by the dome light of the car. He had knocked Jeffrey down and I was honking the horn—" She paused. "I wasn't, like, honk, honk, honk, like I wanted him to get out of a crosswalk. I was leaning on the horn, and he tried to grab my hands, but Jeffrey kicked him in the knee."

"You're a good team."

"Thanks," she said, sipping her coffee. It tasted like the burnt end of a day-old pot in an unpopular deli, but it was hot.

"Do you think we were involved in this?" she said.

"It really is too early for theories," he said, looking in the direction of the forgotten sunset, but attuned to her posture. "And on some level, I'd say you were pretty clearly involved," he said. "Now your husband is the victim of assault. You're witnesses to apparent arson. You may be able to identify a murderer. But do I think you killed anyone? Not at this time."

"Would he have killed us?" she finally asked.

He looked back at her. It came through in patches, the fact that she was scared.

"I don't know," he said. "He could have just snuck off instead of attacking you, right?"

"I guess so. His truck was up the road."

"So we assume he *thought* he had a reason to go after you. I don't know. If the arsonist was the murderer, there's a good chance he wasn't thinking straight. That's usually what happens. People don't know what the hell they're doing, by and large. Someone kills someone else, fifty percent of them panic, the other fifty percent go around boasting about it. Either way," he said, "it creates a certain visibility."

"So you think maybe he thought he had a reason to kill us," she said.

"Well, he didn't. I mean, he didn't use a weapon. Even with fire trucks coming, if he'd had a gun or something he could have been very quick."

"Jesus," she said.

"Sorry," he said. "So, listen, why *were* you and Jeffrey out there?"

"Taking a last pass at the house before we went home," she said.

"Brooklyn?"

"Yes."

"Well, it's getting late now and I don't know how long Jeffery's going to be in there. We need to take formal statements and show you some photos. The fire chief needs you, too, because they investigate arson."

"We both have work tomorrow," she said. That sounded absurd, even to her, coming off the shock of the murders, and the fire, and the attack, and the fire trucks, and all the attention. And inside her, although she didn't feel vastly different, was an ever-present hot coal—the knowledge of new life brewing, sharing space between her head and her abdomen—and that was shocking too.

She burst into tears.

Gerow waited. It had to happen some time. It had nowhere to go but out. She cried for a couple of minutes, threatening to stop and then picking up again, the tears working through her.

When she was done, he had a handkerchief and offered it. She looked at it.

"Eww," she said.

He laughed. "Yeah, I s'pose so," he said. "It's clean, though." She took it.

"I'll fix that," she told him, and blew her nose, loud.

"Anyway," he said, "I was going to say that we can help you get a place to stay. If they let your husband out soon, we might be able to get your statements and have a talk with the fire department investigators tonight, but it's likely to be pretty late. Who knows?" he said "We might even catch the guy who attacked you and have you ID him. We had a call out within five minutes—there's a good chance we'll get him."

"Did you identify the bodies?"

He hesitated. She'd read about it next day, anyway. In fact, he was surprised they hadn't got a reporter out to the hospital yet.

"One of them. He's a minister. Been missing for two months from a town in Pennsylvania. Couldn't get a dental match, but we were able to find a fingerprint ID."

"What about the other one?"

"No, not yet. White male, mid to late thirties, about five-nine, light to medium build. This was the one in the pond. Couple of tattoos that should be helpful. We didn't find anything in missing persons, and we don't have a real good facial image to show around. He was, you know, in the pond for a long time."

"How'd they die?"

"They were both shot, I'm afraid. I really shouldn't say much more than that. We do try to hold back some details that only a perpetrator would know. Often helps solve these things."

"Couldn't it have been a murder-suicide?"

"Ah, well, maybe. For that to be true, you figure the Reverend would've had to be the killer, given the nature of the wounds. And they've swabbed his hands for firearm residue. But, thing is, we haven't found a gun. Or the car they came in, if they did."

The glass doors slid open. A man in scrubs came out, stopped nearby and lit a cigarette. They went silent. After a few moments, he got it, walked along the sidewalk to the other side of the doors.

"Maybe someone came and took it?"

"Maybe. That would require a certain mindset, though, wouldn't it? Say it was a hunter came along and found two bodies and a gun—most would leave everything as is and call the police." He drained his coffee. "Only a *special* person would be likely to want a gun bad enough to just take it—remember, this is a traceable gun used in a murder—and not call the police. And what are the odds someone like that was house-hunting?"

She smiled. Weak after the crying.

"Did Angela have anything to tell you?"

"She was very helpful, but who knows? Maybe something she told us will have something to do with it, maybe not."

Serena sighed. "Why the house?"

"Can't say. The evidence guys were in there a long time. They'd swept it, dusted for prints. Took some track casts on the road and the clearing. They didn't find anything obvious that tied the house to the crime."

"What about the owner?"

"You're pretty good at this," he said.

"Why are you humoring me?"

"Cause I think you got screwed on the house, maybe," he said. "Costs a lot to build a new one."

"I'm imagining some scenario where insurance helps make it cheaper."

"Really? I thought you were imagining the crime, trying to solve it."

"That too."

"Busy, huh?"

"Yeah."

"Well, listen." He shifted his weight off the wall he'd been leaning against. Time to wrap up. He was pretty sure she was on his side, now. "We don't usually solve these crimes through sleuthing. It's not Sherlock Holmes sitting in a room. It's a bunch of detectives going door to door in the victim's neighborhood. Searching computers. Asking the siblings where they were that day. Checking out known associates. And, eventually, something makes sense, or we get a physical match to some piece of evidence. That's what's going to happen here."

"And the guy who attacked us?"

"Got enough on him to charge him with assault, and most likely arson. The fire guys will get that evidence. Something about him will make him for the murder, or connect him to it. And we have a helicopter out there and a bunch of cars looking for him. Lots of white pickups getting pulled over tonight."

"Okay."

"Oh, by the way," he said. "Reporters are going to want to talk to you. I'm frankly surprised there's no one here yet."

"How would they know me?"

"They listen to the scanner. They're usually helpful, don't print too many things we ask them not to. In your case I think we can protect your privacy. It helps that you aren't local."

"Yet," she said.

"Yes, yet. Anyway, I'd appreciate it if you and Jeffrey kept any comments to a minimum. Like I said, they usually try to help, and they'll probably assist us with the pickup truck search if we don't have the guy by the time they go to press. Of course, there was some press coverage when the minister went missing, but that investigation hadn't led anyone out here yet."

"So what do I not tell them?" she said.

"We've already asked them not to print your name, which really is for your protection, in case that misguided individual who attacked you stays out of our hands and thinks he needs to get to you. Far as I know, they don't have your name yet. I'd say, given his existence, that you want to tell them as little as possible. Look whoever it is in the eye and tell them you don't want them to print your name."

"What are we supposed to do, go into witness protection?"

"Trust me, that guy is hiding or running. And if he's dumb like I think, he's not going to find you. Also, NYPD might be of assistance in keeping an eye out in your neighborhood. I used to work in the Bronx. Lots of the crimes up here sorta grow out of the city."

"Those terrorist guys were from up here, right?"

"The Newburgh bombers? Yeah. They weren't exactly masterminds, though."

"They got the munchies on the way down to blow up that synagogue, I remember."

"Yeah, stopped at a rest stop on the Thruway. So, you see what I mean. That case was handled by a bunch of agencies, including the state police and the NYPD working with the FBI. So we'll make some calls down to the city before you go home and make sure you're safe."

She sighed again. Leaned her weight off the SUV. "I want to see how many stitches he's getting," she said.

The doctor couldn't tell them. Jeffrey was in radiology when they got back inside. The woman at the desk told Serena he'd be back soon, that the doctor figured they'd need to give him a couple of stitches for the cut on his chin. His ribs didn't seem to be fractured, but they were checking to be sure.

Gerow went back outside, phone pressed to his ear.

Serena sat in the chair by Jeffrey's bed, half-watching the soccer match. There was a no-cell-phone sign in the entranceway to the ER, but the staff didn't seem to have read it, so she figured it'd be okay. She had a voicemail from her mother and a missed call from her friend Ellen. Although the temptation to start telling the story had hit early on, subsequent events had made it less desirable. And now she wasn't sure she wanted to talk about it with anyone except her husband.

That thought wasn't even cold when the curtain at the end of the alcove slid aside, and a chubby short guy with glasses and an across-the-shoulder black bag peered around it. He saw her there and smiled. He spoke very quietly, respectfully.

"Hi there. Are you Serena?"

She almost said no, but realized that Gerow had been telling her to make friends for her own protection.

"That's me."

"I'm with the *Caller-Dispatch*. Mind if I ask how you're holding up?"

"On the record?" she said.

"Uh, not really, that one."

"I'm okay," she said. "My husband's fine too, they're just making sure his injuries aren't serious."

"That's good," he said, and she thought he seemed truly relieved. But who knew?

"I do have some other questions about the last couple of days. Can we talk?"

"We're talking," she said, leaning her head back and closing her eyes. Then she remembered Gerow's advice and opened them again. She looked at the reporter. This time she did turn it on. Her eyes got big, she tilted her head down a little, furrowed her brow, and raised just her eyes to his.

"Mister...?"

"Uhh, Gilbert," he said. "Oscar."

"Mister Gilbert, my husband and I think we might be in danger. Can you promise me something?"

"Sure."

"Can you promise not to print anything that would identify us? It's just that—well, I'm scared."

"Oh. Oh," he said. "Yes, of course, no—we wouldn't do anything to put you in jeopardy," he said. He laid a hand over hers for a moment. His pudgy fingertips were cool. "Have you talked to anyone else from the papers?"

"No," she said.

"Well, I'm just trying to put some pieces together, and your identity isn't news. I—at least not yet. I'll keep it under wraps," he said.

She whispered. "Thank you." Then she did close her eyes and lean back. "I'm listening," she said.

He took out a tape recorder and asked questions. Serena left out how much she'd wanted that house, and she left out the baby, and the name of the B&B, but beyond that she gave the story. They'd been house-hunting in the area and saw an open house sign, then found two dead bodies back in the woods. After talking to the police, on their way out of town, they'd swung by to take one final look at the place, and saw it go up in flames. Just then they'd been attacked by a man, but he had run away at the sound of sirens and driven off in a white pickup truck.

"Had you been in the house?" he asked.

"We didn't have an appointment or anything," she said. "We didn't get a chance to see the inside."

"Would you recognize the guy who came after you?"

"Yeah, I think so. Maybe don't print that?"

"Sure. We don't really need to make that point in the paper."

Jeffrey came back in a wheelchair during the discussion, and sat quietly through the end of it, nodding occasionally. He was able to supply that their assailant had been wearing leather work boots. Gilbert asked if they knew anything about Reverend Peterson.

"I heard one of the victims was a minister," Serena said. Jeffrey raised an eyebrow at her. "Detective Gerow told me," she said.

She turned back to Gilbert. "He'd been missing for a while?"

"Yeah. It was news for a couple of weeks," Gilbert said. "He was popular, had a weekly radio show on a little AM station, ran a church—sort of a nondenominational place—and just disappeared from his house one day. He's got a sister out in Reading, she hadn't seen him, and no one in his congregation had heard anything. Finding him this way was unexpected. Most people thought he'd run off for personal reasons."

"Maybe he did," said Jeffrey.

Gilbert looked at him. "Got a theory?"

"Not at all. My only theory is wanting to go home. Do you mind if we have some privacy? Don't mean to be rude, but my wife and I are not having a great day. If there's anything else, maybe you can call us? We'll give you our numbers."

"Sure," he said. "Not a problem." He shook their hands, thanked them, wished them luck, assured them he'd keep their names "on the down-low," and left, heading out a corridor toward the hospital's main entrance as Gerow came back in through the sliding glass Emergency Room doors.

The detective stopped at the desk for a moment, then walked over to stand next to Jeffrey's wheelchair. "How you holding up?" he asked.

"I'm okay," Jeffery said.

"Detective," said Serena. "Jeffrey here told the reporter that the shithead who attacked us had on work boots. Not sure if we covered that."

"There was a reporter here?"

"Yes, while you were outside."

"What paper? Did you get his name?"

"Gilbert," she said. "Don't remember the paper. It had two names, I think."

"That'd be the *Caller-Dispatch*."

"That's the one."

"Work boots," said Gerow, and looked at Jeffery sympathetically. "Ouch."

"Yeah," said Jeffrey, making an exaggerated wincing face and placing a hand to his ribs.

"Did your phone tell you anything?" Serena said.

"They're pulling over trucks out there," he said. "I know you guys have been through the ringer, but I wonder if you can sit to look at a photo array. If we have the guy we want to know it, and if we don't we want to let these other guys go. The station's right up the street. I've also talked to the fire department, and their investigators can talk to you there. We can also get your statements and hopefully get you someplace to sleep or back home before Christmas."

"Dinner," said Jeffrey. "I'm hungry as hell."

"Yeah," said Gerow. "Dinner first. I just asked at the desk. Sounds like they're ready to let you out in a couple of minutes."

The curtain at the end of the alcove twitched aside. A dark-skinned guy in an argyle vest, blue work shirt and jeans leaned around it. "Hello?" he said.

"Forget something?" said Gerow amiably.

"Huh?" the man said.

Gerow turned to Serena. "They always have just one more question, that's my experience." She smiled back quizzically, then smiled at the guy who'd come in.

He stuck out his hand, still looking at Gerow with puzzled amusement, and said to Jeffrey "Hi there. Oscar Gilbert. I'm with the *Caller-Dispatch*."

"What?" said Serena. "But—" she looked at Gerow, her smile losing a fight with a "what the hell?" expression. She swallowed. "The guy who just left said he was Oscar Gilbert."

Gerow sat for one more split second. And then leapt to his feet, body tensed, gaze focused fiercely on Serena's face. "You're saying *someone else* was in here? How long ago?"

She got up. "Five minutes," she said. "That way," and pointed down the corridor toward the lobby.

Gerow led, Gilbert right behind him saying "oh *shit!*" and Serena kissing Jeffrey on the forehead before she arrowed out of the alcove after them. The curtain billowed in their wake. Jeffrey's shout calling her back went unheeded as she disappeared around a corner.

He got to his feet and followed slowly, wincing every couple of steps.

SEVEN

It wasn't a big building and they were on the first floor. Gerow
reached the lobby in less than a minute, despite being slowed
by an earnest security guard who'd moved aside at the sight of
Gerow's badge and was now following behind Serena, huffing
and saying "Ma'am!" repeatedly.

She kept on, looking down side corridors as she passed
them, but didn't see anyone who looked like "Oscar Gilbert."
Again, she found herself muttering "what the *fuck*" as she ran,
the apparently real Oscar Gilbert a few paces ahead of her.

Gerow was at the front desk in the lobby before realizing he
didn't know what he was asking for. "Did you see a guy—" he
started, breathing heavy, and then said "ahh, *shit*." He turned to
sprint back to the ER, almost running over Gilbert and Serena.
He reared back, grabbed her shoulder and steered her to the
desk.

"Good, okay," he said. "What's he look like?"

The woman at the information desk just inside the front
entrance was kind of old, Serena saw, with downy white hair
styled as high as it could go. It looked fragile, wispy, but crisp
and lofty with chemical help. The poor woman's eyes were
wide, her mouth open, and a hand at her throat.

"Short, bald, chubby, glasses, white," Serena said, panting.

"Did you see anyone like that come through here about five minutes ago?" Gerow said, leaning forward wolflike over a little ceramic pot of flowers, trying to hypnotize the answer out of her.

"I don't— think so," she said, hand to her throat.

Two security guards joined them. "What's happening here?" said one.

Gerow spun. "We're looking for a suspect, white, bald, heavyset, glasses. How tall?" he said to Serena.

"About my height," she said.

"Age?" he snapped.

"Forty?"

He turned back to the security guards. "He was here within five minutes. You—go that way, check side corridors between here and the ER. You—call the parking lots and tell them, then do a perimeter of the building. I'm outside."

He turned to Serena. "Go back to your husband until I come get you."

A third guard had hustled in from another corridor. Gerow caught his gaze and waved him over, showing his badge again. "Take this woman back to the ER and make sure she and her husband are safe; there's a suspect in the hospital. Stay with them until I get back."

He whipped out his cell phone, hit a speed dial number, and headed into the parking lot barking orders.

The guard turned in the direction of the ER and said "Ma'am?" But she stayed still, watching the door slide shut behind the policeman. Gilbert was looking back and forth between her and the darkness outside. He came back to her, and she let the guard guide her back into the hospital. He pulled out his radio and spoke to someone.

70

Gilbert said "Just so I'm clear, someone said he was *me?*" Serena looked at him as they walked. He smelled like cigarettes and had pulled out a digital recorder, but it wasn't on.

"He said he was from the Caller-Whatever, and when I asked his name he said Oscar Gilbert," she said.

"I'll be damned. What did he ask you?"

"He asked about what we saw. He asked what I expected a reporter would ask. Who the fuck *was* he?" she said.

They came upon Jeffrey, who had almost made it to the lobby, and Serena ran to him. She held him, not squeezing. He put his face at her neck and nuzzled. "I love you," he whispered.

"I love you too," she said inside the little chamber created by the curtain of her hair.

He said "I've been thinking, on my way over here."

"Yeah?" she said. It was quiet in here, just the two of them. No one was pulling at them or anything.

"I was thinking let's not move up here."

She laughed. "This is a crazy fucking place," she said.

"I can't keep up," he said.

"Me neither. But I've been thinking too."

"Uh-oh. And?"

"Let's figure out who killed those guys and fuck them up."

"Oh, Serena," he said.

They broke their embrace and let the security guard, who was paranoid now, looking left and right, hand on a stun gun at his belt, lead them back toward the ER. The reporter kept pace, and an orderly appeared with a wheelchair for Jeffrey. He let himself be pushed.

Nothing else happened. Nothing except that Jeffrey and Serena spoke to the reporter, gave him the same story Serena had given the impostor, and she added some details about the impostor, but asked him not to print them.

Gerow came back after fifteen minutes, striding in with the head of security, both of them trailed by a pair of troopers. Gerow shed his entourage and joined Serena, Jeffrey and Gilbert. He ran his hand through his hair.

"This is getting ridiculous," he said. "Let me just confirm something absolutely. There's no chance that the guy who said he was Gilbert was the same guy who attacked you, right? Totally different descriptions."

"That's right," said Serena.

"We're getting the security tapes from the hospital, so we'll at least be able to see this guy." He turned to Gilbert. "That's some balls on the guy, huh?"

"I think he's wasting his time. Pretend to be me? You're gonna pretend to be somebody, you want to make it count. Strictly amateur."

Gerow said to Serena and Jeffrey, "so, what'd you tell him?"

"You mean besides our cell phone numbers and names, and the fact that we would recognize the guy who attacked us if we saw him again? Nothing much besides that," said Serena.

"And the workboots," said Jeffrey wearily.

"Yes, workboots. Detective," Serena said, "Seriously. What the fuck?"

"Uhh, yeah," Gerow said. He paused. "Clearly this is more complicated than we thought. Two victims, and at least two conspirators. I mean, unless that fake reporter was a real reporter pulling some kind of scam, or a blogger with a police scanner or something. There's some chance he has nothing to do with the case."

Jeffrey looked at him with a level, deadpan gaze.

"Although, yeah," Gerow said, "that doesn't seem likely. We're putting more resources on the case. If that helps."

"It doesn't help much," said Serena. "Wait," she said. "What was the minister's name, the— the dead guy? Or, wait. Was it Peterson?"

Gerow's mouth opened. "Yeah," he said. "Did—?"

"That guy knew it. He said the name, talked about his church in Pennsylvania."

Gerow's hands started to twitch. He wanted his cell phone, he wanted more cops. He forced himself to relax.

Gerow turned to Gilbert. "You have what you need for the minister story and the fire?"

"From these two, yes, I think I'm good. Although I'm going to prove my identity now."

Gilbert produced a plastic ID card with his name and photo on it that said *Caller-Dispatch* in an old English font. It had a magnetic stripe on the back, and an address in Middletown with a request to return it there if found. He also handed them each a business card from a small stack in his pocket with his name and "Reporter" after it, same logo up top.

"For all we know," he continued to Gerow, "you could be a nut with a police scanner."

Gerow was already walking away, cell phone to his ear.

Gilbert turned to them. "So, I'm the real thing, but I guess you already knew that. I'll tell you right now, this is pretty unusual, what's going on here. I've never been impersonated before. You guys have never found dead bodies before. Jeffrey, have you ever had someone attack you before?"

"No."

"So I can imagine you guys are tired and kind of nervous."

"Yes," Serena said. She was sitting in a metal frame chair—pleather over foam—next to the bed where Jeffrey lay ("my ribs hurt when I sit, but standing and lying down are okay," he'd said). A fleecy pile of outdoor clothes lay in her lap. She kept checking for security guards, saw them, could see Gerow off by the front doors, occasionally pacing in front of the sensor and making them open and close while he spoke into the phone. Cops came and went from the front. She saw Deputy Hatch once.

Gilbert stood. "All right, I'm going to call my editor and go make Gerow's life hell. You might hear from another reporter from the *C-D* as well, but I'll make sure to introduce her by phone first. The fact that my name is now in the story might make it tricky to cover it. Thanks very much for all your help. I hope everything works out for you."

Serena let him shake her hand from her seat. "You're welcome," she said. "Remember now—we're pals. Keep our names out of it. Not that it matters now."

"It matters. I'm not happy about being impersonated. So now you, the police, and I all have personal stakes in this. Good night." He went to the exit and stepped outside with Gerow, who was still on the phone.

Serena added Gilbert's number to her cell phone contacts.

The doctor came back with Jeffrey's chart. "All right," he said. "Here's a sheet with some instructions for taking care of your injuries. Here's a copy of the medical report we fill out when a patient is brought in by the police." He peered at the stitches on Jeffery's chin again. "Is the numbness starting to fade?" he said.

Jeffrey nodded. "But it doesn't hurt badly."

"It will, but only when you talk, laugh, chew, or breathe."

"Great."

Serena stopped the doctor. She pulled out a business card. "Here," she said. "I recruit for health care in New York, but we might be looking to relocate here."

"Your company might?" he asked, looking at the card.

"No, my husband and me."

"Oh, yes, I heard you were house-hunting." He looked at her. He was young, possibly as young as she was, she thought. He had cafe au lait skin and a pencil moustache and eyes that protruded a little bit. He was very skinny. "The fall air can be nice, if you don't mind all the murder and arson."

She chuckled. "Anyway, if we do move here, I'd be in a position, either though my current company or another, to help the hospital with staffing. If you can pass that on to HR, or if you're thinking about a move, give us a call."

He pocketed the card, thanked her, told Jeffrey to call if he had any questions, and went on. Gerow had been waiting by the front desk, and now he approached.

"Good news," he said.

"They caught him? Them?" said Serena hurriedly.

"Oh. Ah, no. The good news is that if you can stand another hour, we'll take you to the police station, have you look at a lineup, get your formal statements, and let you go. If you want to stay in the area tonight, Deputy Hatch has been assigned to get you to a hotel."

"Deputy Hatch!" Serena said to Jeffrey.

"A good man," said Jeffrey. He closed his eyes.

Serena draped herself over him, avoiding his ribs and chin. They paused, breathing one another in. She stood again.

"Nothing happens without coffee and something very good to eat."

"Done," Gerow said.

"And information."

"Pardon?"

"I want to know the names of the owners of the house. I'd like to know what Angela told you about the people she's showed the house to. Tell me about when you worked in the city, about the number of policemen assigned to this case, and about who's in charge. Tell me everything they know about this minister."

"Okay. I can tell you a lot of that. Just remember. Me, cops. You, citizens."

"And pie."

"All right, Mrs. Gale. Pie."

"Then what the hell are we doing standing around here? Let's go see the pickup truck drivers."

EIGHT

It was none of them. They put them through a series of lineups of four men each, none of whom were their attacker. On lineup number three, Jeffrey recognized a man, but it was the officious trooper, Officer Fine, dressed for Sunday football watching. No one else made an impression.

Their dinner came from a restaurant called Riccardi's. Baked ziti, garlic bread. They ate between photo arrays.

They gave statements. A detective who was not Gerow asked Jeffrey into a room to take him through his side of the story. He called it an interview room, but it had a one-way mirror on one side and a table that was bolted to the floor. Jeffrey looked at it. "For real?" he said.

The man said "We don't like anything that can be picked up."

Jeffrey immediately found himself imagining what it would be like to sit here being asked these questions if he had committed a crime. Before too long he was starting to feel as though he had. At least the door was open.

As far as he could tell, he told the guy everything. After the first minute, another investigator came in and sat down to listen and take notes. "This is being taped," they told him. He laid it all out.

They were back at the beginning, back again to the first set of statements they'd already given. "We were driving from Poughkeepsie," he said. "Spent the day in Manhattan on Saturday, and we'd taken off Monday so we could see the area up here on a weekday."

They'd stopped in Krumville, had that excellent lunch. Then Bone Hollow Road, the "for sale" sign, Angela's soccer-mom face. He didn't speak about, but did remember, the light through the trees. The way the clearing meant something, and the path down beyond it meant something further. How could he speak about that? No, instead, he told how they'd seen the water down there and the path. Then the bodies.

The two men were polite, patient, conversational. They apologized for covering the same ground again, but explained that, given the new circumstances, anything they could hear might be relevant. They worked like the harrier hawks he'd seen on a David Attenborough special, circling as a pair and diving in to drive him around a fact until it was laid bare and examined from every side. For example:

"Approximately how far from the bodies were you when you saw them?"

"Maybe fifteen feet."

One cop got up and walked away from them, outside the conference room, into the main office, until he was a little way away. "Here?" he said.

"Closer."

"Here."

"Yeah, that seems right."

"Call it twelve feet."

"Okay."

Then the other guy: "now you say you were behind your wife at this time. Did you have a clear view of the bodies?"

"Not at first. She fell on me."

"How'd that happen?"

"When she saw the bodies, she backed up. I was right behind her."

"So she was, what, ten feet from the bodies when she saw them?"

"Uhh, probably more like eleven."

They wrote it down.

They spent a lot of time covering the periods of time when Jeffrey had been on the ground; when Serena fell on him, when he'd been knocked down the next night.

The guy had come at him from behind, and he was backlit against the fire. Then there was the kicking. Jeffrey hadn't, in fact, gotten a good look at his attacker's face, from down on the gravel, the brief flash of the dome light catching the upper part of the bastard's face when he looked down in surprise at getting kicked. He'd been limping when he ran off, Jeffrey now remembered.

Pie, and midnight, arrived during the second half of the interview. They showed Jeffrey a computer application with a library of eyes, hairlines, goatees, noses, asked him to build a face with them. He worked at it; they came up with something, but he wasn't sure. "That's okay," they told him. "No one's ever sure, unless they know the person we're talking about."

They showed them a bunch of different white pickup trucks. They narrowed it down to a big American make based on outline, but they'd been distracted and weren't sure.

The pie was okay. Apple, of course. Not hot, though they offered to microwave it. Jeffrey paced slowly while he answered questions. He explained about the ribs. His split lip hurt too.

The fire inspector was there. Where had they seen the fire first? What had happened? Did they smell anything? Hear anything? Was there an explosion? Had he noticed any odors on his attacker, seen any strange stains on his clothing? How far had the truck been from where they were parked?

There were breaks; he and Serena talked, left voicemails for their bosses, made out a little. They compared notes on the pie. They agreed there was better pie out there. They talked about the cider donuts they'd gotten in Accord, how much better those were.

Gerow came in a couple of times, his long face tired. He had reading glasses he wore down on his nose, taking them off, putting them up on his head, depending what he was doing. He was encouraging, thankful.

Back in the room, they got around to the hospital. They showed him a still image in black and white; a partial facial shot of the "reporter" who'd showed up. He was leaving the ER, looking down at the floor, mid-stride. Jeffrey was pretty sure it was the impostor, yeah. His face he'd recognize for sure, he told them. He'd talked to that guy for a couple of minutes. They built a face on the computer, and it was…okay. Slightly moon-faced. They monkeyed around with it some more, but it was hard to pin down. At some point they decided it was good enough.

"Where's our car?" Jeffery asked them. It was in the parking lot. It had been gone over pretty thoroughly; they could take it with them tonight. "It's a rental," he said. "We were going to have it back today."

They offered to write a note; the rental company would have a form. They'd give him a copy of the statement he was making now.

At some point, it was enough. Gerow brought Serena into the conference room. He handed them their fleeces, gave Serena her corduroy coat. The big deputy from the day before stood nearby.

"Well, folks," Gerow said. "Let me just say I'm sorry about all this, but your help is absolutely vital to what we're doing here. Now, like I said, Deputy Hatch can get you to a hotel out by the Thruway; we can have someone drive out in your car if you want. And we'll have a trooper in the lobby all night, as well."

They went for it. Hatch ("Glenn. Please," he'd said) drove them in the back of a patrol car; they went to a large, well-lit Holiday Inn near the Thruway. A trooper followed in their rented car and another trooper followed that.

The deputy carried their bag to the front desk. They had to pay for the room; the cops didn't have a budget for that kind of thing, apparently. Hatch came up with them, walked the hall, looked around the room, checked out the window. He seemed satisfied.

"I've got four more hours on my shift, so I'll be down the lobby if you need anything."

"Thank you, Glenn," Serena said. He left.

They were alone and it was around two. The room was okay. King bed, gray wallpaper, river scene over the bed. A flat screen TV. Jeffrey lay down.

"Get up," she said. "Teeth. You won't get up if you don't do it now."

He complied. "Fucking teeth," he said. "It's like every day with these things."

In the bathroom Jeffrey was surprised to see his hair hadn't turned white. His eyes were a little bloodshot, sure, what he could see of them under the lids that kept threatening to close. He hadn't shaved since Friday, either. He regarded himself for a few moments.

"I look like shit," he said. She was in the other room, already brushed, changing into boxers and a t-shirt.

"Yep," she said. She came to the doorway, leaned against it. He looked at her, at *the mother of his child*, he thought again. There were gray swoops beneath her eyes and the lids were puffy. She let her head tilt to lie against the doorframe, closed her eyes. "You're still handsome," she told him.

"I love you," he said.

She let a hand rise and reach around for him, not opening her eyes. She got his shoulder and squeezed it. Then she pulled herself forward, wrapped her arms around him with great delicacy, so careful of him. She pressed her length against him, up his left side, leg to leg, her hips against his thigh, belly against his hips, trapping his left arm against his torso, burrowing her face into the spot where his neck met his shoulder.

He worked the toothbrush slowly, watching what it did to his new face, careful not to open his mouth and stretch the wound at his chin.

"My Jeffrey," she said. She paused. "I wanted to kill that fucker."

He stopped brushing. "Oh, hon."

"He hurt you."

"They'll catch him."

"If I'd had a gun, I would have used it."

"Me too," he said. "I thought he was trying to get into the car," he said. "To get you."

"You kicked him."

"Yeah." He smiled. It hurt. He looked at the hurt happening in the mirror.

They went to bed. That vision—bandaged chin under swollen lip, red-rimmed eyes, all framed by a hobo's three-day whiskers—accompanied him to sleep.

NINE

Serena woke up happy, the dream-memory of a tiny hand stroking her hair. Diluted sun shone through the separation in the heavy drapes. She couldn't help a momentary thrill at the thought of another day off.

Jeffrey was snoring lightly. She slipped out of the heavy hotel-covers and padded to the bathroom. Took off her t-shirt and looked at herself in the mirror. Turned sideways. Everything looked the same. She tried to round out her belly, arching her back to help the effect, managed a little pot belly, but it didn't look like anything much, really. Her boobs, she knew, would get bigger, and...painful? She didn't remember from last time. She did remember that her aunt, back in that summer, hadn't seemed out of sorts at all, except over her boyfriend, whose eventual proposal had filled the whole family with relief.

The memory of the pregnancy test—of this one. She had a shot of it on her cell phone, blue line blurred. Retrieving her cell from the dresser top, she took another look, shaking her head. Seemed like another world, that blue line. Her memory of the day she'd done the test was fading, and little had changed for her physically.

She'd done it at work, assuming she was going to throw out the results, but when it came up positive she suddenly wanted to hang on to it. She compromised by taking a picture and throwing away the plastic. She'd sent the image to Jeffrey's cell but called him at work before he'd had a chance to look at it.

"You sitting down?" she'd said.

"You pregnant?"

"Look at your phone," she said. He looked.

"I guess I'll be having some champagne tonight," he said. "Should I get you some fizzy apple cider?"

She sent the image to her mother, to her sister, and to Ellen, with text saying "Shhh." They called, there was cooing.

After work, bursting bursting, she and Jeffrey met at the Astor Place subway stop to go home, and held one another. They made out a little. She could smell everything—him, the crisp air of September, coffee.

He gestured at the big book shop around the corner. "Should we get some books?"

"Not yet," she said. "I don't want to read about what I'm supposed to worry about."

"You've got nothing to worry about," he said. They went back to Brooklyn, and it was on that ride that she started to notice things. It started with the train floor—something she'd looked at thousands of times in her five years in the city. It wasn't that it was dirty, because it was dirty, but not as filthy as she might have thought. It was that she could feel her feet shrinking away from it inside her shoes. In the corners there were viscous, gray deposits, accumulated goo that no amount of pressure washing could dislodge. She had to force herself to grasp the pole for balance as their train—the train packed to the gills with people from every corner of the world—swung into the 7th Avenue station. And those people! And Flatbush Avenue! She grabbed Jeffrey's hand. He squeezed. She looked at him. His eyes were shining. He leaned in. "I know this will sound stupid," he said as they walked along. "But I'm proud of you."

Here she was, upstate, just three weeks later. They'd always talked about a country place, and those searches on realty sites and up in the Berkshires and the Litchfield Hills had been indulgences in fantasy—it wasn't as though they had the money to buy a place and keep their apartment. But something about this latest journey had really begun to sink in. It was that summer she remembered, she guessed. There was a pull here.

She looked back at her phone. The blue line was still there, although blurry. So her breasts didn't hurt and hadn't gotten bigger. She hadn't gotten sick from the subway in the last couple of weeks. She was taking a daily horse-pill multivitamin her doctor had prescribed. Her doctor. "Anything bothering you this week?" she would ask at her next appointment. "Actually, doc, yeah. You see, I found a couple of dead bodies up in Bunglefuck and then we surprised the murderer setting fire to a nearby house, and now there's some kind of gang stalking us."

She smiled. That little hand stroking her hair, that had seemed awfully real. More real than the impostor reporter touching her hand in sympathy. More real than the house that had burned down.

A little flutter of nausea made itself known, but it seemed like nerves more than anything else. She took a quick shower, threw on jeans and the same t-shirt and made the hotel coffee packets, opting for volume by doing both the caff and decaf. Jeffrey woke up to the smell of it.

"Home today?" he said.

"Yeah. I'd say we've outstayed our welcome."

He stretched, angled his head down to peer at his ribs. The bruise was big. Fortunately it wasn't foot-shaped. He felt stiff, but it would only hurt if actively pressed, or if he twisted or jostled. "You thought we were welcome?" he said, and patted the bed.

She sat, and Jeffrey petted her with his eyes closed. He parted his fingers and slid them into her hair against her scalp, then gently made a fist of a handful of hair, a gentle squeeze. Her own eyes closed and she tilted her head back. Her lips parted. He did it again. She leaned down to kiss him, conscious of his cut, then lay beside him and put her jeans-clad leg over his hips. She ran her hand over his torso, along his neck, rubbed the bristles on his cheeks. They kissed again, and he pulled her t-shirt out of the waistline of her jeans and soon enough her jeans were beside the bed and it was after eleven.

"Good thing we had that pie," Jeffrey said from the shower. "I'm starving."

They packed their bag and went downstairs to eat something. A pass through the lobby revealed a state police cruiser parked just to the side of the front entrance, a wide-brimmed Stetson hat visible inside. They waved, he waved back.

The food was lunch, but that was okay, and they ate wraps and fries, checked out, walked outside and stopped off at the trooper's car.

Jeffery leaned in. "Hi there," he said. "I'm Jeffrey Gale. This is my wife Serena."

"How you folks doing today?" said the cop, eyeing Jeffrey's chin. "Everything all right?"

"Yeah, we're okay. We just checked out, and we're planning to drive down to Poughkeepsie and take a train back to the city. Detective Gerow said he was going to make some calls?"

"Yep, the Investigator asked me to tell you that he's been in touch with the precinct house in your neighborhood and that you should check in there with a Sergeant Bunting."

"Okay, great."

"I'll tag along to make sure no one follows directly after you. Do you need to make any other stops?"

"No, we're good."

"Okay then. Investigator Gerow also said that if you think of anything you forgot to tell us, to call him right away. And if you feel threatened in any way, under any circumstances, call 911."

"Right."

"Okay, and last thing. He said to tell you that there are still plenty of desirable properties in the area that he bet Ms. LaPorta'd be glad to show you."

They thanked the officer, got into the rental, which seemed no worse for the wear of having been swabbed and dusted for prints. There was no fabric missing from the seats, no signs of struggle, nothing to indicate that Jeffrey had cut open his chin on top of the door frame. Nope, it was still peppy, they were back in their fleece, with faces pointed toward home.

Jeffrey faced backward as they neared the highway. The entrance ramp was a single lane leading to two toll booths, and as they pulled in the police car behind them turned on its lights and slowed to a crawl. He watched, but all that happened was that the line of cars behind the police car stopped, too. He watched the scene as they pulled through the booths, entered the southbound lanes, twisting his neck as they wended around a cloverleaf, and kept his eyes on the flashing lights until they were out of sight behind them.

"Home," he said. "We'll call the place and ask where to drop it off, pay the extra."

"It's kind of nice having a car, isn't it?" she said.

"Yeah," he said. She looked good driving, he thought, and felt for the lever to tilt his seat back.

He'd noticed this before, coming back from the Jersey shore, or a couple of times from trips out to the North Fork or the Hamptons. On the way out, the men drove. On the way back, on the Sundays, it was the women driving, and the men reclined their seats and shut their eyes. Men drank too much.

On a Tuesday, though, it was mostly trucks.

TEN

Killing the minister and the redneck had been nothing compared to posing as the reporter, Baker reflected, cutting between striated hills on a two-lane road, driving into a Pocono sunset. That had been hard. That had taken balls, he thought. And going back to work on Tuesday had taken balls, too. He had no doubt that someone would point him out, say something, put something together.

It had hit him pretty hard in a bathroom stall an hour after lunch. He dropped his wool suit trousers and sat down and was overcome with an expectation that the door was going to get kicked in, hitting him in the knee, and four cops in riot gear were going to pile in. It seemed real. He clenched, powerless to get up, watching the door, imagining pairs of thick-soled combat boots gathering along the bottom of the flimsy partition, picturing the point man doing one of those Hollywood countdowns, wrapping five fingers into a fist and giving the go sign.

It didn't happen. He moved on, but the SWAT team dogged him the rest of the day. It hit him again picking up coffee at a gas station about a mile from the office. His fear wasn't about the murders. It was about the impersonation. He knew that didn't make sense—he wasn't going to jail for pretending to be a reporter—but doing it like that, walking into that hospital, with the cops around, unarmed, nothing but a tape recorder and a couple of questions. Fucking *cojones*, man. He hit the steering wheel and grinned. A day later and he could still call up the adrenaline.

Don Baker's job consisted largely of being seen only when it made sense to be seen. He made it a core principle of his job not to exist unless it was to do business. He was on the payroll, sure, and he got the benefits, and he had two places to live. He even carried the corporate credit card. He was legit. But with so many gray areas in his unwritten job description, it didn't pay to leave a trail. He liked to move soundlessly across the information landscape. Hated toll booths. Didn't like cell phones.

There'd been too many times when a straight-ahead job had swerved, just a bit, into slightly unethical territory, and he'd wished his name hadn't been on the hotel registry. But those had been small-scale things, nothing anyone would ever care about, much less look into. A payoff here, a planted memo there. Despite a little unease here and there, he'd just gone ahead and done them. But as time got on, he began to do more of his legitimate work on the sly. Encrypted his emails. Logged into the work system from libraries. Borrowed wireless. Kept his conversations short. Stocked up on pre-paid cards. Amassed cash.

The wheel slipped between his fingers, long drawn-out S-curves in the Pennsylvania back country, the sun sinking lower ahead.

He hadn't even known he was preparing, but when the time came that Baker had really had to do something very, very illegal, it had seemed...natural. Top of the hill, sighting down, the redneck had brought the guy right where he told him to. There was open space at the edge of the pond, so he knew he'd have a shot. The two sessions at an Ohio shooting range, the separate cash purchases of the scope, then six months later the rifle, used, from a hunter in Vermont. All that was tight. Pulling the trigger? Almost nothing. It was necessary, and he was at peace with himself over that.

But pretending to be Oscar Gilbert, fuck. That was a gamble. It disquieted him a little, because on the drive east to Kingston, he'd worked up a cover. He had meant to say he was from the *Record*, and he meant to say his name was Carl Jones, and instead he'd blurted the *Caller-Dispatch* because it was on his mind. And when that clean, good-looking girl, that Mrs. Gale, had asked his name, the Carl Jones cover disappeared and Gilbert's fucking face popped up in his mind and it was nothing to smile and say the guy's name and ask his reporter questions, nothing to defend himself with but the smile and the recorder. If one of them had known Gilbert. If a cop had been there. Well, he'd waited till the one cop walked out, then moved. But he could've come back. Risky. Crazy.

Crazy like a fucking fox, he thought again, the grin returning.

He'd walked out with more than the recorder, of course. He got that couple's cell numbers. In another day he'd have their address, their jobs, families. He didn't know what he'd need, yet. They didn't know anything. They weren't likely to be trouble. 'Course they could ID that *other* asshole, that panicky weak sister, but he wouldn't be around long enough to implicate Baker.

He hadn't walked out. Run out, really. He'd walked calmly through the hospital then jogged around the corner and up the street to his spot. His car was unticketed. He checked his watch as he ran and held his cell phone to his ear, laughing good-naturedly. He made sure to say "Okay, okay, I'll be there! I'm on my way there right now," with a laugh. Pure method acting!

No idea if anyone was around to hear him. He was just a guy heading out to meet a friend for a drink, or going home to his wife.

Then boom, straight away from the hospital, not dumb enough to pass the front doors, not fast enough to attract attention, no camera pointed at his car. He'd kept his face down in the hallways, hadn't spoken to anyone in the place, tried to look like a sad relative when anyone caught his eye. He knew he wasn't a rock star, knew his face wasn't going to make any calendars. He'd used that before—it was partly how he'd gotten where he'd gotten—but he'd never used it so directly. Sometimes he'd had to avoid notice in a general way, but he'd never had to evade a lineup or a wanted poster. He had driven east out of Kingston, crossed the bridge over the Hudson, then gone south on country roads till he crossed the other way, going west on I-84, no toll booth this way. Switched off that onto route 17 outside Middletown, then did it again a while later to go south on 81 into Pennsylvania. No pictures, no tolls after that first bridge.

This was new territory for Baker, but he was digging it. He was *into* it. He could fucking do this. Driving again, now after his first day back at work, he pulled up to a yield sign at a fork. No one behind him. He tilted the driver's side visor down a little and flipped up the cosmetics mirror cover. Somehow when you did this kind of thing, saw yourself as a badass, you couldn't *not* do a Clint Eastwood squint. He did that. Watery blue eyes, baby smooth face, but he forced a couple of crow's feet to appear. He tightened his lips. Thought about Gilbert.

Soon. Cautiously, slowly, but soon.

He got where he was going, a bar in a town called Rundee up in the coal mining hills of central Pennsylvania. Twenty-five miles from where he lived. Rundee had its very own traffic light and this bar, called the Rundee Pub. There was a convenience store where two state roads met. The bar had a pay phone that worked, near the bathrooms. Baker bought a half-pint of lager, left it on the bar a couple stools away from the only other patron, a rumpled guy in a feed cap he'd seen there on his last visit, and went back there with a pocket full of quarters. He dialed a cell number.

"What?" That thick-sounding voice.

"It's me. Did those friends of ours catch up with you?"

"They ain't gonna find me. I hid the truck. I don't use my real phone. You, they might find. Me, no."

"Well, if you aren't ready to get together with them, you're not ready. That's cool. So, listen, I was wondering. I know you introduced yourself to that young couple. What was that?"

"I didn't *introduce* myself to anyone. The fuck you talking about?" He was breathing heavy, as though exerting himself.

Baker sighed. "I mean you made contact. Did they have something you wanted?"

"I came out of that job I was doing—for YOU—and they were standing there. The chick saw me before I realized there was anybody there. I thought the guy might go for me. He was turning around, so I clocked him and got out of there."

"You'll be happy to know I chatted with them." This was it. There was one person alive that Baker could tell this to. He wanted a reaction.

"How?"

"After you introduced yourself, the husband thought he might want to talk to medical professionals."

"What? That pussy. I didn't even hit him hard. He fuckin' nearly broke my knee, though."

"Yes. Well, while they were there, I walked in and just asked them a few questions."

"Are you fuckin crazy? The cops?"

"Yes, some of our friends were there too."

"What'd you do, put on scrubs or some shit?"

"Something like that," he said.

"Fucking crazy, man. What'd they tell you?"

He'd gotten a reaction, but the whole thing was wasted on this asshole.

"They thought you were handsome. When you checked out their car, they had a few moments to make an impression. They also admired your ride, but they didn't remember what kind it was."

"Sounds like I'm still clear," he said.

"I think you might want to keep off the roads in that ride of yours; it's a deathtrap. And you might want to avoid the post office."

"Yeah, yeah, I got another car, I ain't stupid." His breathing sounded like he was walking.

"I'll leave that one alone. Where are you?"

"Fuck that. Someplace comfortable, someplace where 'our friends' don't hang out."

"All right, I don't want to know anyway."

"I figure you and me got just one last thing to talk about."

"Yes, that's right. I've got the candy you asked for. Where do you want me to ship it?"

"I got a place. It's a hotel."

"Okay, that's fine. Where?"

"Arkville. You know it?"

"No, but I'll find it. What hotel?"

"It's not in the phone book. But you go there and you ask for the hotel, they'll let you know. It's abandoned. Called Schlesingers." He had trouble saying the name, Baker noted. *Slessinners.*

"Why there?"

" 'Cause no one goes there. Been shut for twenty years, half of it burned down five years ago. Jew lightning. You can get in easy, and you can leave it in a bag under the counter, and it'll get picked up and we're done."

"Sorry, what was that? *Jew* lightning?"

"Yeah, it's an act uh God. The heat from two insurance policies rubbing together." He sounded like he'd stopped walking.

Baker smiled at the irony—the arsonist as judge of others' crimes.

"Okay. Schlesingers it is. Sunday, it'll be there in the morning. I don't want to see you."

"B'lieve me, you an me both."

"Well don't let's get personal. We're partners, after all. I just think it'd be wiser not to hang around together."

"We're done after this."

"You don't want any more work? I mean, there might not be any, but you do *such* a good job."

"I know how you like to pay. I know how you paid the last guy."

"He gave me reason to distrust him. You haven't done that."

"And I ain't gonna. Slessiners, Sunday morning. It'll get picked up sometime after noon."

"Okay, fine."

"You can trust me, but I don't trust you. So lemme tell you this," the thick voice said.

"Yeah?"

"I know your name. I know your license number. I get mine and I lose that information. Something happens to me, or I don't get my—what'd you say, my candy?—they get found."

"See, now? That's not how partners talk."

"Was that last guy your partner?"

"I thought so."

"Well, he probly did too. See ya never."

The cell clicked off. Baker went back to the bar, said something about the Steelers to the rumpled old guy down the bar, got a laugh. Drinking his beer, he caught his face in the barback mirror over the whiskies. He gave it the Clint. A badass. In an inconspicuous mid-priced suit.

The bartender and the old guy watched him leave, and the old guy said "that little fat guy thinks he's hot shit, huh?"

They both laughed.

ELEVEN

For a week, Gerow worked phones, went door to door. His bosses let him keep the investigation, which was at its heart still a murder case. He assigned an investigator under him to liaise with the fire investigators. He had a Sheriff's homicide detective working with him, Deputy Hatch had been assigned to support—just so the county could keep its hand in—and there were four other state guys. Troopers backed them up.

Finding the minister's body made a stir with the local sheriffs investigating that one out in Pennsylvania, and a team came out from there and looked at the body and notified the minister's only family—a sister in Reading. Now it was a double murder, everyone's boss got on the phone with everyone else and they made nice and agreed to share.

They sat down with Gerow and his detectives. They brought the files and took him through the case. They had piles of evidence. Some of it hadn't been revealed before.

Everyone's heads bent over the big table in the conference room. Stuff started to go on whiteboards, up on the wall. One of the detectives was keeping a spreadsheet cataloguing witnesses, victim's known associates, statements, license numbers, locations, times, dates.

The arson, and the impostor at the hospital, changed things. This was a conspiracy. Two different suspects, one at the house, one at the hospital. Two victims. You had four guys now. It started not to look like a Pennsylvania thing. It started to look like something they hadn't seen before. Drugs started to suggest themselves. Drug networks spanned states and had multiple players. What else?

The guy was a minister? They asked.

The sheriff's guys looked a little uncomfortable. "Yeah, that's right."

"Anything there?"

"What do you mean?"

Gerow said it. "Boys? Girls? Women? Men?"

"You ask that after you ask if he's a minister?" one of the sheriff's guys said.

Gerow said "Seems like you throw a rock in a seminary, you hit a pedophile. Just asking."

They produced a file. Nineteen-eighty eight, James Peterson had been named in a sex harassment suit. He'd been an executive at Anthrol National in the eighties, a PA coal company. Had a fling with a female junior member of staff and tried to keep it going after she was done with him. Made things tough for her, bad enough that she eventually got her father the lawyer from the big Denver firm involved. Anthrol caved, paid a settlement, fired Peterson. The woman took the money and quit, her final gift a memo revealing that the company's much-touted new longwall cutter for anthracite, supposedly a promising development that had briefly raised the company's stock and implied a comeback for anthracite mining in select areas, was a complete dud.

Peterson had started a franchise of a knife-selling business—one of those pyramid-type things—that didn't last. Got more involved in his Lutheran church. Did pharma company sales. That lasted a little longer. He moved out of his house and into an apartment over a shut-down store on the main street in Messerbergh.

Mid-90s, he got a minister's card out of the back of a magazine, rented the downstairs storefront and put up a nylon banner that said "New Community Church." There was a flier explaining its mission of "spiritual fellowship and good deeds." He seemed to have enough money saved up from his pharmaceutical job to keep it open. He recruited a few congregants from his former church. A few more dropped in. Their schtick was to visit former coal workers who'd stayed after nearly everything had shut down, and they'd help them do yardwork. Raked leaves, clipped hedges, mowed lawns, shoveled snow. The aged recipients of this assistance would stop by the church on their way to the drugstore, drop a little of their social security, meager pensions. Their kids, those who'd stayed, would call him and thank him, send a check now and then. In 2003 he'd moved the operation to an actual rented church, formerly Methodist and now empty.

By all accounts, the church and its minister had been well-regarded. They got in some watered-down bibles, had some books on Buddhism, encouraged people to speak out like the Quakers. Peterson preached, but he wasn't a firebrand. Cobbled together his services out of traditional ones he found on the internet, plus some Khalil Gibran, Apache wedding blessings, Richard Bach, St. Exupery. They didn't do communion. He presided over a couple of weddings; there wasn't a lot of that kind of thing going on out there. When he disappeared the church and he were in the black, pulling down around thirty-six thousand a year. A lot less than Anthrol or the pharmaceutical company had paid, but the guy seemed to've truly taken to it. They hadn't turned up anything wrong in the finances or anywhere else.

"Any more trouble with women?"

"No, no more trouble. We talked to two women who'd dated him; the last relationship broke up in '05 when she moved for work and he didn't want to come because of his flock. We didn't find anyone who said they had anything going with him when he died. We found a fairly normal porn stash. Straight. Some magazines, some movies. We wondered the same as you, but nothing turned up."

"Any enemies?"

"The Lutheran minister never forgave him for siphoning those first few customers, but he wasn't exactly rabid about it. Wanted to welcome him back. I think Peterson liked the leadership action too much to think about it. We talked to the former employers at the pharma company. He was an okay employee, made enough in sales to keep his job and pay a mortgage. We talked to the harassment victim. She's in San Francisco, working for Pacific Gas & Electric, hasn't thought about Anthrol or him in years, she told us."

"Anyone in the congregation draw suspicion?"

"A couple struck us as a little off. There's a state prison about fifteen miles away and once in a while a former inmate takes up residence. In fact, the church was actively helping out three guys who lived in a group home in the next town over. AA ran a meeting there, and these guys were in that. They're big participants in the raking. There was nothing to indicate recidivism; they were druggies, all seemed clean. Though you never know what someone gets into, inside."

"All those inmates accounted for?"

"Former inmates, yes, they've basically been around town for the last month, the congregation confirmed it—course they can't account for every minute, but none of these guys mentioned any out of state travel or anything. Two of the church members who had keys have been running the show over there, keeping the lights on. Congregation chipped in to pay the November rent."

"How long's the drive from there to here?"

"About four hours each way."

They moved on. They were still a negative on the other body, the floater. No dental match, no print match—although getting a print hadn't been easy. The toe prints had been better, although the boots had split and filled with water and algae, and that had been hell on the skin. The PA sheriff's guys looked at the photos, couldn't draw anything from them.

The killing had happened at the site. The shooter had fired from a higher elevation—one of the two small hills that flanked the pond on the southwest side. They didn't find anything up there, but the trajectory of the bullets matched. They recovered the bullets. Thirty-thirty deer rifle. No match to anything in their databases. They shared the ballistics reports with the PA guys.

They'd been dead for about three weeks when found. Peterson had last been seen October 6. His car wasn't found in Messerbergh, nor at any of the train or bus stations in a thirty miles radius, and the state troopers hadn't found it anywhere either. Records showed it at a toll plaza on the Pennsylvania Turnpike east of Messerbergh, but they hadn't turned up any other records.

"'East of Messerbergh' leaves a whole lot of territory to cover," said one of the PA detectives.

They switched from the murder to the aftermath. The sheriff's guys from PA wanted to know what about the couple from Brooklyn?

"Nice kids," Gerow told them. "No sign they had had anything to do with the murders or with the arson. We sniffed the car, no sign of accelerant. They had an alibi until about fifteen minutes before it started, and that was about the travel time they'd've needed to get there."

"What's the alibi?"

"They were in Accord, at the police station with me, and driving around with a realtor looking at houses."

"That's right, you said they were house-hunting. Guess that hasn't worked out. Where are they now?"

"Back to Brooklyn."

He told them the fire was started inside using gas rags in the living room. Entry gained through a broken back window on the back door. Tracks inconclusive; they overlay the prints of the evidence team. Those guys had photographed and preserved everything when they arrived, but they muddied up the yard and they were unsuccessful at isolating the new set of lug soles. Firebug might've had the same make as one of the evidence guys; they were all wearing brand name boots.

They talked through the fire, then it came back to the couple, to the attack.

"You're sure they're clean?"

"I know, it's weird. You look at the bodies, then the arson, then the attack, and then we haven't even touched on this, they say they had a guy come in to the hospital while I was right outside the ER, and impersonate a local reporter. He drills them for information and does a runner."

"Holy shit. Did that really happen?"

"They're not from here, but they gave a real reporter's name. Sure, they could have picked it up off the Internet, I guess. But then the real reporter—a guy I know—comes in a minute later and they don't blink. Then he introduces himself. They freak. They say a guy was just here claiming to be this reporter. Why would they make that up?"

"Why would they burn the house down?"

"She said something about insurance, but that was about rebuilding, not in connection with them buying."

"Insurance. But they didn't—"

"Right, they don't own the place. Their story makes sense, I think, but it says things about the case. They say they came up house-hunting, happened across a place with a for sale sign, saw the pond and went down there, saw the bodies. Next day on their way out of town they swung by a last time—they liked the house, see—but it's just in time to see it go up. Then they get jumped and the guy runs off. We take them to the hospital, and some guy claiming to be a reporter asks them questions."

"Same guy?"

"They say definitely not."

"You don't see them as being involved in any of it?"

"I don't see why, much less how."

"Okay. What about the impostor?"

"Unknown. We got shots of a guy walking the hospital, but he passes out of range of the last camera on the parking garage right after he leaves. No other sign of him. Don't know what car he had or anything. Face is unclear in the footage. The couple says they'd ID him for sure if they saw him again."

Gerow's phone rang. He checked the screen: a New York number, not one in his contacts. He bumped it to voicemail.

He leaned back. "So?" he said.

"Were they killed at the same time?" asked one of the deputies.

That sparked another round of discussion. Seemed unlikely they'd've been there at different times. Had the second one found the first dead while the shooter was still up on that hill, then been killed as a witness? You'd have a shooter lounging on the hill aiming down at the pond just waiting for whomever came along. Interesting theory.

How'd they get there, even?

On the back side of the hills were more birches, maples, oaks, a gentler slope down to a road about a quarter-mile distant. Lots of deer trails, some unofficial but obviously human-trod hiking paths. From the shooter's probable position on the southerly hilltop you had a view of the little mud beach at the pond, but you'd have to be looking. Shooter had to've had a scope. Even with it, ballistics had found two more bullet strikes in the soil of the water's edge. Probably more in the pond muck at the bottom, but they didn't have a metal detector that'd work under water and the bottom was all sticks, mud, pine needle litter. The water was so tannic it had stained the floater's skin brown.

They sat for hours, drawing pictures, creating lines from event to event, question marks around the floater, around the arsonist, around the impostor. The case was looking big, but they had so little. They'd gone up and down Bone Hollow Road knocking on the doors of the widely-spaced houses. Only a couple of those were occupied year-round. Of the ten houses on the road, most were vacation homes. The owners of the two that had been occupied hadn't heard anything unusual. Gunshots? Yeah, they'd heard gunshots. What day? Oh, most days. More on weekends. Back in October, say week of the fifth? Yes, definitely. What day? Most days that week. Deer season was still about three weeks away, but you had turkey hunters now.

They'd called the owners of the house, three children of the deceased mother. They were dealing with insurance now. Two of them were planning to come up this coming Friday; the other was in Seattle and hadn't returned the cops' calls yet. They were all alibied up; hadn't been up near the house in months, could account for practically all of their time for the past month—at least chunks of most days. Work, home, social lives. The cops asked would they please do that.

The fire department's investigators and the police evidence guys had gone back into the burned house, tagging, sampling. Between the fire and the water, a lot of stuff was gone. If there'd been paper evidence somewhere in there, it was gone. They dug under the foundation. They had a team there now doing demo on the remaining sheetrock and paneling, pulling up remaining floorboards. The second floor was a wreck you couldn't walk into; the county had loaned a cherry picker and they were using that to angle into the upstairs rooms and dig around.

Gerow's phone rang. Area code 610. It joined the others in voicemail. He'd given out his number to the investigating teams and was gathering leads through the message box when callers were passed on to him.

They'd gone over the evidence photos and reports from inside the house many times. Two predominant sets of prints in the house, but there were a few more pairs. No matches. Owners, occupants, realtors, prospective customers. The former owner was the mother, she was dead, not a suspect.

Angela LaPorta had given them a list of about a dozen prospects who'd come to look at the house. Detectives were calling them this week, had a couple of hits. Some were from the area and had agreed to be interviewed. Couple were dead numbers.

They had a field trip out to the location; everyone trooped down through the clearing to the water. They sighted up to the shooter's location. Others went up that way, scanning the ground for shell casings, cigarette butts, anything missed by the evidence guys. You couldn't see the house from atop the hills.

Gerow thought about what he'd said to Serena Gale. Shoe leather. Door knocks. Computer hard drives. They were generating paper, electronic files. The database was getting fat; their guy could sort the thing by any number of fields. You could tag each player, every witness, with keywords and view a list by keyword.

They kept at it.

TWELVE

Their black ink cartridge had been out, but Jeffrey went to the office supply store on Flatbush, and they'd printed out everything they could find. Serena put down the final sheet. "Not much," she said.

Jeffrey put down the page he was holding and picked up the last one. "Nah, not that much. What are we hoping to do with this stuff, again?"

It was a short stack of pages. It was Wednesday night. The day had been surreal.

They'd gotten home at three the day before. The rental agency had told them to drop the car on 7th Avenue by the natural-foods grocery. It was ten degrees warmer here. Strollers everywhere. They got Thai. Saw the neighborhood regulars. They ate tom kha gai and curry and dumplings. They walked home full and tired. They had called the police as instructed, let the detective know they were home. They entered their block on Carlton, and as they turned off Prospect it got quieter. There was a police car across from their building. They crossed the street and stopped a couple feet from the car window. There was a woman uniformed cop there, on her cell. She rolled down her window.

"We're the Gales," said Serena. "We spoke to Sergeant Bunting at the precinct."

The officer—nameplate Diaz—nodded and spoke into her phone.

"Walk us in?" Jeffrey said.

"Ooh, yeah, good idea," said Serena.

Diaz agreed, radioed that in too, took a radio unit on her belt along with the panoply of gear. The belt sat low and Officer Diaz was short, but she had hips that could take it. She followed them.

Serena opened the downstairs door, a Medco lock and the older, lower lock with its scratched and aged brass. Jeffrey had the bag and Serena's purse.

Diaz's gear was a bit of an orchestra as they entered the spacious tiled lobby. It was grand in size, but empty of adornment. Her gum chewing and jingling echoed. "What floor are you on?" she said. *What flaw yon?*

"Third," Jeffrey told her. The elevator was there. It was slow; you hit the button and it considered your request. Its every move, from the sliding open or shut of the door to its eventual ascent or descent, gave the impression of grudging acquiescence.

The elevator opened at the top of the stairs with their brown-painted iron railing; they went for the brown-painted door on the left. It was shut. Sounds of television came from behind the right-hand door. A door closed on the fourth floor. Nothing was changed.

Serena unlocked it. She turned to Diaz. "You first?"

Diaz rolled her eyes, opened the door and saw the light switch. She flipped it. The light went on. She opened the door the rest of the way and walked in. They followed.

She turned. "Everything look okay?"

It didn't, but nothing had changed. It looked small. The air was still. The ceilings were high; way high. The room they were in was big, and a hallway went back to a kitchen and a bedroom. Bathroom was off the hallway. There was an old light fixture on the ceiling.

"Yeah," Serena said.

Their stuff was here, and it looked somehow shabby. Particle-board chic. There wasn't a good window in this room, just one out on the air shaft. Bit of a bummer, but the bedroom and kitchen had windows that looked over the street and across the alley to the next building.

Jeffrey placed their duffel on the floor and walked back to the bedroom. He called out as he entered the hallway "would you like some tea, officer Diaz?"

"No thank you," she said. "You guys okay? We're going to have people come by periodically outside. You can call the station and ask for Sergeant Bunting any time you have a question, but remember to call"—*cawl*, she said it—"911 if you see anything out of the ordinary. Then call the precinct directly."

"That's great," Jeffrey said. He poured water in the kettle, turned on the stove, and came back into the living room. "Thank you very much."

There were no messages on their answering machine. Diaz walked through the rooms once with them and said "don't worry about anything." She left.

"Feels like a Sunday," Serena said. Jeffrey gave her tea. "See?" she said. "Tea." She put it on the coffee table. Hex-head screws held it together.

He laughed, sat next to her on the couch. The couch wasn't disposable, at least.

"Bedbugs," she said.

"What?"

"Bedbugs. It's a scourge. The city's lousy with 'em."

He understood. She was going someplace in her mind, the way she sometimes did. His job was to keep up, help her work it through. Advocate for the devil. "Okay, but Thai food."

"Sure, Thai. But apple cider donuts."

"Touché."

"Can you fucking believe we have to go to work tomorrow?" she said.

"I have a doctor's note," he said.

"Does it still hurt?"

He touched the place he'd been kicked, seeing how much it could take. "Not as much. Definitely don't want to get elbowed on the subway."

"What do you think?" she said. "Is it like the Mafia or something?"

"The Mafia? Why?"

"Well, there's so many of them. At least a couple. But they got a guy into the hospital. How'd they do that?"

"I don't know."

Serena leaned her head back. The lack of outside light was bugging her. "Shit," she said.

He sipped tea. He looked at mail from Saturday and Monday. "What, honey."

"Names, Jeffrey," she said. "Names."

He dropped the mail, leaned back and closed his eyes, resting the tea on his knee. "Never name your kids on a Sunday," he said. "It's as important as never go shopping hungry. Look what happened to the Addams Family."

"It's Tuesday. Most productive day of the week."

"Even worse. What's the most creative day of the week that's still respectful of tradition?"

"I don't know. Charlesday?"

"Almasday?" he said.

"Idaday?"

He saw a pun float by, grabbed it. "If I'd a day for every shitty name I thought of, I'd have a whole year."

She laughed for a second, then sighed. Then said "First things first. What the fuck are we going to do?"

"About which thing? We have lots of things going right now. Should we be making lists?"

"Broad categories."

"One," he said. "Baby. Two. Moving. Three. Murderers on the loose."

"Wait. *Two* is moving, and *three* is marauding killers?"

"Well, we are planning to move, right?"

"Yeah, but—" she said. She could feel her mind getting ready to race. It wasn't *racing*, no, but it was getting in gear. She shifted on the couch.

He turned to look at her directly. "And we're not planning to bother those murderers, right?" he said.

"Define bother. We might spot one in a photo ID, or testify against the guy who knocked you down." She traced the cut on his lower lip with a gentle finger.

"It's not like we can tell the cops anything. They'd have to have their eyes on the person first, *then* they call us. If they have one in a lineup or a photo array and just need us for ID, dude is already on the list. And we can't put them there. Logically, there's very little reason for anyone to care about us."

"I guess." She looked around the apartment from where they sat on the couch. She let her eyes unfocus a little, and felt something crystallize in her thoughts. *Steer into fear*, she thought.

She said, "It seems to me that if we're right—if it's down to the baby, the moving, and the murderers—there's only one of the three we can do anything about in the short term."

"Agreed," he said. "So what do you want to do? We can look at Realtor.com or call Angela LaPorta."

"I was thinking we could go to that town where the Reverend was from."

"Serena." He set down his tea cup. "That doesn't make any sense at all."

"Why not?"

"Because we're not cops. Can we have a process check? I thought we just agreed we weren't going to bother the criminals. What's the goal? To get killed?"

"Payback," she said.

"Payback? For this?" He pointed to his chin.

"Partly." She got up and walked around the edges of the rug. She navigated the two armchairs, the flatscreen TV, the plywood-housed component stack. A silver lamp on a long stalk that leaned out over one of the chairs.

"And what else?"

"They burned down the house."

"It wasn't ours."

"It could have been. It could still be."

"What could still be?"

"That spot. With a house on it. Maybe that house." She had her back to him, standing before a bookcase loaded with Penguin classics and their old college texts. She turned her head over one shoulder, looked back at him. Slowly wiggled her hips, gave a little ladylike leer. "The path," she said. "The pond," she said.

He remembered. The way the light had entered that clearing.
You couldn't burn that down. You couldn't kill that, he thought.

. . .

They watched some TV. He opened a beer. She went to bed
early. Jeffrey called his mother, told her some of it. She told them
to come out and stay at their place. He declined. By the time they
got off the phone, it seemed like their apartment again. But he
checked the lock three times. Flipped the anti-push bar. Checked
the window lock in the kitchen where the fire escape was.

His second beer brought him to Letterman's opening
monologue. Dave talked, Jeffrey remembered running up the
path away from the pond. He thought about what Serena had
said, about calling the dead guy's sister. He couldn't see it.
What would that accomplish? He picked up the papers again.

It hadn't been that hard to find the owners' names. Just enter
the address into the Ulster County tax map database, click the
tax lot number, and there it was. Harrison. Siblings, Angela had
said. The mother died.

Maybe Serena would compromise. Tracking down the
homeowners was just savvy shopping, wasn't it?

Unless that would piss off the killers. He thought about
that for a couple of minutes. If the owners of the house were
involved, and they called? The place had been on the market
for months—over the whole summer realty season. They were
holding out for a decent price. Maybe they were just holding out
for a real offer. And now, with nothing there, what could they
possibly be holding out for?

Of course, calling one of the owners might mean that the
cops would hear about it. That wouldn't do. Gerow seemed

like a sharp guy and a good guy. He treated them well, but he didn't seem very patient. Jeffrey thought they'd narrowly missed falling under suspicion a couple of times. Something in the detective's eyes.

What would it mean to be a suspect? Beer number three helped him picture it. It felt a lot like he felt right now, unable to go to sleep because he knew someone was going to kick the door in or break the window and off him. He'd read *Crime and Punishment* in college. Didn't remember most of it, but he had the gist. So what was this? *Innocence and Paranoia*? What did you call it when you hadn't done the crime, but the person who did thought you could hurt them? And wanted to hurt you? Whatever it was, he didn't like it.

It was an old schoolyard terror. Kevin Weiss waiting for him by the fence, fifth grade. There had been shoving at recess, and threats in the hallway going back to class. It outlined the rest of the day in a bright framework of fear. It rose to near panic a couple of times. If someone had asked him what he was afraid of—but no one had, his friends giving him sympathetic looks— he would have said "getting beaten up." But it wasn't that, as much as it was just the waiting. Being trapped. This was Kevin's game now, and Jeffrey wasn't running the show.

But a plan formed, one he knew wouldn't work, and he was first one out of class at the bell. He turned right, heading toward the exit that let onto the bus lot, instead of his usual left out to the sidewalk and the half-mile to home. Kevin would be waiting for him there.

Brendan Fitzpatrick and Frankie Rosetti followed him, and more of Kevin's friends fell in around them, and they sent one of them to get him. So when Jeffrey came out, the Italian and Irish kids in their Jets shirts were arrayed around among the lines of kids piling into buses. They talked comically tough and herded him, until he was facing Kevin over there by the fence.

After that it had been easy. They shoved him, and he was beaten before he even got there. Kevin pushed him and said real tough guy stuff like "you're not so tough now, are you?" But Jeffrey wouldn't punch him. Frankie took Jeffrey's hand and swung it for him. "He's soft," Frankie said. Jeffrey stood there, didn't say anything. His face was red. "I'm not gonna fight," he said.

"Cause you're a chickenshit," Kevin told him. He pushed the center of Jeffrey's chest. "That's right, isn't it?"

"I just don't..." he choked a little. "I just don't believe in it," he said.

They let him go. There was a little chasing, but he didn't run. One of the smaller kids punched him in the back as he walked away, not hard enough to hurt. Jeffrey didn't turn around. The buses weren't even full before it was over—half the kids had to get on anyway—and he walked home.

His hand was gripping the neck of beer number four pretty tightly, and Letterman was deep into a conversation with Woody Harrelson.

"Fuck that," Jeffrey said.

He picked up the sheaf of papers again. There were some Google searches that Serena had done—two articles from the *Times*. State Police investigator Bill Gerow highlighted in the text, speaking about solved cases. A picture of him, fifteen years younger, among others behind DA Morgenthau, with a cache of weapons on a conference table. Textbook cop quotes, appreciation of colleagues, "tireless efforts," "keep the people of the city secure," one appearance of "bad guys."

There was a copy of a citation for service, apparently from his twenty-year anniversary and retirement. Dated '04. Gerow still looked like New York. Fine gray hair, long pale face threatening to go to red, pale blue eyes. Gray suit, when he'd seen him last.

There was something enviable about Gerow. Surety. Confidence. An ability to say something and mean it. A lot of people didn't have that. They kept talking, looking for the thing they meant, or meaning nothing and saying too much. It's not that Gerow was reticent. No, he had plenty to say, especially when more and more shit kept coming down. But when he spoke, nothing was wasted. It was practiced, and probably came from a lot of years thinking logically, asking liars to tell him things, and digging into what the liars said to come around to the truth. After twenty-five years largely spent listening to lies or inconsequential prattle, you probably learn to limit your own contributions in that regard.

Jeffrey flipped through the pages. There was an article about the minister's disappearance from the *Patriot-News*.

It was a thin packet. Jeffrey went to the desk pushed up against the wall behind one of the two armchairs and pulled out a manila folder. He thought about the label for a minute, staring at the pen tip. He wrote "Krumville" and put the sheets in. It was midnight. He turned on the laptop to review the weekend through maps and satellite imagery. Accord, Krumville, Bone Hollow Road. The hospital in Kingston.

He went in to find her snoring, brash and brassy, arm flung up and resting partway up the wall behind the head of their bed.

At work tomorrow, he'd reflected, they would cluster around him to hear his story and see the evidence of his lip. That would be hard to decline, that attention.

. . .

And so it was. For both of them, the next day, a day back at work, had been tough. Serena had been distracted; she hadn't told anyone about her pregnancy yet. The books, her friends, her mother all said to wait three months. So there was that. There was the nagging thought of working at that mixed bag of a hospital. When she was a kid she'd had Legos and an erector set. That hospital was like a Lego building with an erector set annex, all hodgepodge. If the city was big enough to have a hospital, it was big enough to have health care human resources management. They'd need recruiters.

But she was in New York at her small firm's office on lower Park Avenue and that was where the work was now, so she alternated periods of concentration and focused attention to phone calls and resume evaluations and handling advertising copy with spells of complete stoppage—an image would rise up. The boots at the water's edge. The roar of the flames. The flesh-crawling sense memory of the fake reporter's sympathetic hand on hers. Her manager had come by during one of those and asked her if anything was wrong.

"Zoning out," she said, and told her boss some of it. And the crowd gathered.

She didn't warm to her story. It wasn't as she'd pictured it would be, a rowdy tale told loudly, with embellishment. Right now it seemed both frightening and unreal. They comforted her. They gasped when they heard about the bodies. Her boss asked if she wanted to take the afternoon. No, that was okay. She turned back to her work. As the memory of the place faded, after a night in her own bed, her sense of threat faded too. But that could be dangerous. Relaxing her guard might be precisely the wrong thing to do.

The work day ended. As she took the subway home she remarked, without anxiety but with precision, the ground-in gum on the train floor, the invisible layers of *contact* around the steel poles. The *usedness* of everything. Was that because of the baby? Or was that because of the way the promise of that pond off in the woods had seemed so fresh, so pristine? She was having trouble distinguishing.

They ate burritos at the kitchen table, and Jeffrey pulled the Krumville file from his computer bag. He'd copied the set and had jotted notes on one, kept the other clean. They shared the marked up copy. He waited till Serena had read everything. They talked.

There was a window here, fire escape to the alley. They could talk and look out and see a patch of sky and the tops of a couple of trees—the scrappy ones with pointed leaves that sprang out of trash and corners. Jeffrey had looked them up once. Ailanthus, they were called.

Serena put down the last sheet. "I know who'll know who the owners are," she said.

"Who?"

"Amy Berenson, prop."

"The B&B lady?"

"Yeah."

"And?" he said.

"And we can find them, and talk to them about the house."

"But why? Why not just work through the realty lady?"

She said "What's with all this 'lady' stuff?"

"I don't know. They seem like ladies."

He looked at her across their little table, with its plastic salt and pepper shakers, from the disposable picnic set they got for Prospect Park in the summer. Everything here was temporary. She was holding her phone, looking back at him, one eyebrow up. His eyes went to her chin, her nose, each eye. She let him.

For some reason, his mind went back to the hours in Minneapolis, sitting numbly at the table in the hotel ballroom, sleetbound, paralyzed, unable to help her across the thousand miles between them, and unable to close them. The men passing him while he stood in the carpeted hallway, going out to smoke. The smoke rising into the clear winter air.

"Okay," he said.

And she did. She got Amy on the first ring, and booked a room for the upcoming weekend. Looking at more houses, she said. And she did one of those things they taught you in sales— let the other person say what they wanted to say. Which in Amy Berenson, Prop.'s, case, was to inquire about how they were doing after their ordeal. And one thing led to another while Jeffrey watched Serena work the phone, until she got a name. Rhonda Harrison, the daughter. A masseuse in the city.

There were a jillion Rhonda Harrisons online, but the one they were looking for was an LMT, and there she was. They left her a message. Calling about the house.

Thursday morning, Diaz was parked across the street, which was nice. They left together, late, and waved to her. Serena sent Jeffrey around the corner for donuts and coffee and walked to the car.

Diaz rolled down the window. "How you doing, sweetie? Actually, let me come out there." She got out of the car, stepped to the sidewalk, cracked her back. She looked up at Serena.

"Any trouble?"

Serena smiled at her. "No, we're good."

"All right, that's good."

"Of course, that doesn't mean I'm not worried."

"Well of course you are! Some guy comes and attacks you? It's crazy."

It was weird, Serena thought, standing here talking companionably to a uniformed cop. No one walking by looked up, of course, it being New York, but it was new just the same.

The radio squawked and Diaz held up a finger. Unintelligible static spewed out. She listened, then relaxed.

"Not for me." She smiled brightly at Serena, looked her up and down. "You ever been mugged?"

"Me? No."

"I have friends who did, and two of them took self-defense classes after, and they said it helped. Made 'em feel more, like, in control."

"Oh, yeah, I could see that," Serena said.

"Yeah, you might think about it. Of course it's still dangerous, you know? You have self-defense training, but you still have to defend yourself, right?"

"I hope not. That's what I've got you for." They laughed. Then Diaz said "still, though, here's one thing. You ever have to hit someone—here, show me your fist."

"My fist?"

"Make a fist for me."

"You're not going to arrest me, are you?"

Diaz smiled wryly and said "no, sweetie, I'm teaching you to make a fist. Good, you put your thumb right. Okay, listen—you ever need to hit a guy comes up in your face? Remember, you didn't hear this from me," and she cocked an eyebrow.

Serena, arm half raised, hand in a fist, said "sure, yeah, of course not."

Diaz said, miming as she did, "You come up from under and use your legs, and just come up—" and she demonstrated an uppercut. "Right here," she said, and tapped the point of her chin. "Make him bite his tongue. And then, sweetie?"

"Yeah?" Serena said, bemused, still absently holding her cocked fist half up, eyes wide, looking into Diaz's face.

"Then you run like hell and call the police." And she put her head back and laughed, and was still laughing when Jeffrey came down the block with coffee and a couple of donuts.

She got back in the car and showed them that she already had some. They gave them to her anyway, handing the cardboard carrier through the window, and she laughed again and rolled off down the block.

And it was just the two of them again. Serena had Rhonda's number with her, written in a notebook she'd broken open for the purpose. They'd talked about how this should go. About how pissed off Gerow would be.

"What if the owners of the house had something to do with the murder? What if it's all an insurance scam?"

"The whole thing? Like, a life insurance scam for the two murder victims and then a homeowner's claim to top it off? I think if any of the Harrisons were beneficiaries of Peterson, the cops would know it by now."

"Okay, but the fire," she said.

"That would be kind of nuts, with the cops there. Unless one of the kids was involved and needed to hide evidence."

"Kids?"

"The home owners. Kids of Mrs. Harrison."

Gerow called Jeffrey at 10am and asked if he could email a couple of pictures. Gerow stayed on the line while Jeffrey opened web mail.

There were three images. Two mug shots, men in their forties, hangdog faces, both with goatees, neither of them his attacker. The third was a glamour head shot, guy in a dark suit and a tie, smiling without showing teeth. Nothing familiar about any of them.

"Who's the suit?" he asked.

"One of the owners of the house. Michael Harrison. Just wanted to eliminate the homeowners."

"Speak of the devil. Serena and I were just talking about whether it could be an insurance scam. When is it not too early for theories?"

"You have a theory?"

"No, you told us not to."

"But if you did."

"Still no."

Eleven o'clock Thursday morning, Serena called Rhonda Harrison and left another message. Serena sat at a desk in a semi-open office suite, her boss in a fishtank against the wall and two colleagues within earshot. The place was frosted glass and white-toned fluorescents and potted plants, cherry-tone wood accents and countertops. Sterile, clean. Reminded her of the subway, somehow.

She got up, left the suite and went to the elevator. Walked out of the lobby, out of the bubble into human traffic, the noise of Park Avenue in the thirties. Went for a coffee.

Her cell rang. It was the detective.

"Can I send you a couple pictures?" he said.

"I'm not at my desk, but I can take a look and call you when I get back."

"That's fine. Call me and I'll send them while we're talking."

"Okay. Say, detective?"

"Yeah?"

"I called the daughter, one of the homeowners. Rhonda Harrison."

"Mrs. Gale, what are you doing that for?"

"It's about the house."

"What did she say?"

"I left a message."

"Listen, Mrs. Gale, I haven't had a chance to talk to her myself for more than a minute. She's coming up here tomorrow. So's one brother. Can you lay off until I've had some time with them?"

Her stomach lurched a little. She checked her watch. It was eleven fifteen.

"You don't think they know anything, do you?"

"At this point, I know little. The fake reporter adds an unusual degree of complexity. I'm starting to think he was just a nutcase or a rival reporter trying to dig something up. Speaking of which, has Gilbert been in touch?"

"Not so far."

"Well, that's good. The less he talks to you, the better. Means he's leaving you out of it. His paper never ran a piece on the missing minister except what came over the AP, so he's probably working that. Now let me ask my next question."

"What's that?"

"When are we seeing you and Mr. Gale again? They do a nice Halloween parade in Accord on Saturday morning. I wouldn't be surprised to find that you two made it back up here."

"We don't have plans to."

"That's good."

She got it, she really did, but she was feeling needled. "No, actually, we've been talking about going out to Messerbergh, in Pennsylvania. I thought we could say a homily or whatever."

He sighed. "I guess what I don't understand," he said, "is what you hope to gain."

"I just want to kick that guy's ass who burned down the house." She sidled over to a garbage can at the corner, phone to her ear, coffee in her left hand.

"Mrs. Gale, I don't want to kick anyone's ass. I want to make sure that criminals are punished for their crimes and that good people stay safe. You can help me by answering questions about the criminals, and by being one of the good people who keeps herself safe."

Her stomach flimmed. Then it flammed. She said "I'll be back at my desk in five minutes. I'll be able to look at those photos."

"I want to be clear that you—"

She said "gotta go," and hung up and held her coffee out to the left and her phone out to the right, then took a bow into the garbage can. That helped.

THIRTEEN

Jack Grant stood on a stepstool, arm stretched high into the rafters, his fingers brushing the canvas wrap cover on a Browning over and under twelve gauge. He stretched another inch and caught a fold of canvas, then dragged it toward him off its perch, which was atop several leftover pine planks from the paneling. There was dust on the whole shebang.

He got it close enough to grab and hoisted it down, letting go the beam and stepping down in one movement, big booted foot hitting the boards.

The shack was small; a kitchenette and a bunkroom and a shitter that was just a toilet. You washed your hands in the kitchen, although Jack didn't worry about that. Definitely not at the camp.

He put the gun on the only table and unwrapped it. The stock was oiled walnut, and the metal was oiled too. His hooded sweatshirt had a tube pocket across the front. He emptied it of shells. About thirty, he figured. He didn't intend to use any, but figured he would if he had to. This Baker guy was a prick for sure.

After all, he'd killed Jack's brother. You were supposed to hate a guy for that.

But Jack had hated Cyrus as much as you could hate a person. You only took so much shit from a person, even from family, before you wrote them off. So he didn't hate Baker, particularly, for shooting Cyrus Grant. And hey, if this worked out, he'd have the twenty-five hundred for torching the Bone Hollow house, cash free and clear. And a place to go in Syracuse, Monday morning first thing.

So he wasn't mad, so much. But when a guy like that was around, you packed. And the bird gun was the best he had handy. He couldn't go back down the mountain, not till Monday—at least not in the truck. That couple had seen it, had seen him.

The good thing was, the prepaid cell had signal up here. And there was canned meat enough, a wholesale case of it, and some white gas for the stove. If you fried that shit you could eat it. So he could bide till Sunday and pick up the cash, coming down into Arkville the back way down from behind the hotel, never even get into town, no cops to see him, nothing. Less than a mile through state land to the front desk of Schlesinger's and the bag, shotgun ready.

And backup not far off. That was next.

He loaded the gun, then went out to stand in front of the cabin. He took a Bud with him and his cellphone.

Some of the most memorable beatings from Cyrus had happened right here under the overhang out in front of the place, and that was before Cy had gone real bad. Once he was real bad he never took after Jack any more. But that last time Jack remembered, Cyrus had just got the Confederate flag tat on his left bicep and Jack had said something stupid about it, something about rednecks and "yawl," and gotten his ass kicked pretty good for that.

Jack chuckled and drank some beer. The screen on the phone showed two signal bars. He looked to the right and could see a couple miles down the valley toward the state highway that ran through the heart of the Catskills. The road along Dry Run ran up another couple of miles, camps and larger houses coming off it like spokes.

The cell tower on the north side of town was visible from here; it was on a little lot that bordered the old hotel grounds, in fact.

Nights this week he could hear the steam whistle on the Haunted Train Ride. That thing they did up there this week every year. The heat-up old train drove a mile of the old track out of town then went back, backwards. Some kind of theater company hung props in the trees and played screams out of loudspeakers, lit smudge pots out in the woods and hired local high schoolers to dance around them like savages. It was pretty funny, funnier if you went fucked up, which Jack had been known to do on occasion.

He called Charlie Pedrango. Charlie wasn't his oldest friend, but he was his baddest friend. And for five hundred bucks, give or take, he was pretty sure Charlie would hold a gun on Baker if Baker was still lurking around when Jack got to the hotel. And if Baker didn't do the drop, well, Jack and Charlie could talk about what to do about/with/to Mr. Baker.

Charlie's voicemail picked up. "Talk to me," said the outgoing message in Charlie's graveled voice.

"Charlie, it's Jack on Thursday. I'm working on something I thought you might want to help me with. Call me back."

FOURTEEN

Serena buzzed the place on 88th near the corner of Columbus. It was one of the gray modern brick buildings she supposed had been built in the 50s or 60s—between the era of stone and the current era of glass and steel that was getting steadily weirder. "Healing Hearth" it said on the buzzer.

Expecting a Scandinavian-style place with blond wood and clean lines, she was surprised at the throwback nature of Rhonda's shop, and of Rhonda herself. The lady was slender and pretty and had gray hair pulled back in a neat ponytail, and after that everything went to hell. She was bedangled like a gypsy fortuneteller, with earrings tugging at her lobes and a sequined headband covering her hairline. She had on a kaftan or a muumuu or a drapery and one thousand necklaces. Her wrists were probably setting off the magnetometers at Newark this minute.

In the instant before Rhonda grabbed her, Serena could see that the waiting room of the healing emporium went on in the same style. The wallpaper was richly patterned and textured. There were a lot of candles. The smell of sandalwood incense came out with Rhonda. The centerpiece: a fat vertical rock sawn in half to reveal chunky purple crystals lining a hollow interior. Sitting in the grotto, a little jade Buddha.

In that instant Serena noticed Rhonda appraise her. Rhonda covered it with a gasp of *total empathy*, but the eyes flicked efficiently and coldly—hair nails shoes face—until they landed on Serena's. Then she launched herself forward in a tinkly rush and buried Serena in her arms, pulled her close, and held on like the place was sinking.

Serena wasn't surprised. When she'd spoken to Rhonda after lunch, she'd picked up a heavy *vibe.*

"This is Rhonda, how can I help you?" Her voice was airy, soft edges. A fairyland voice.

"Ms. Harrison, my name is Serena Gale, and I'm calling about the house you're selling up in Krumville."

"I'm sorry, who are you with?"

"Oh, uh, no one."

"If you're calling to tell me it burned down, I'm afraid I already knew that."

"No, sorry, that's not it. I'm— my husband and I had been there to look at it, and we liked it very much—"

"Oh, dear. You must be the couple who found those poor people." She threw a lot of music into it. Uuup and dowwwn went the trilling voice.

"Yes, that's right."

"Oh, you *poor. Thing,*" she said. "You must have been absolutely *terrified.* I know I would have been. How do you feel now?"

"Ah, well, I'm okay, I guess. A little nauseous. Nauseated." Jeffrey always made a big deal out of that one.

"Of *course* you are. Oh, darling, that's just terrible. Your equilibrium must be completely thrown off. Now what can I do for you?"

"I was calling about the house, actually."

"What's left of it, you mean. Nothing lasts," Rhonda said.

"I was wondering what your family's plans were, if you had figured that out yet."

"My brother and I are meeting there tomorrow to look at the damage and talk to the police and the realtor. We'll know more then."

"Can we speak on Monday, maybe?"

"Of *course,* sweetie. But first I'll want to see you, today. I'm concerned about you. I can hear the stress in your voice. And your digestion is affected as well. What time can you come? Before seven?"

"Six, I guess," Serena said. "But I don't have money for—"

"Shush!"

The appointment was made. And now Serena was in her arms. The hug was very long and completely silent. Serena made a mental note to check her pockets after.

She was carried on a draft of incense through a beaded curtain and into large room with a massage table in the center. It was candlelit. There was less junk and tchotchkes here, but the walls were lined with anatomical diagrams, herbalists' charts, and illustrations from India.

Rhonda sat her in an overstuffed armchair. She had tea waiting. Rhonda poured. She sat before Serena and leaned forward. She clasped her hands dramatically. Sixty bracelets made a sound like wind chimes.

"What kind?" Serena said, lifting the tea and inhaling.

"My own infusion. I start with chamomile and pennyroyal and go from there. It's perfect for digestion and stress."

The hot liquid slopping over the rim stung Serena's hand as she put it down. "This is pennyroyal tea, you're telling me?" The cup clacked on the table at her elbow.

131

"Well, yes," Rhonda said. Then her eyes widened. She tilted her head back and laughed. "Oh, dear. Oh, Serena, the look on your face." She composed herself, leaned even further forward, gathered Serena's hands. "How far *along* are you, darling?"

"I found out two weeks ago, when I was late."

"Oh, sweetie. That clears up the nausea. Now, listen." The fairytale whisper-voice, rich with undercurrents of compassion. "The tea is perfectly safe. Someone would have to drink it for days to have the effects you're worried about. Although I completely understand if you don't want some. "

"Yes, well. Okay." Serena's tea stayed where it was.

"Now what about your stress?"

Serena told her everything. She was fearful of talking about her pregnancy; she knew that anything could happen at such an early stage. But there was something about Rhonda. It was as though once the pregnancy was out there, in the room, everything else was inconsequential. And oddly, although the woman had offered her a poison—possibly, as she claimed, in a harmless dosage—it was easy to tell her everything once she knew. If there was information Serena was trying to keep hidden from a potentially hostile world, it was this. Not how much she knew about who had killed who or burned down what. Just this. I'm going to have a baby.

At the end, Rhonda said "I think you and Jeffrey should come up tomorrow. My brother Michael and I can talk. We're going to see the realtor also. And Serena," she said, again putting their hands together in a single bundle, "my mother would have wanted you to have that house."

FIFTEEN

When Victor Generro was twenty-two, he had broken the nose of a rival ad salesman on a weekly newspaper in rural Colorado and gotten off. He'd never looked back. As CEO of WestGen Minerals, he ran an aggressive shop, stood up to larger suppliers of natural gas, the press, enviros, and politicians, and hired a lot of lawyers.

"Get it done." Generro's voice came through the earpiece of Baker's phone. "No footnotes. I'm counting on you, Baker."

It wasn't a huge company, but it was still rare for him to talk to someone at Baker's level. The guy had caught his attention a few years earlier at a refiner's forum, one of these industry meetings where the drillers get together with prospects and try to undercut each other on price and flash their technological superiority.

At the meeting, Baker had had some slides touting WestGen's accuracy in projecting well lifetimes, meaning they could shave their landowner contracts pretty fine, meaning they had a couple of basis points' advantage over some of the bigger outfits who standardized contracts across larger numbers of properties and figured it'd all come out in the wash. A couple of the highest-paid guys—and one woman—in the company were the ones who were on the money on the volumes they projected for a given region, or even particular wells. Leaner and more accurate, WestGen had been first in on a couple of good territories, willing to put in a wildcat well and give it their full attention where a massive outfit couldn't. Slightly wider margins on those contracts, plus first-in status meant high profits for WestGen, good pricing for their customers.

But at WestGen's size, a mid-level guy wasn't going to pack quite the credibility punch the refiners and brokers were after. So Baker's boss had made a request up the ladder, and Generro's eastern territory president had asked him to sit in. Baker still ran the slides, did much of the talking. Generro's silver hair, chin cleft, crows feet, tan, and expensive watch juxtaposed against his wildcatter's hands did a lot. But it had definitely been the slightly paunchy, intent guy talking through the graphs that had won the day.

It was Baker's passion for getting it right that seemed to resonate. The guy could lose himself in the numbers a bit, get excited about *why* it was that people would be willing to let WestGen into their land, puncture their soil, delve into their mineral rights, and why the subtle differences—hundredths of percentage points—in costs made it reasonable to buy from WestGen. He'd squint up at a graph, walk really close, talk like no one else was in the room. Like he was a scientist discovering something, in a movie. And it didn't look like an act.

Generro believed in building talent. He'd talked a bit with Baker afterward, pleased that he wasn't an MBA but had started riding shotgun—at fourteen!—on his dad's oil deliveries. Little Cinderella thing going on there, then. He put Baker into the acquisitions organization, where the guy took to quoting Glengarry Glen Ross and making a name for himself. Thought he was Ricky Roma, and honestly, he wasn't too far off. They didn't make him take the sales trainings, didn't expect him to cut up at conferences. He just had to deliver. And he did.

Periodically, Generro would check in with the guy, which seemed to mean a lot to him. The boss had seen that before, that sense of connection to power making someone feel bigger, so he cultivated it. He had the impression that Baker's mind was always on the prize, on *the good of the company*, on getting it done. No footnotes. Generro liked that one, had heard it quoted from another CEO, and it was kind of perfect for a guy like Baker. Give the guy a sense of purpose. Generro played it tough, played up the roughness of their work. Baker had never laid pipe, never run a drill, but Generro could tell that that side of the business appealed to the guy. The man's-man nature of it. So he played up the Glengarry stuff, the tough guy sales stuff. Motivational.

The contracts came in, that was certain. Baker had a good hit rate, one of the best in the acquisitions group, even in some of the muddiest territories—hard sells, entrenched competition, tough regulators. If there was bribery going on, Baker was smart enough not to hint at it. If there was pressure of any kind, Generro didn't know and didn't want to. For ninety-nine percent (and ninety bps) of cases, the pressure came from simple economics: your valley is farmed out and your coal mine closed. Your thirty acres can hold two 4,000-foot wells. There's your annual income for twelve years. Sign here.

From his office, looking out to the southwest across line after line of folded hills, Generro had precisely the view he wanted. His office was on the second floor, where the building was stacked highest against the top of one of those ridges, the sharpest edge of the thing tamped and tenderized, tamed into a flat surface for laying in a foundation. But he had the right view. Blue mountains fading into distance, even a couple of well sites visible among the fields. He liked to point those out to visitors now and then. And the money came. Precisely how he liked it. A little reward, and a little pressure. Got results every time.

Of course Generro knew that pressure sometimes made cracks. But they were hard to see under that green and brown and blue landscape out his window.

SIXTEEN

The location: the driveway of a convent in northeastern Pennsylvania. There was a reservoir of natural gas under this part of the mountains. It was hard to get at; not economically feasible, really, unless a driller used horizontal hydraulic fracturing, which was slightly problematic.

Baker hit END on his phone. Talking to Gennero always gave him a charge. There was a guy who got things done.

The nuns had to understand. WestGen wanted only to help them, bring in jobs, provide energy, and take a deserved, but modest, profit. The pseudo science they were citing in their objections to the proposed plan was the work of rabid ecoterrorists whose only goal was to stop development of any kind, without regard to whether it was necessary or safe. They were an insurgency.

But the nuns bought it. Some of it, anyway. They claimed that water wells were poisoned by the hydraulic fluid. They claimed that the gas wells were obtrusive and loud. They claimed that the burnoff of gas raised the levels of particulates in the area. These were women who had supposedly run away from the world, people who supposedly spent their days in solemn prayer and tending gardens and— what the fuck, he didn't know, *knitting*—but here they were packing municipal meetings and writing letters and standing behind congressmen who were holding up their fingers and declaiming against any harm to the communities within their districts. Don't get him started on *those* pricks. Riding the good sisters' tidal wave of bullshit to get more leverage so they could make bigger demands. This game he hated. He wasn't a lobbyist. He didn't want to play the game, balance the scales, give a little to get a lot. He was charged with one thing: put the fucking well in the ground, and get the product out. That was his bread and butter.

Baker got out of the car and folded his cellphone in half and put it away. He ran a hand over his thinning hair. Shot his cuffs. Checked his breath. This one, he figured, was going to happen. It was dicey, but momentum was on their side. They'd been through a battery of site reviews, environmental impact statements, public comment periods, and God knew how many convoluted hours of backroom shit with Wagner, Cappolo, Kneisel, and the rest in Washington, hashing out ongoing campaign contributions, checking and re-checking the legal limits of gifts, getting Cappolo's wife on the payroll of a lobbying firm one industry over, and the quid pro quo *that* had entailed. So now, in addition to his own boss, the CEO, Baker was forced to answer calls from some fucking Iowa congressman's son-in-law who knew fuck-the-fuck-*all* about natural gas.

Baker pinned it squarely on Peterson. These nuns would have rolled over in a heartbeat if it weren't for that hippie motherfucker. The data on the Clearbrook leaks would have remained where it was, the town and its citizens fairly compensated.

Thank God—no, he thought, walking up the long gravel drive to the doors of the main building on the convent campus— thank *him* that he'd taken the initiative with Peterson. Because

138

while this one was practically a done deal, that next one, the New York one, was not.

At least the check in his briefcase would be welcome at the convent. You had to jump on this kind of thing, pay it down, work company reputation, work the press, shell out more dosh to regulators, town guys, every fucking kind of layer of local shitbird. But never show that you were in a hurry. They'd see a bead of sweat on your forehead and they'd say "of course, there is the matter of a stakeholder survey," and you were out another mil. No, instead, you sent your CEO to break ground on the new children's development center, or you gave a hundred grand to the local scholarship fund. You endowed a nursing home.

Peterson. That had been such a break in the fucking grind. His own gig. He paused in the shade of an enormous copper beech halfway up the drive, let his mind drift back to the kick of the rifle against his shoulder. Such freedom. Once he'd decided to off Cyrus Grant as well, it had suddenly shifted everything to him. There was no lawyer to consult. No sign-off to get from the boss. He could just... do this... and it would close a loop and get him closer to putting in a whole new moneymaking system. All him. No footnotes.

The stakes for the Catskills deal were even higher. He'd been promised a bonus for getting this one in place. More than anyone else at the company, more than Victor Generro himself, this was Baker's deal. Even if his name didn't go across the documents, even if the project would be named after its location, you could have called it Baker's Wells. He was accountable. So he was running the thing his way. Bang. Bang. Bang. Bang.

As it did every time, replaying the scene infused him with focus, control, confidence. When he started back up the drive toward the massive door of the convent offices—built in 1872, he knew—his stride was a perfect blend of purposeful gait and playful stroll. Any swagger was completely gone. This was as much an impersonation as playing Oscar Gilbert had been.

There was a bell pull. He pulled. Just inside the door, a bell rang. He waited, studying a little crucifix on the door with a bemused and respectful smile. He thought raising his eyes to heaven would be a little much. These women weren't stupid, after all, just misinformed. He could help them.

The sister he'd last met at a town council meeting opened the door. She was beefy, mannish, clunky black shoes showing beneath her gray habit. Big hands. She shook his. "Please come in, Mister Baker," she said, and gestured him into the front hall.

The entry hall carried all the way through the building to the back. It had a stone tile floor and a vaulted ceiling with a staircase going up the right-hand side to a mezzanine. At the back, a couple of large windows and a glass door in the middle looked out on fields and an apple orchard. He could see figures out there on stepladders, bushel baskets on the ground. On *his* ground, he almost thought.

Instead, he said "getting in the harvest, I see?"

She followed his eyes. "Oh yes. We use half and donate half to the food bank."

"Mrs. Jennings must appreciate that."

"You know the Pike County food bank?" she said.

"I've done some work with them through WestGen," he answered. They entered an office that sat directly on the line between organized chaos and plain chaos. There was ol' Jesus on the wall.

Funny thing. Baker didn't have much use for religion, although he'd gone to church most of his life. It was good for networking, and the atmosphere was comforting. But now look at him. He'd killed a minister—a dime store phony, for sure, but the guy ran some kind of church—and his boss had just ordered him to screw a bunch of nuns. He was at a convent, for Christ's sake. Speaking of whom, there he was, eyes looking out from the picture at the viewer. Frank, compassionate. Baker recognized the expression; it was the one worn by every successful televangelist at the moment they asked for the money, painstakingly copied from paintings like this one. Baker looked him in the eye, thought *yes Lord, money's coming right up, Lord*, and sat down.

Sister Margaret had gone around the desk and cleared a space, then pulled her chair in close. Baker took the seat opposite and put his briefcase down beside it.

"Thank you so much for agreeing to see me," he said.

"Of course, Mister Baker. When you said you could present more information on the safety of the hydraulic fracturing process, we were happy to take a meeting. The data from the Clearbrook site were of concern."

"Naturally, Sister. Sorry, do I call you Sister?"

"That's fine."

"I would be concerned if I read the Clearbrook article, too, without the additional knowledge of the industry and the process that I have. And that's because the report you're talking about paints a dire, inaccurate, picture. I mean, to read the report you'd think that the water there was poisoned and that everyone had left the area. We have thirty wells, and there is still a community of healthy people at Clearbrook. The study implies that the hydraulic fracturing process destroyed the town."

Another nun came in with a tray of tea things.

"Would you like some tea, Mister Baker?" Sister Margaret said. Dancing, dancing, dancing.

"Thank you, yes," he said, and he smiled.

"I admit, the report I saw about Clearbrook did seem pretty grim. It was especially odd because I Googled it and didn't find anything in the papers about it."

"Don't worry—there were a lot of reporters on the case. What they found was that the quasi-scientific findings of one biased hydrologist who lived locally were not compelling enough to cover as a story. Now, that's not to say that *nothing* happened in our operations there. I can tell you what did happen, if you like."

"Please do."

"What happened was that on April 16, 2008 a small quantity of the water produced in the drilling process escaped into a containment pond—dug by WestGen for that eventuality—and created an odor that was perceptible to the people of the community. A local hydrologist tested *that* water. He did a perc test on the soil around the containment pond. And unsurprisingly, he found industrial chemicals in the water and surface fractures in the soil that allowed for its escape."

"Why is that unsurprising?"

"For the same reason we put in the containment pond. We've done such extensive testing on the area that we had identified that risk zone, leased the property and obtained legal easements, installed the containment pond, put up a fence, posted the perimeter, and were monitoring the water in it ourselves. We responded within hours of contamination, about fifteen minutes before anyone reported odor."

"Then why the report?"

"I'll tell you frankly. Mister Taylor, the hydrologist, was already doing very well in royalty payments made by WestGen for property he owned. However, he had always felt that he wasn't getting as much as he deserved, based on the acreage of his property."

Sister Margaret moved a pencil on her desk "My concern, and his, from the report I read, was that the same thing could happen elsewhere, someplace without a containment pond."

Baker nodded with a tight smile. *I hear you.* "I won't deny that it *could.* But I will state this: WestGen has never had an uncontained leak, not in any one of our one hundred and fifty gas and oil operations in the United States, whether using hydraulic fracturing or other methods."

"Is that right?" she said.

"That's right, ma'am. You can Google your fingers blue on that one, you won't find anything. Even a big corporation like WestGen can't beat the Internet. If there was something to be found, you'd find it."

His story was bullshit, of course. The water, chemicals and microbeads forced into the shale during fracking shoved out all kinds of nasty shit. Sometimes the water hit the surface— although you couldn't call it water at that point. Sometimes it was sludge, sometimes it smelled like formaldehyde, sometimes it had oily residues in it. Sometimes it pushed out into wells drilled for—well—for other purposes. Like for babies to drink. That was a bummer. They'd had to cover up a drinking water well explosion and settle with two other families, instituting gag orders and sealing the court papers. There had been the aquifer in Montana—his eyes flicked to the portrait of Jesus in silent thanks that he hadn't been involved in that nightmare.

It was so hard to keep a lid on this stuff, and it was never perfect, but as long as the gas kept flowing you could convert a small percentage of it to the money and information required to grease the machine. The one piece of truth in Baker's story was

Taylor. Fortunately the greedy fucker had been amenable to an enhanced royalty payment for mineral rights and had backed off. He was boiling his spaghetti in Poland Spring now.

"There's a reason for that, Sister. As a corporation, we have as much at stake as the communities where we work. That's why we line our wells with concrete. Why we monitor emissions at points all around our gas projects. Why we don't use benzene or toluene in our operations. Why we test groundwater and work with families and water authorities to ensure the complete safety of their product."

"I've heard some pretty bad things about the process, this 'fracking.' "

"There have been issues in some states, it's true. And there are allegedly problems with a well out in Dimock, you may have heard of that."

"Yes, that and Clearbrook, that's what brought us out to the meeting where we spoke."

"Okay. I don't mean to sound crass, but the company in Dimock isn't WestGen. And I can't speak to their problems and potential missteps. What I can address is how WestGen conducts itself."

He picked up his briefcase and opened it on his lap. He sorted through, with the leather top pointed at Sister Margaret. She sat patiently, stolid, but he noted the nearly imperceptible lean toward that case. What did she think was there? Money? Information? Answers? It was.

He pulled out a glossy folder with the WestGen logo on it, and a picture of a wind turbine set in an impossibly green field under an impossibly blue sky. He held it, gestured with it, generating little puffs of wind while he spoke.

"I know people will speak out against the industry as a whole. But in our defense, on the face of it, it doesn't make sense. Sister, WestGen has invested tens of millions in finding these deposits and in developing the technology to get at the gas safely. We know we're not above the law, and in one hundred six years we've taken responsibility for any adverse effects of the industrial processes we conduct. Given that investment, and our responsibility, why would we risk everything by cutting corners?"

It sounded so clean. So pristine. Who could argue? Truth was, there was money in the mix. Money forced into the cracks and fissures of public opinion, wedging its way into miniscule fault lines and forcing them open, continuing the flow of permission.

In the field, WestGen deployed massive pumps. Like alien fire hydrants on steroids, they looked, forcing salt water and ceramic beads or sand into fissures in the Marcellus shale. In the nun's office, Baker pulled out an envelope. He placed the folder on the desk.

"In there are a lot of articles and papers, some technical, some less so, that back up our position. And here," he said, placing the envelope on top, "is a gesture of goodwill."

"A payoff?" she said, but with a smile, not ironically, not rancorously.

"Let me be clear: No. Strings. Attached. This is something I was able to personally arrange with our charitable foundation, since you're a 501(c)3 and WestGen works very hard to give back to the host communities where we play a role.

"No, Sister, the real payoff for your order is going to be the royalty payments you'll be receiving in four months' time. This is a corporate contribution, above board. In fact, you'll see in the folder there is a short press release we'd like you to approve citing the contribution. We like to put charitable work in our annual report. The publicity folks get a charge out of it."

He smiled.

She smiled.

He stopped selling and got the hell out of there and no nuns got fucked in the literal sense during the making of that particular sub-sub-sub deal.

Baker called in and updated Generro. "Ninety-five percent closed on the nuns," he told him.

SEVENTEEN

He had one stop to make. He hammered the gas home to the little rented ranch house, the country place, two hours south and west.

Once there, he prepared for his next trip, out to New York, Arkville, where he would deal with Jack. He dug into the cash box in the fire safe, pulled out the stash. He liked to take out cash from ATMs on his corporate card and pay with that. He reported every dime, of course, but still managed to keep a lot of small bills he got back as change. Today he grabbed three grand in tens and twenties, packed a gym bag with a couple of changes of clothes, pulled out a good old paper map of New York and found Arkville on the little grid, then located it on the map. His eye tracked east and south from there to Krumville. He folded the map, put it away again in the study among all the other US maps, alphabetically. Nothing sticking out to show he'd been using it.

While he worked, Baker thought about Jack, this fucking guy who'd gotten hold of Cyrus Grant's cell phone. Cyrus had been just a little too smart for himself. That hadn't ended well for him. And now some friend of his, some last smart move on Cyrus's part, had added to his to-do list.

He'd been surprised by the call.

The prepaid phone he'd used to talk to Cyrus wasn't supposed to be ringing. He thought about dropping it into a waste water lagoon, but curiosity won out. "I had a friend who gave me this phone and told me to call you," someone said. A male voice, kind of…thick. Like something about the guy wasn't particularly nimble and his clumsiness came out in his voice. A dis and dat kind of guy, but not Brooklyn. Country.

Baker's heart actually did a little dipsy-doo. "Oh yeah? What about?"

"He put a few things in the house you might want to not have found."

"I doubt it."

"Just telling you what he said."

"You know the house he meant?"

"Bone Hollow Road," the thick voice said.

Fact was, he'd been in the house. He'd let that realtor show him around in the summer using an assumed name, an excuse to case the region; they'd looked at four houses together. He might've touched things here and there, but who knew? He was pretty sure he couldn't be tied to the house. But he needed to get this guy on the payroll, give him the same thing he'd given the other guy.

Baker had paused. "What do I call you?"

"Jack."

"What is this friend to you?"

"Just someone I know."

"Jack, do you care about that house?"

"Not really, no."

"Want to make some money?"

That had been in September. The idea was to wait to torch the place—no need to call attention to the mess out back. But attention had found it. That couple from Brooklyn. And that had started to get funky. Jack had called him, then gone ahead with the plan, hand forced. But the cops had been in there all day after the murder was found out. If there really was evidence, he could be screwed.

And then Jack called one more time, told him he'd been seen. And Baker thought he might have a shot at finding Jack, through them.

He sighed, remembering, wrapping the loaded rifle in a blanket.

It was just another one of those deals. You kept a lid on it best you could, you kept working it. Nothing was perfect. He'd only met Cyrus Grant once and doubted there was any evidence, but this guy Jack claimed to know his name and license plates. Why say it, if it was complete bullshit?

Dammit. If he could shoot Peterson again, he'd go ahead and do it.

The minister's only tangle with fracking had been with a different company, but he'd learned his lesson. Three of his congregants were complaining about drilling operations abutting their property, and Peterson had weighed in, once, four years earlier. Loudly, publicly, at one county environmental board meeting. And their case got swatted away pretty quickly. This in a place dying for want of coal mines, towns shutting down, a generation of unemployment, flight to the cities.

Peterson's sole contribution ended up being five minutes in front of the microphone at that one meeting. It got buried in the post-meeting coverage, a fracking-friendly feature article in the Harrisburg paper, the Dimock debacle; all that washed Peterson's little rant aside. Third page of the search results, who was gonna look there?

He'd got Baker's attention, however, and Donald Baker was paid to know who his enemies were. Baker looked in at the church and chatted up one of the congregants at a bar in Messerbergh a few days later. He got a sense of the operation, then filed it all away.

But not long after Peterson's disappointing showing in challenging the drilling up north of Messerbergh, some kind of Marcellus Shale Robin Hood had emerged. Sure, there were a couple of high-profile guys making noise about fracking in the enviro-media, and those humps in Dimock had been dumb enough to leave sludgy water lying around where a news station could get pictures of it and talk to homeowners who didn't like the royalties they were getting. But there was more than that, too. If you knew the details of specific gas operations, you knew that some of what made its way into blogs and into the periphery of the newspapers was stuff that wasn't easy to know. Here and there information welled up through fissures in the corporate PR strata and sat stinking in the sun. There'd been pictures, too—one of a guy setting fire to the stream out of his garden hose. Jars of brown shit that could have been real output for all Baker knew. Some reports of WestGen and other companies' own test results. Someone had put the hydrologist onto that leak at Clearbrook. Someone had gotten the Clearbrook report to the nuns. Executive salaries from the quarterly investor filings were trumpeted, along with average royalties. An uneasy balance— this skullduggery was soaking into the consciousness, but no major stories had broken over it.

He had an instinct, and went back to that bar a couple of times until he saw his friend again. He bought her a couple of drinks and talked about gas drilling. He talked about Peterson. She said yeah, she'd overheard him talking about permits for

Liberty, New York one time. She'd heard the word "fracking."
She slurred a bit at this point. "Like Battlestar Galactica," she
said. She laughed. Baker didn't know what she was talking about.

You take that, and you take the leaks and the snapshots,
and Peterson's history, and you put pins in a map, as it were.
It culminated with Baker calling a town councilman in Liberty,
New York, where the next project was slated to go. The guy's
receptionist—he was a private-practice lawyer—answered.
Baker said "It's Reverend Peterson," and the guy got on and
said "Hi there, Jim, great to hear from you."

He'd hung up.

If you look at all that, and if you're a guy who spends every
day fighting to get people to see things your way, you realize
you've got a crusader who has to be dealt with.

And James Peterson had been one of those who couldn't
be pushed. Baker had gone to a service, once. While the
congregation was singing along to a hymn played by a tattooed
guy on an electric guitar, he'd slipped an envelope under the
apartment door upstairs. A check from WestGen's foundation
made out to the church. It had appeared back at the office two
days later in a larger envelope, "no thanks" written on it.

Well, okay, both sides had tendered a statement of principles.
Trouble was WestGen's hands were a little tied. Peterson
couldn't be pressured publicly because he never did anything
public.

Baker's art was the art of the clampdown, and he'd been
moving faster and faster at this Whack-a-Mole shit, and the
Catskills piece was huge and hard to keep in line. Websites were
springing up. The rednecks up the hills there were emboldened
by a successful campaign to keep a power line out of their
backyards. Christ, they'd been emboldened since they beat Con

Ed in the 60s to save the top of that mountain they wanted for a hydro battery. And now GE had folded to the crunchies, been made to clean up the whole goddamn Hudson.

It had been remarkably easy for Baker to come around to what had to be done. James Peterson was one mole. And Baker was the one holding the hammer.

Finding the right place that summer hadn't been hard. It had to be far away from him, and far from the nearest WestGen operation. He knew some of the back roads in that part of New York from his endless legwork. He'd seen the house on a drive. It had stuck with him, somehow, with the path out the back, down into the woods there. When he'd been there the woods had been black-green, impenetrable. The few maples set amidst the birches and hemlocks had been in full leaf, the deer trails the only breaks in the underbrush. No houses back behind there, just woods and Roosa Lake.

He'd driven around behind those two low hills backed up against the west side. Found a deer trail, or a trail used by local high school kids, hunters, who knew? It arrowed up through somewhat open woodland, over scree in places, roots and stones making a bit of a staircase in others. After a half mile it leveled off, a tree-covered dome, with a little meadow at the top, some exposed rocks there. On the far side of those, looking down east into the little scooped-out bowl below, he could see the edge of the water. That would do.

. . .

Now, Baker finished packing. Sandwiches, soda, water. He didn't want to stop for food. Fewer eyes. The gun would go at the back of the trunk, inside the lining, filled out with some rags to flatten it out. He got back into his car and pointed it east.

The rest of it replayed itself as he drove. He remembered it had been his own foolish idea, and another impulse, to get Cyrus Grant involved. Peterson wouldn't negotiate, but Baker hadn't been sure whether he was weak or not. The minister didn't have a corporation and lawyers to back him up, but he was playing this asymmetrical game, and that gave him an artificial strength. If Baker wanted help he needed someone bad who wouldn't know the guy. He wasn't really thinking this until he came across Cyrus.

It had been at a Denny's right off Route 17 in New York on his way down from Vermont after getting the gun. Eleven at night. Baker had gone into the men's room and surprised a tatted-up hoodlum trying to tie off in front of the sinks. He wore a white t-shirt with the sleeves actually ripped off, had a death's head down one arm, a blue-ink rose on his neck, a Confederate flag on his left shoulder—for some reason that one was depicted dripping blood. The guy was lean, but his muscles looked like bridge cables. Stringy hair and hollow cheeks. He had a length of latex hose around his forearm and was holding a hypodermic in his teeth.

The door had swung shut behind him by the time Baker took it in. He stopped for a second, surprised but not shocked in any kind of moral sense. Just—wow.

More surprising, perhaps, was the guy's reaction. He looked directly at him, deadpan. Not threatening. Not anything. Just staring out of the severest pair of eyes Baker had ever seen, needle in his teeth, teeth showing like a death's head himself. This motherfucker was *dark*.

"Sorry," said Baker, and stepped over to the urinal. He was calculating. He knew how he looked. It was part of his whole MO. Nebbishy. Thinning dark hair, sport jacket over a travel-wrinkled button-down shirt and jeans, tassel loafers. This guy would see him as a mark. Which he might actually be, despite the rifle in the trunk of his car.

He watched the guy's reflection shoot up in the flat disc of the flusher on the urinal in front of him. Watched the plunger on the syringe sink down, drive the brown liquid into the vein. When the guy untied the tourniquet he leaned forward on his elbows and hung his head.

Baker zipped up and turned around. "Can I ask you something?" he said.

"Whuuuuut," came the answer from the depths of the sink.

"You ever kill anyone?"

EIGHTEEN

A Confederate flag dripping blood. That was this guy's trademark tat, and it'd taken them a while but they'd found someone who knew it. Late Thursday a sheriff's deputy talking to an ink guy in a parlor on the main street in Monticello got a confirmation: they'd done it for a guy named Cyrus Grant. Gerow figured they had their John Doe. That had been confirmed when the minister's car was found out back behind Cyrus Grant's house in the hills outside of town.

They had a couple of detectives on the Cyrus Grant trail now, and it was a hot one. Every single piece of information that came in created new ripples of surprise with one main theme: you mean to say *this guy* wasn't in jail? It didn't figure. From the tattoo parlor it was easy jumps to a dealer already in the Otisville pen who'd sold him heroin. Two guys who were willing to say, once they'd been told he was dead, that he'd beaten them up for money owed. Four arrests and no convictions for assault. As of Friday afternoon, he was looking good for two unsolved murders, one of them a bargain-basement white-supremacist type up in the hills around Livingston Manor who'd been talking to the Southern Poverty Law Center and disappeared one day. It was unanimous: Cyrus Grant was a bad, bad guy.

He had a brother, but they didn't run in the same circles. The brother was known to be a bit of a thug, but Cyrus made him look like a banker.

The brother lived in Olivebridge. Gerow liked it. Eight miles from the Bone Hollow homicides. Gerow led the crew that went. Jack Grant wasn't home. Jack's DMV records came back. He had a big American-made pickup. It was white. That was enough for a warrant and they were due to have it by Friday night.

But first, Gerow thought that Friday morning, over a cup of his wife's coffee, first he had the Harrisons, Michael ("Call me Mike") and Rhonda, brother and sister. They were coming up from the city together and they were all due to meet in the police station at Accord, close to the house so the Harrison sibs could meet with Ms. LaPorta and their insurance adjusters and inspectors. Busy day for the Harrisons.

NINETEEN

Jeffrey had been against the whole thing. "Honey, we are going to get arrested if we go there and talk to Gerow with these people," he said.

They were sitting up in bed, he in his drawers, she in her work clothes. She'd come back from Rhonda's place pacing the apartment, telling him the conversation, wired. But yawning. Exhausted. She'd told him about throwing up again. She had stopped at Barnes & Noble, had *What to Expect When You're Expecting* with her, had been reading it on the subway. She was on schedule, feeling like shit.

She wanted to sleep. She didn't want to brush her teeth. She didn't want to go to work the next day. She'd been pacing back and forth.

"You're obsessed," he'd said.

She stopped. "Aren't you?"

"With you, yeah. But not with them. Not with those dead guys. Not with escaping from Brooklyn."

"What do you mean, escaping from Brooklyn?"

"I mean escaping from Brooklyn." He was sitting up. "Look, I didn't want you to go meet Rhonda in the first place. I don't want you out of my sight while freaks are roaming around in the woods upstate burning shit and posing as reporters."

"I'm safer in Manhattan, at Barnes & Noble, than I am here."

"I feel like a target," he said. He got up, went to her, put out a hand for her shoulder. She made a new move, a twisting, full-body rejection. He hadn't seen that one before, in all their fights.

"Obsessed," she said. "With...escaping."

That move. He couldn't protect her. She twisted away. He had to protect her.

"I don't know, maybe not escaping."

"And yet," she said, her voice light. "You said it. Obsessed. Escaping. Something we agreed on was to raise our kid someplace besides here. And now one of us is *escaping*. As opposed to doing what we said."

"No. I want to leave too. But we're running so fast to get out of this place—" he gestured around the apartment "—shouldn't we think more about what we're running into?"

"I'm looking forward, Jeffrey." He hated when she said his name, like she was reminding him who he was supposed to be. "I'm running toward something I want."

Tears came down her cheeks as she faced him. There was, inside her, a huger truth than she could speak. It had started when she miscarried, but it had felt older than that. It had first come to life on that September 11, when she'd watched the television over and over, and felt something so fundamental shift within her. Something had given way, clattered down through the struts that held her up, clattered down and made her entire—soul?—sway as though in a wind.

After the miscarriage, the shrink had given it a name. Even given it a number. Generalized anxiety disorder. Anxiety! Sure. Anxiety, of course, made her think of a nervous person biting her nails.

That was not this. This was, at its worst, a sense of sanity slipping away. She'd hear a song sometimes, and three hours later realize it was still playing in her mind. Or she'd check a lock three times. And then this sensation of panic welling up in her mind, a panic that rose to the point where she felt like she had to run, but which kept her rooted to the spot she was in, and then rose higher. What if she ran, but into traffic? What if her mind slipped past the point where she was herself? The terror could feel, between two heartbeats, absolutely bottomless. What if they found her in Central Park, covered in blood, dead kids in the bushes around her, unable to speak? Worse, what if she *could* speak, *could* remember every single thing she'd done? What if she was crazy?

That progression of thoughts could come to her sitting on a train, packed into one of the tunnels, on her way to work, between the *ding* and a door sliding shut. She remembered counting her pulse the whole way home from work on the train one night, counting off beats in fifteen-second intervals, then multiplying by four. For thirty-five minutes. It was sixty-eight pretty much every time.

She wasn't crazy. She never lost it, whatever *it* was. It was the threat of losing it that hovered there, off the edge of her consciousness, out in a zone someplace from which it sometimes made forays when work was stressful, when she stayed up too late and over-caffeinated next day, when they fought. She went to a gym for a while, that was okay. She dealt. There was a bottle of pills she'd half-finished in the last six months. Exercises from the shrink. Even a couple of self-help books.

But here was the thing. This *disorder*, whatever it was, came with a gift.

This fear was the worst *they* could do.

This was the worst *they* could do, no matter who the *they* was. The hijackers. Then, later, when it was herself and Jeffrey that she blamed for the baby. For their dead baby—she was the *they*. That was the worst she could do. That was the worst he could do. It was bad. Plenty bad.

Yet...here she was. Still able to taste soup. Still able to hold down a job. Still able to love, most times, this man. The gift could hit her just like an attack—in a quiet moment, a realization that the future pooled out from this moment. That, bone-deep, everything short of death was life, and life was survivable.

Serena didn't know how to say these things. They were burned into her: panic and peace, superpower and weakness, sides of a coin. Jeffrey knew it, knew her, watched her and sometimes tethered her at the onset of a panic attack (that time in the housewares store, looking at pillowcases), once watching as she talked to a homeless person and stayed intent and relaxed to hear his story.

She couldn't describe it. But she could say what she wanted. Because she knew.

"I want you and us and a baby in a place that feels right." She went into the bathroom.

He got undressed, got into bed. She came out, eyes dry. They continued. They sat on the bed.

"So maybe we'll get arrested," she said. "We haven't done anything wrong."

"It morphs into something wrong when we interfere with a police investigation."

"Then we won't interfere."

"What time are they going up there? What about work?"

She had him. It was becoming a reality in his mind. She wanted to paint him a picture of their day, but a different word came out.

"Obsessed," she said.

"How was work?" he said.

"What?"

"Work. Today. How was it?"

"It was...I don't know. It was okay."

"Did you sign anyone?"

"No. I was kind of distracted." She paused. "You asshole."

"*Obse-heh-esssed*," he sang.

. . .

In the morning she felt like shit, as though sleep hadn't happened at all. They rolled out at eight o'clock, spotted no police, and took the subway to Manhattan. Rhonda's car was a BMW and she kept it stabled in a garage around the corner from her place. They walked the block. The city in the morning, in the fall. Wind, gray skies, a scent that paradoxically always reminded Jeffrey of spring.

They'd brought bagels. Rhonda smiled tolerantly and declined. "Gluten," she said. Jeffrey rolled his eyes at Serena behind Rhonda's back. She'd eaten at five, she told them.

Jeffrey ate his bagel and lay in the back. Rhonda talked. She drove as though her association with the car was very casual, and what happened beyond the windshield concerned her peripherally—perhaps later she would tell friends about it at a gluten-free dinner—but was not as important as telling Serena how to raise her fetus.

"And Jeffrey," she said at one point, staring into the rearview and braking to avoid a column of backed up early weekenders on the Henry Hudson, "you are involved. You understand that?"

Serena turned and looked at him over sunglasses. "Honey? You understand?"

161

He sat up. "Involved. That's me. Rhonda, when was the house built?"

"In the eighties. My parents were psychiatrists and bought it as a weekend place. We kids spent parts of summers there, but we were mostly in college or just out. Alan's the youngest. He spent the most time, but he hasn't been back in years. Lives in Seattle."

"Did you burn it down?"

Rhonda dug an elbow into Serena's ribs. "I like him," she said, and started singing along with the radio. Serena mouthed *stop it* at him over the seat, smiling, and he lay back down. His ribs didn't hurt. He'd made an appointment to have the stitches out of his chin on Saturday. Maybe they could swing by the hospital in Kingston, get the same guy.

Rhonda crossed the George Washington Bridge and steered them onto the Palisades Parkway, along the river. The clouds were low and flat, and up here, looking down on Westchester through the thinning leaves across the gray water, they felt high. The city receded. Jeffrey's bagel was gone. Hills loomed ahead. The car topped a rise at an exit that said Mount Ivy and they saw the hills close, entered them. They wound between forested slopes. Rhonda took them to a traffic circle and went out of it heading west. The road carved its way through a last hilltop, through a cut in the rock, and Jeffrey, sitting up again and looking out onto the landscape, felt as though they had crossed through something important.

Beyond the cut they could see ahead a vast valley stretching west. A long mountain ridge lay to the right across the gap, gold and green. Down below they could see the Thruway snaking, a toll plaza, a big mall. They descended in a single lane behind a long line of cars. The road hugged the side of the hill. Jeffrey looked further to the right, saw the range of hills marching off over his right shoulder. Ahead of them it stretched south, fading into distance. In the drafts here at the edge of the mountain range there were dozens of huge black birds soaring.

He tapped Serena on the shoulder. "Eagles!" he said.

Rhonda glanced. "Vultures," she said.

At the bottom they got off the narrow highway and into a brief snarl of traffic lights before getting onto the Thruway north. He felt it again. They were now Someplace Else. Jeffrey lay back down.

"Are we meeting your brother there?" Serena said.

"Yes, I'm supposed to meet him at the diner in Accord and go to the police station together. I think you and Jeffrey should go to the realtor's office."

"I'll call her."

"Good idea. I think Michael and I ought to talk with the police first, before they know I brought you up."

"I'll be curious to hear what you think of the detective in charge. His name is Bill Gerow."

"I've spoken with him. Tell me about him."

"Tall, long face, gray hair. He used to work in the Bronx. He seems like a no-bullshit kind of a guy. But you get the feeling he knows things about people. About how they work."

"I'd say that's right. After he's through with my brother and me, we can all talk to the realtor and the insurance adjuster. We're supposed to meet them together at the realty office. Before you meet Michael I'll have to talk to him about what you told me. I can do that at the diner."

Serena left a message for Angela LaPorta, saying they would be stopping by with the Harrisons.

"What's your brother like?" she said to Rhonda.

"He's an absolute darling to anyone he doesn't work with. He's an absolute shit once he puts on a suit and wants to make money."

"What about the house?"

"That falls in between. He and I are close. I'm on your side. We'll see where he falls after I talk to him and after he meets you. I'm going to tell him you're pregnant."

"I'd rather you didn't. We're not telling anyone."

"It'll help. And the information isn't yours anymore, is it? That's how information works."

"That's not how manners work, though."

"Don't worry, Serena." She reached out, squeezed her hand. Bracelets slid down and rested against Serena's wrist. "I'll wait for the right moment. Remember, my mother and father were psychiatrists, and I'll know when to clue him in."

"So were his. He'll know what you're doing."

Jeffrey leaned forward between the seats. "I can't hear shit back here," he said.

Rhonda smiled, patted Serena on the wrist, and resumed singing.

They got off the highway at New Paltz and cut through the town. They watched the sheer walls of the Shawangunk Ridge approach, wound up through it. He looked behind them and saw the vast valley below again. They rolled down the far side into another wooded valley, narrower. Ahead of them, to the north, the taller mounds and terraces of the Catskills loomed.

The car pulled into Accord. Rhonda parked on the street. "See you at the realtor's office in an hour," she said.

When they walked in, a tall guy in a denim work shirt was getting up from the chair beside Angela's desk. She was still there, her face pale. They both turned toward the door.

"Deputy Hatch!" said Jeffrey and Serena in unison.

His voice was quiet. He almost, Serena thought, sounded like he was talking to himself. "Well, well, well," he said. "The Gales." He sighed. "He's not going to like this."

He turned back to Angela. "Thanks, Ang. I'll be in touch." He touched an imaginary hat brim, turned, and headed for the door. He stopped before Serena and Jeffrey.

"We just—" said Jeffrey.

"I didn't—" said Serena.

Hatch held his hand up, stopping word-traffic. "Here you are," he said. "Everything okay?"

"Yes."

"All right, then. I've got to go across the street. If I see Investigator Gerow, I'll have to mention that I ran into you."

"Of course," said Jeffrey.

Hatch touched the space in front of his forehead again, made his large, placid way across the street and disappeared into the police station.

They turned to Angela. She was composed again.

"What was that about?" Serena said.

"Glenn's married to my cousin. He was just catching me up on some family news."

"Are you okay?"

"Yes, I'm fine. But wait—" she got up. "What *are* you two doing here? I'm supposed to meet the Harrisons and that insurance adjuster."

"I met Rhonda Harrison yesterday," Serena said. "We got her name online and called."

"Why?"

"We're trying to figure out how we can get that property."

Angela leaned back against her desk. "There are hundreds of properties within twenty miles of where we're standing right now, with houses on them. Habitable houses," she said.

Jeffrey roamed the office, let Serena explain that she didn't want a habitable house, that she wanted a home and she was pretty sure she'd found it the previous Sunday.

She had a couple more houses she thought they might find interesting, and they humored her, looking at grainy pictures on the computer while they waited for Rhonda and Michael. Angela was jittery. She left the office, cell to her ear. She came back, sat down with a big sigh.

Serena looked at Jeffrey and went over to her desk. She leaned forward. She channeled Rhonda.

"Sweetie," she said, and put her hand on Angela's hand. "Sweetie, what is it?"

TWENTY

"Jack Grant? He's got a hunting camp outside of Margaretville," the woman said. She stood on the front steps of a trailer up the road from Grant's place. She had on sweat pants and a big pink hooded sweat shirt with some kind of abstract floral design coming up off the left side and across the belly. It was stained. She was smoking. She had white-blond hair. She leaned against the doorframe. A friendly pit bull nosed around the cops' feet. There was a chain-link pen in the back with nothing in it. Two cars parked reasonably neatly next to it.

"Do you know exactly where?"

"Nah, he never said. Outside of town there, though, up in the mountains. Goes up there deer season, sometimes on a weekend. He in trouble? He never did nothing down here that I heard about."

"No, no trouble," said the sheriff's detective. "His brother passed away, though, and we're afraid no one's informed Mr. Grant. Do you have a number for him?"

"I don't. Just see him taking out the garbage sometimes, we don't talk much. How'd his brother die?"

They gave her a little, left her with questions, asked her to keep it to herself. They could practically hear her get on the phone and start jabbering as they drove off. That was a lit fuse, right there.

TWENTY-ONE

Gerow was sitting with Rhonda and Michael Harrison. He'd just finished concluding that they had nothing.

The brother was big-time but he wore it okay. He'd arrived in a Range Rover, had on a country outfit, khakis and rich man's boots under some fleece and a polo shirt. He was a little shorter than Gerow, thicker around the face. He had executive-model hair that Gerow was pretty sure wasn't a toupee.

In his years with the State Police in the Bronx, Gerow had seen some weird shit go down with Wall Street—there was the Greenwich millionaire he'd arrested who liked to stop in the South Bronx every Wednesday on his way home for a foray into the urban wildlife. They'd busted an apartment for prostitution on a tip and snagged him with a crack pipe in his pocket and a shitstorm of excuses that culminated in an attempted bribe. There were a fair number of busts around the stadium, sweaty Yanks fans from the straight life buying dope off cops, lots of traders into that. There was one case he'd headed, a Wall Street executive shot in his car because he wouldn't surrender his wallet. Part of New York. He didn't miss it.

In any case, Michael Harrison didn't match any profile in his experience in terms of murder or arson. Guy like this was an embezzler, maybe, or might order a hit out of jealousy. *Maybe* he'd off a business rival. But connecting him to Cyrus Grant and the storefront minister? You'd have to go to Mars to make a connection.

Rhonda he didn't think would be able to burn her way out of a paper bag, much less kill someone. She rocked that zany vibe, decked out like a junkyard, draped in a thousand yards of fabric. She had strong hands, though, he remarked on shaking with her.

She'd held his too long. She'd turned her head and looked at her brother while she held onto Gerow. He wanted his hand back. She didn't want to let it go.

"Detective Gerow used to work in New York, Michael," she said.

"Is that right?" he said. He smiled at Gerow, looked at his sister's hand, gave the detective a miniature *what can you do?* shrug.

"He knows a lot about how people work," she said. She turned her eyes back to Gerow. They were brown. "You're married, Detective?"

"Twenty-five years last March," he said. He put his hand on her wrist and guided it gently off his own. For a split second she resisted, and just before he was able to form the thought that he was going to have to *pry* her fingers off him, she let go. She didn't just let go, though. Her fingers *slid* away from his, trailed away, floated away at the end. He suppressed a shudder.

She hadn't pursued the marriage line. They'd spoken for about a half hour. Gerow and another cop talked to them. Who would have burned the place down? What was the insurance situation? Neither of them claimed to have been up to the place in the last year. The mother had died a year and a half ago. They'd both come up and chosen the local realtor to show the place. An estate service had come and taken everything from books to clothes, done a broom sweep, sold what could be sold. The parents hadn't been collectors. Lots of books. Their father had been a fly fisherman. He had a few nice rods and books, some rare flies, all of which went to a dealer in the city. And that was it. To their knowledge, the house had been closed since, except for realty showings and a couple of cleanings that Angela LaPorta had arranged.

Gerow had a switch and when it flipped, the interview was over. It was the "nothing here" switch, driven by instinct. It flipped.

At that second Gerow's cell rang. "Gerow." He listened. Got up. Said "hang on," and put the phone down at his side.

"Folks, if you'll excuse me, something's come up I need to attend to. I think we're all set, and the detective here can wrap up with you." He nodded to the other cop and took off, getting details out of the handset at his ear.

He went into the squad room and got the attention of the detail. "Gents, we have a probable location for Jack Grant and it's got a time limit. The neighbor who gave us the lead is likely to talk. I want three cars. We're going to Arkville. It's about an hour."

Rhonda and Michael heard part of it as they left. "Michael," she said, taking her brother's arm. "I want you to meet the most darling couple. They're at the realtor's." She pulled him across the street.

Gerow headed for the back entrance. He spotted Hatch. "Glenn, I know you're off shift, but I'd like for you to join if you're able."

"Actually, Bill, I was looking for you. Cyrus Grant was my second cousin. Possibly third."

Gerow stopped, the sound of his shoes echoing to silence in the small space. "Whoa. You *knew* this cat?"

"Hadn't seen him in years. Only just found out an hour ago that he was the John Doe. I had to tell Angela."

Gerow remembered now that Hatch was married into that bunch, too. "Jesus. Your family been here long enough?"

"Back to Dutch days on mom's side."

"Glenn, you know where the brother's hunting camp is?"

"I do." He paused, thoughtful. "Looking for Jack?"

"I make him for the arson."

"Ahh, shit." Hatch looked at the linoleum. "That's what I get for taking a day off." He looked up. "Let's go."

TWENTY-TWO

So Angela LaPorta was distantly related to one of the murder victims and to Deputy Hatch. Small world. Serena wasn't sure what to make of it.

Serena didn't know, of course, that the dead guy had a brother. Angela knew that. She even knew the dead guy's brother drove a white pickup truck. But she didn't know the cops were looking for a white pickup truck. There were too many twos and twos to put together to make four, and everyone had their two in a separate pocket.

Jeffrey had come back with two chicken salad wraps from the diner and was about to reenter the realty office when he saw the Harrisons coming back from the police station. They'd be able to get back out to the remains of the house. Angela had okayed it with the police and the fire inspectors.

Serena came out to the sidewalk to greet them. Her boobs hurt. She couldn't look at any more pictures of houses. Angela worked the phone inside, business and family gossip.

"Jeffrey," Rhonda said, and she guided Michael's hand into his. "This is Michael. Michael doesn't follow sports." She turned to Serena. "Darling, that Bill Gerow is fascinating, isn't he?"

Michael greeted Jeffrey. He said "Jeffrey, good to meet you."

Car doors slammed across the street. A bunch of state troopers were leaving the local police station in a rush, getting into cars in the small parking lot that adjoined it. Jeffrey looked over Michael Harrison's shoulder. He saw Deputy Hatch's blue work shirt among them. Cars were jockeying for the chance to get out. Jeffrey saw Gerow hop into a marked cruiser with a uniformed cop. They maneuvered to take the lead. There was a bit of a clusterfuck.

"Keystone cops," Serena said.

Angela stepped out of the office and looked across. She looked nervous. Her cell was in hand. Serena turned back to her. "Angela?" she said. Angela was fixed on the action in the parking lot. She made a fist. She bit her knuckle.

Serena got it, snapped her attention back around to look at the station. "Oh, shit!" she said. "Jeffrey, they're going after someone!"

And right then the lead car pulled out, Gerow in the passenger seat. Serena saw his eyes cut left to take in the little cluster of onlookers across the street. She saw him do a double take. She saw him lean forward, across the driver as they completed the turn out of the driveway. She saw him fix her with a glare. She felt the glare in her solar plexus. She saw Gerow twist in the seat, his glare a beam of pure anger, trained on the little group of people on the sidewalk outside the realtor's office as the car sped off. Trained on her.

Something rose up in her. She was already in danger, as far as she knew. She'd been in fight or flight mode since finding those bodies, but the switch had been stuck on flight. She wanted some fight. She felt cornered, her back to that goddamn house on Bone Hollow road, hunched protectively over her belly, and she wanted some *fight*. Gerow wasn't letting them in, and she knew—of course she knew—that there was no reason they *should* be in. But she wanted in.

Fuck it, she thought. *This was the worst they could do.* "Rhonda," she said. "Give me your keys, would you, *darling*?"

Rhonda's car was peppier than the rentals they'd been getting, Jeffrey noticed as he negotiated the curves. It wasn't a problem to follow the caravan of police cars, flashers visible through the trees. They blew past the Country Inn and swept onto a state highway that curled around the western edge of a big reservoir. They went north, and west, at a good clip.

"Where do you think we could be going?" he said. He and Serena were alone in the car. Rhonda had cheerfully handed her the keys, as though she expected it. Nothing ruffled Rhonda. She was a nutcase, Serena concluded.

But she had a nice ride, and Serena's curiosity was more than she could bear. When she'd seen the cop exodus across the street, her first thought was that they were heading for the house. *The house!* But no. They blew past the turnoff to Bone Hollow, continued on. Those cars were moving. Jeffrey wasn't the most practiced driver. He'd grown up in suburbia, of course, and had had a car through college and for a couple of years after that. They rented a fair amount. He was doing fine.

She was going to throw up again. The chicken salad wraps sat on the seat next to her.

"I can't even imagine," she said. "A meeting of the society of fake reporters? The murderer's club get-together?"

He smiled at her. "Gerow is going to be *So. Pissed.*"

"Totally pissed," she said.

Her husband put the hammer down.

TWENTY-THREE

It was worth it to Baker to come out here and pay the guy twenty-five hundred. That wasn't so much to part with. But only if it would solve the problem. And he wasn't convinced it would. Trouble with a guy like Cyrus Grant, and presumably with the kind of people who'd be friends with him, was that they didn't have much else going on. If they found a little money, they'd want more. They'd try the same thing again, and again. If Jack thick-voice thought he could lever more money out of him, he'd just call back the next week. He might *say* that he'd forget Baker's name and license plate, but information didn't just go away. And people lied.

The play still eluded him. He wanted to get there early, though, and he wanted to case the spot. Maybe he'd just drop the bag and skedaddle. But he doubted it. He needed to know Arkville anyway. He'd be back this way pretty soon sniffing out the resistance. That town councilman, for a start. There was a congressman from these parts who was a problem. Grew up in the Movement, this guy. That was all okay. These were the usual challenges. These were the things he'd been dealing with since he rode shotgun in his dad's oil delivery truck in Jersey in the 70s. There were always people who didn't want other people to make a buck. Rivals. Cheapskates. And there were parasites, somewhat easier to deal with. Fortunately, decades of working the work, working his way up through it, had given him an eye for the patterns and the pressure points.

The trip was about six hours from his place. He could have driven it straight but he wanted a place to stay, someplace far from town. He spotted the right place near the state border. He got out of the car. Could feel the Marcellus Shale beneath his feet, deep here. Further east and north, out by his destination, there were outcrops of the stuff.

You had to pay out in a perimeter around the operations. Of course, landowners right on the deposits got the straight royalty, but leverage extended outward in roughly concentric circles from the actual area of impact, and that was the zone you had to grease. In the case of the Catskills, because some genius had put in an aqueduct a hundred years ago, they had to worry about New York City. It was all WestGen could do to handle the fucking state legislature. *Those* fucking guys were a bottomless fucking pit. You paid them, you never—ever—stopped paying. They could smell a dollar at any depth and would drill till they had it. Add New York City to the mix and you were well and truly underwater.

So, research, research, research. Who were the players? Who were the players who could give him the players? Maybe this Jack fellow wasn't a complete idiot. Maybe there was a proposition there. He wouldn't mind a pair of boots on the ground. Although these boots had kicked someone who could recognize them.

He wondered where Jack lived. That whole area just south of the mountains was a warren of roads, old farms, little crossroads towns with a convenience shop and a gas station, here and there a gourmet restaurant tucked into a nook for the weekenders, cheek-by-jowl with trailer parks and gun shops. The cities were east, along the river. Easy to hide out there, but probably hard to stay hid.

He did his usual unobtrusive thing: fake name, wrong license plate, and paid cash at a motel on the edge of town. He put on sunglasses and a Yankees cap. In his experience, that was camouflage anywhere within a hundred fifty miles of New York City. Then he went to see the sights.

It wasn't a great day; the overcast was near-solid. Not too windy, at least. Last leaf-peeper crowds. Halloween decorations everywhere. There was a big banner over the street for a haunted rail ride, signs pointing to a historic train station. He heard a steam whistle off that way. He could blend, that was good.

He got a pre-made sandwich, some water and a Chamber of Commerce pamphlet, read about the history a little. Western edge of the borscht belt. Big old hotel on the east side of town. Schlesinger's.

The steam whistle went again. Baker realized he was part of a small mob gravitating toward that side of town. There was an old rail yard over there, he could see, converted into a fairground. Couple of big tents set up. There was a popcorn cart, some cotton candy for sale, stalls with the same crap you could find at any one of these kinds of events. Fork-and-spoon wind chimes. Soap.

A black-and-orange draped stage bore a bluegrass band plinking away, dressed up like scarecrows. Couple of old people sat there in the front row, hearing aids presumably turned down. One guy wearing his American Legion hat with WWII decor. Some fleece-clad couples with strollers, a woman with expensive sunglasses and high heels yelling at a curly-haired little girl who was trying to take the old vet's cane. "Emma! EMMA you put that down! Emma!" She looked around for her husband. Absent without official leave.

The whistle went again, and Baker saw a big painted-plywood board with Haunted Train Ride times. That was a two-minute warning. What the hell, he thought. Maybe he could case the Schlessinger property from the train. He joined the press for last-minute tickets and climbed into the vestibule of an old passenger car.

The cars bore logos of old railroads from around the country. They were just boxes with seats at this point, minimally maintained. This was no Pullman luxury retreat; this was strictly Point A to Point B stuff, and points A and B were about a mile apart. Between two of these cars were a couple of open-deck flatcars with double-sided benches running down the middle, chain link around the perimeter to keep the toddlers aboard. The map showed the haunted train went out along the Schlesinger's property, stopped at the old hotel station and then reversed down the track.

The steam engine pulling the thing was actually a diesel, painted black and fitted with a whistle and an old-timey stack that blew exhaust, not coal smoke. They'd pinned a big plywood painted death's head on the front. A banner ran along it: Haunted Train Ride.

"Not real haunted, is it?" Baker turned. A guy stood next to him, five-year-old hanging from his sleeve. The guy gestured at the daylight.

"Ah, yeah."

A woman leaned across Baker from the other side. "It's been running for a week. I hear the nighttime ride is the one to see. They do ghosts and stuff in the woods."

Baker smiled, said "excuse me," worked his way out of the vestibule into the car proper. Tinny speakers overhead played that creepy organ piece, but it was nearly impossible to hear over the parents barking orders and the children disobeying them.

The last person was pulled aboard, doors slammed, and the train lurched away from the platform. It crept out of the station, the crowd from the last ride still jammed up outside. Heads turned to watch the steam and follow the motion of something so big, so close. Looking down from inside, it really felt like pulling out of a busy train station on market day might have felt back when people did things like that. *Shit*, Baker thought. *This is almost fun.*

The decibel level in the passenger cars was astounding. As he stutter-stepped his way along the aisle, waiting for clear passage and guarding his gonads from troops of pre-teens and toddlers, Baker wondered if there was an evolutionary benefit for little people to scream constantly. The lions wouldn't be far off, he thought.

He broke out into one of the flatcars. Better. Still packed, but the sound dissipated into the mountain air. The train left the confines of the yard, crossed a road at grade level. Everyone waved to the cars stuck at the crossing. "Suckuhs," said a heavy guy decked in Yankees gear with two kids standing in front of him, faces pressed against the chain link. "Suckuuuhs," the kids said. They high-fived.

One thing; there were cameras everyplace. Video cameras, cell phones, little digital point and shoots, a few serious-looking dudes trying to wield big telephotos and tensely begging their wives to fend off the kids for a second. Losing battle, that.

Baker pulled his cap down and kept his back to the car. He positioned himself on the north side, where he'd get the best view of whatever the old hotel had to look at, the old station.

They exited the built-up side of town and pretty quickly went along an embankment into the woods. He looked right and saw a black fabric archway held up by a cherry-picker over the tracks, painted to look like the gates of hell. A big fanged devil's mouth. They passed through and were in trees on both sides. Mummies hung from them, electric red eyes. Screams played out of loud speakers. Sinister Dracula laughs, *muhwhawha*. Kids pretended to scream. Adults jostled them, said "boo!"

It was fine. They went along that way; tarry smoke drifted across the track from small fires back in the woods. Black-clad figures wandered around with medieval weaponry. Baker wasn't sure what the theme was, overall, but it had atmosphere of a kind.

He got his look at the old hotel, spread out across a hilltop a quarter-mile north of the tracks. It looked mostly intact to him. Big, sprawling, part of it a low-slung concrete wing, the central portion a big brick and stone thing with two towers in front. Looked like the burn damage centered where the newer wing joined the older portion. He could see chain link and razor wire. No Trespassing signs. Its old driveway was breaking up, its paint faded.

Cheap jet fuel took care of that place, he thought. *Was burned before Jewish lightning ever touched it.*

By the time they stopped and began to back up, he had a plan.

TWENTY-FOUR

Jack handed the spliff to Charlie. They were standing under the overhang outside the cabin. Charlie had on a canvas work jacket and paint-spattered carpenter's pants. He had on work boots. He had a shaved head and a little tuft of goatee under his lip, with two deep lines down the sides of his face. He looked like a bird of prey. Charlie inhaled deep.

"Guy's got twenty-five hundred, he's got more, am I right?"

"Yes, you are."

"How much more, and how do we get that? That's what I want to know."

"I don't know, man. I got a pretty simple set up. He's just gonna leave the money at the hotel desk and then I'm s'posed to go there and get it. I told him Sunday noon, but I'm planning to stick it out till late Sunday night. This guy aced Cyrus and another guy, and I don't want to give him another notch in the bedpost, you know?

"What the fuck's that mean?"

"You know, like, when you kill someone."

"Bullshit. It's when you fuck someone, dipshit." Charlie toked again.

Jack held out his hand for the joint. "Anyway," he said. "It's not complicated. But I figured I should have some backup in case he's still around. And you're good backup."

"Fifty-fifty, you said," Charlie said.

"No, *you* said. *I* said five hundred. You don't have to do anything but stand there with a gun. You do that anyway in three weeks. Someone pay you twelve hundred bucks to go hunting?"

"This guy's such a badass, I'm taking half the risk. He's a ninja or some shit like you think, I'm liable to get my ass shot. Or have to shoot his. That's worth something. I'm the kind of guy who gets paid what he earns."

"If you get shot, I'll give you half."

Charlie laughed. "That you will, Jack. That you will."

Dick, thought Jack. The pot was hitting him. Bit of a rush to this batch.

Pedrango *was* a dick, and didn't care who knew it. He was the kind of guy who'd walk into a place and say shit like that, talk about himself. "I'm the kind of guy who..." he'd say. He could follow that up with any bullshit he wanted. It was usually "...don't like to be lied to" or "...don't take any shit" or "...says 'I'm okay, you're okay,' but don't try to fuck me." Jack thought maybe Charlie Pedrango had trust issues.

He had 'em even worse since Iraq. Jack and him had been buddies before, but Jack had work and Charlie didn't, so he'd joined up. He'd talked about it one time. Four kills. Knew six guys who'd died, three in one incident with an IED. He didn't seem much changed by it. He didn't seem to have flashbacks, it wasn't that PMS shit. He was maybe just a little less patient. He'd done his two years, got out just before stop-loss.

Before, he'd been the same badass. He and Jack fought in bars. They stole car batteries from time to time. They robbed an office supply store after closing once down in Kingston for dope money. It was the time Jack had been out with Charlie eating speed at an old quarry that stuck in his mind, made him think Charlie was his best bet to get out of the money pickup okay.

They'd seen a bonfire across the way and staggered through the woods around to that side. There were about eight or ten high school kids, mostly guys, couple of chicks. The local metalheads. They were Jack and Charlie, ten years younger. They were drinking forties and pouring gouts of white gas on the fire. Boys were jumping through the flames.

Charlie and Jack had come out of the woods roaring, scared the shit out of the kids. Girls screamed, guys yelled "what the fuck?" and everyone laughed. Then Charlie froze them. His face went raptor, and he stared around the fire, catching everyone's eyes. Jack had stood behind him, folded his arms, looking grim. Eyes watching the fire dance dance dance. Tweaking.

"All right, everybody," Charlie'd said. "Take everything outta your pockets and put it on that towel." He pointed to a ratty beach towel one of the jumping kids had been sitting on.

"Fuck you," one of the kids started to say, and Charlie pinned him. It really was like a rodent pinned by a bird of prey, but Charlie didn't even move. His eyes snapped onto the kid, his head inclined a little.

"The fuck you say to me?"

Silence.

"That's fuckin-a right. Do it. Purses too, ladies."

They'd run off with eighty bucks, a bag of weed and one unopened forty-ounce, laughing their asses off. They never showed a weapon. They never even threatened anyone. Charlie just wanted it, and he said so, and he got it. It was all attitude, Jack thought. It never occurred to Charlie that it wasn't his.

And that had been *before* the camel-jockey clusterfuck in the middle east. Charlie still seemed as steady/unsteady as he'd been before. Just maybe a little quicker with talk about getting his, about getting what was coming to him. *Five hundred, give or take,* Jack thought.

Take, most likely.

TWENTY-FIVE

Gerow fumed into the phone. "There's no reason for you to be here. You're dangerously close to obstructing governmental administration. That's a charge we can levy against someone who gets in the way of a police investigation. And I will do it. Why did I just see you with the Harrisons? Did that realtor put you in touch?"

"No," Serena said. "The tax maps."

Jesus God, he thought to himself. When it came to fight or flight, it was like this lady's *flight* was broken. Why was he even bothering with this shit? Arguing with a witness? Granted, he wanted this couple on their side; they were maybe a day away from ID'ing Jack Grant, and he needed them for that. He needed them to ID the fake reporter, who he was pretty sure Jack Grant could lead them to. They were central to unraveling this whole—what's the Yiddish word people liked—*mishigas*. So he didn't want them hostile. But there was a fucking limit.

"Mrs. Gale, there is a limit," he said. "Are you in it for the adventure? What's going on with you two? In fact, you know what? Put your husband on."

"My husband?"

"Yes, please let me talk to Mr. Gale. I saw him there two minutes ago, I know he's with you."

"I can speak for us both. Besides, Jeffrey's busy. "

"Busy? What do you mean, busy? This is the *police*." Gerow saw the trooper driving the car glance sideways, his face neutral. The guy's lips tightened. He studied the road. *Ah fuck,* Gerow thought, *I'm gonna hear it over this.*

"He's driving."

"Driving? Where?"

"To look at houses."

Gerow's lie meter sang. He gripped the phone more tightly, tilted it so he was talking straight into the pickup "Let me make something very clear to you, Mrs. Gale. You are *not* to follow us. You can do *nothing* to help in this investigation except what you've already done. I promise you we will do everything we can to arrest the person who attacked you, and who burned down the house you liked, and who killed those men you found. That's *my job.* Yours, I've told you before, is to keep yourself safe and stay out of our way. Do you get me?"

A mile or so back, Serena heard "...person who attacked you, and who burned down the hou...ike...ose...en...oun...*y job*...old... ore...eep..elf safe and...out...ay...et"

He listened, heard her voice, fragments. "...aking...all...o?... orry..."

"God *damn* it," he said, and shut his phone.

Deputy Hatch had shown them the Grant family hunting camp on a map before they left the station in Accord, and the column of cars was closing on it. They had put in a call to the sheriffs and asked for a unit to park out where the camp road met the state highway, so they figured the camp was sealed off that end. No roads showed going out of it the other way. Units were instructed not to approach until the full detail arrived. The guy could be holed up there with scoped hunting rifles and hand grenades for all they knew, or not there at all. Jack Grant could have killed his brother and burned down the house to hide some imagined evidence that hadn't turned up. Gerow was more and more of that mind. They didn't have a mug shot for Jack, or he'd've asked the Gales to ID it. All they really had to tie him to anything was the white pickup, his absence, a rough description matching what he'd gotten from the Gales.

Maybe Hatch had a recent Thanksgiving pic. Jesus. Between these Grant boys and LaPorta having a meeting with the Harrisons and the Gales, the extended Hatch family was proving a swift pain the ass.

But it all still left the reporter thing. What *was* that?

The real Gilbert had stopped at the barracks in Kingston twice in the past week and talked with Detective Gerow. He'd gotten the ID on Cyrus Grant a day after the cops, was chasing down leads for a piece on Grant's career. There was enough in that one for a loooong series. Cyrus Grant had been a living crime spree. Gilbert and his colleagues were working with reporters from Pennsylvania in parallel with the cooperative police investigation, working up a piece on the tie-in to the minister's disappearance.

But what still had Gilbert scratching his head, and where he hadn't made any headway, was the fake reporter. The security pics hadn't been that great. The *C-D* had run the best three-shot series a couple of times in conjunction with stories about the murder/arson. Nothing. Pudgy guy in khakis and a blue polo shirt, black bag with writing pads and a tape recorder, glasses. No great shots of his face. No shots of a car. The sketch hadn't turned up anything. He'd flared briefly into sight and then disappeared.

It made the case a conspiracy. The ground in PA had been dug up, the whole congregation questioned. The three convicts had been a tight focus, but these guys seemed pretty straight. They'd been in jail for non-violent offenses; one B&E, the other two dealing. Out, they'd rented a place together and been referred to Peterson by their parole officers. They had been questioned when he disappeared, and they'd all seen Cyrus Grant's mug shots a bunch of times in the last day or two, and they didn't recognize him. None of the three had ever missed a meeting with their POs; they were well-regarded by the congregants, worked hard on the work crews. Didn't raise any flags

Gilbert had told Gerow he'd keep working it.

TWENTY-SIX

Jeffrey was getting nervous again. Serena's argument with the cop had been weird and cut short.

She smiled over at him, flipping her phone shut. "Yup," she said. "Completely pissed."

"What'd he say?"

"Well, he wanted to talk to you. Like you were going to 'correct' me." She looked down at the seat, pouted, looked up through her lashes. "You wouldn't do that, would you, you big, big man? To little me?"

He took it in with a quick glance, hands tight on the wheel. God, she was astounding and could be utterly ridiculous. "I love you, you goofball," he said.

"You must be hungry," she said, and unwrapped one of the wraps. She made a face and held it out away from her. She turned and opened the window, gulped air, handed it over to him blindly.

"You okay?" he said, and took it, took a big bite, felt pieces of lettuce and mayonnaised chicken land in his lap.

She said "I'm fine," but leaned out and left a stream of barf ribboning back into the wind, striping the side of the car. He started to brake. She did it again. Then she pulled her head back in and turned to him.

"Don't stop!" she said.

He stepped on the gas again.

Serena spit out the window, picked up the other wrap, and threw it out of the car. Closed her eyes and sipped water from one of the bottles.

"Sorry," she said.

"Tell it to Rhonda," he said. The land was rising around the western edge of the reservoir. They merged onto a wider state highway and chased the line of police cars through towns. They had finally entered the country of the high mountains that had hovered before them earlier. The golds and reds were duller now. Leaves blew across the road. The police convoy was drawing away, its lights and powerful engines too much for their intrinsic fear of breaking the law and Jeffrey's inexperience with eighty-plus driving, even in a high-performance car like this one on a dry road with good visibility.

"This is dumb," he said. He threw the rest of his wrap out the window, gripped the wheel more tightly, and floored it. The car leaped forward, the tach rising close to the redline before the automatic shifted up to fifth, and *now* they were into it. He picked up some ground.

"There can't be too many places to *go* out here," he said. He glanced at his wife. She was lolling on the seat, eyes closed, occasionally taking little sips from her water bottle. "Even if they lose us, we'll probably catch up to wherever they go."

"Yep," she said.

"That book said to expect this," he said.

She opened her eyes. "Expect this?" She gestured at the car, at the road.

"You didn't read that chapter, huh? Week four, it says, you may be feeling like chasing cars."

"Oh *waaaiiit,*" she said, her voice singsong. "I don't think that was the book you think it was..."

"You mean I was reading *What to Expect When You're a Dog!?*" he said.

Jeffrey's nerves were stretched. He kept expecting his foot to ease up on the gas, but it kept not doing that. The lights were still visible up ahead. They were close enough that the rare gaps in traffic that the cops opened up were still open enough when they arrived. Cars got back out of the way. Jeffrey flashed the brights, opened a lane, whipped through. It was a matter of attitude, he realized. Drive like it's yours.

He changed his tune a minute later when a delivery truck that had pulled onto the shoulder lumbered back out into the highway directly in their path, at the same time the oncoming lane filled up. Jeffrey slammed the brakes, then pressed down, then *mashed* the pedal while the logo on the back of the truck got bigger and bigger. Rubber screamed. Serena's hands shot out and hit the dash. Jeffrey gripped the wheel. The front end dipped and they skidded an impossibly long time, the car continuing straight like it was on rails. They were kissing distance from the back deck of the truck when the driver goosed it forward and their 200-yard skid ended, the truck infinitely far away, untouched. The driver flipped them the bird. Jeffrey stepped on the gas again.

He flashed his brights at the trucker, but the guy wouldn't give until the next town, a few minutes later, and the road wound too much to pass in the oncoming lane. The driver's voice dopplered "aaaAAAAsshoooole" as they accelerated past him searching for the flashers. Nothing. Shandaken. Pine Hill. Fleischmanns. No clusters of cop cars, no cars stacked in the shoulder as though they'd just passed. They kept on.

It was a few miles past Fleischmanns ("like the yeast?" they'd both said) that they blew into a town with some action. Folks were wandering the streets. Jeffrey slowed. They bumped over a railroad crossing.

"Ooh, bars," Serena said.

"I don't think we should be—"

"On the phone, Jeffrey," she said.

"Gotcha."

"Huh," she said. "Three missed calls. Three voicemails."

He slowed alongside a family cluster, fleece-clad tourist types like themselves, but with less puke. "Excuse me?"

Dad came over to the car. "Yeah?" He sniffed, then eyed the stripe of yellow down the silver door panel.

"Did you see some police come through?"

"I heard them," the guy said. "But I didn't see which way they went. I think along here," and he pointed down the main street. Main Street.

"Thanks." They moved forward again. He pulled up again at the next corner.

Serena was looking back at them. Daddy, Mommy, girl, baby.

"Look at that, Jeffrey," she said.

He looked in the rearview. "What?"

"A family of tourists."

"Yes. A tourist family."

"It's just cute, that's all."

"Oh." He looked again. He pretended to break into a sob. "I love them so fucking much," he said.

"Dick," she said, and put her hand on his thigh. "I want crackers."

"Okay, we'll get 'em in a sec. 'Scuse me," he said out the window. A mother and her daughter sitting on a bench. The daughter was eating french fries out of a cardboard boat with a wooden skewer. The mother stayed put, said "yes?"

"Did the police just come through?"

"They turned right up at that corner," she said.

"Thank you." He went thataway.

They made slow progress that way through town, stopping at every turn and asking, but eventually petered out at the end of a street that went out of town up toward the mountains. There were options here, and the crowds were non-existent, and they'd lost five minutes. The trail was cold. Jeffrey pulled to the edge of the street—there were no curbs here—got out, and listened. He heard nothing. He looked up ahead, but from below the views weren't clean. At night maybe he'd be able to see the lights bouncing off the sides of the ridges, but now they were lost in the reds and yellows of the mountainsides.

"Dammit," he said. He leaned into the car. "We can wait at the edge of town for them to come back," he said.

"Crackers," she said.

"Well, they're certainly not the hippest guys around, but a couple of them were African-American," he said.

"Jeffrey. Crackers," she said. She meant it. He took her into town to a diner. They got her some saltines and he had a grilled cheese. She ate three crackers, then a pickle and all his french fries and a milkshake and some of his grilled cheese.

They didn't notice the chubby Yankees fan in the sunglasses who marked their entrance to the diner, who lingered until they came out, who followed them the block to their car, who memorized the license plate, who stuck around to see where they went next. The town was filling up with twenty-somethings getting rowdy for the nighttime ride of the Haunted Train. Lights flared at four o'clock. The mountains cast shadows while the sky stayed light.

TWENTY-SEVEN

They reconnoitered at the base of the valley road leading up to the camp. Hatch stood with Gerow and the sheriff's guy who'd been staking out the road the last hour and a half. No white pickups had come or gone. Couple of other cars, one blue pickup with a gun rack and two guys in camouflage, out for turkey. There was state land at the head of the valley. There was no road over the ridge, but there were ATV and snowmobile trails up there.

Glenn Hatch had only been there once, six years ago, but he knew the spot. It'd been some uncle's place. Jack had gotten it because he was the hunter and he'd put in some years there.

"I could call him," Deputy Hatch said. He checked his own cell. Bars.

"You have his number?" Gerow asked.

"No, but my mom would," he said. "Or, she'd have his mom's number."

"How many of you are there, Hatch?"

"Thanksgiving's pretty big." He looked up the mountain. "Although this year it's gonna be weird."

Gerow considered it. "We could call in a SORT team. But they like to shoot. Those MP5s don't pay for themselves unless they get shot off. Cousin or not, I hate to call those guys."

"What's the play, Investigator? It's your case."

The hills rose either side of the road. They were gathered on a small flat spot. There was a tiny cemetery across the road, set back and set off with rocks painted white and with American flags. The stones and stars were taking on an evening glow, down here in the trench between Stone Ridge and Fox Ridge. Behind the cemetery they could hear the rush of a creek. The last house of the residential district was a hundred yards down. Flashers were off. The overcast was breaking up and the breeze was freshening. Staties were putting on their jackets. Men were checking their guns.

Gerow ran a few scenarios through his head. The SORT option—Special Operations Response Team—was really heavy, and he liked the plan with the least flying lead. "See if you can get his number. Call him up and don't tell him we're here. Ask him where he is. Tell him about Cyrus. Tell him you'd like to talk to him at the Accord police station. Don't mention the arson. Don't tell him a white pickup was spotted at the scene of the killing."

"I can do that."

Hatch went back to his car to call where it would sound indoors. The detective briefed the detail on the current plan.

It took fifteen minutes—Hatch's mother told him she'd have to call him back—before he got Jack's number. He signaled Gerow, who joined him in the cruiser. Hatch dialed.

"'Tsup?" his cousin said. He spoke from somewhere under his tongue, Hatch remembered. Jack always sounded like his next word would be "duh," but he never quite said it.

TWENTY-EIGHT

Baker stayed invisible. He saw the cops go past at two thirty, blazing through town silently but with flashers on. SWAT team! He tensed, then forced himself to relax. No, no, not for him. He was camouflaged, he knew that. They were state cops and Sullivan County sheriffs. He'd watched as they turned off the main strip. His map was in the car and he couldn't check it to see what options lay that way, but he suspected they weren't going far. There just weren't many places to *go*.

He entertained the idea that it had something to do with him, but he didn't hang onto it long. There was nothing he could do either way, he supposed. Could they be onto Jack? He wasn't convinced that Jack lived in Arkville. For a drop, you set up a place that couldn't be tied to you. Didn't you? That's what Baker had done, the few times he'd had to do anything like that. It was more likely a hunting accident. In any case, he himself wasn't expected till Sunday, supposedly, so he wasn't worried. It wasn't as though Jack could finger his location now, even if it was him they were after.

In fact, Baker thought, the cops probably had Jack pegged for the murders, if they knew anything about him at all. That pretty girl from Brooklyn had seen his face and could ID him. They'd seen Jack's truck. Who else would torch a murder scene but the trigger man? Jack's ass was hanging out on this one, far more than Baker's.

In any case. Baker's plan was in place. He had a hot ticket for the Haunted Train Ride into the mouth of Hell. He was going to hop off the train on the first nighttime ride, do the drop, then jump back on for the return trip on the second one. And he still hadn't decided whether he'd stick around for Sunday morning someplace quiet with his .30-30, looking for Jack.

He was thinking thoughts like these as he headed back to his car for another layer of clothes. And Serena's face, paler now, but unmistakable, loomed out of the afternoon, coasted past him on a crowded sidewalk. She looked drawn. Her husband held her elbow. Baker went on instinct. He kept walking, heart hammering—SWAT team!—till he reached a corner and turned in time to see them go into the diner whose windows faced Main Street.

Ahh, shit. This made no sense. Were they with the cops? Was this a setup? His mind automatically looked for precedent, a recognized pattern. A logical explanation. None came to mind. Baker was at a loss. He suddenly had a feeling that this was no longer his gig.

He didn't like that. At the very least, their presence here suggested that the cop caravan that had rolled into town had something to do with the case. The case? *Him*! Shit, shit, shit.

He crossed the street, walked back down until he could see into the diner. He watched Jeffrey—that was his name—and Serena take a seat. He saw her tear into a packet of saltines. They raised menus.

Baker tried to avoid jogging back to his car—makes you visible—to grab a jacket and think. Diner time was, what, twenty minutes minimum? In general he had plans in place for eventualities. Scenario planning, they called it in the big WestGen national conference. They were asked to brainstorm various energy-related scenarios on a large scale and smaller scales. So in the event of a leak, say, or an accident at one of the sites, a certain routine kicked into place.

Here, he had nothing. He could've planned for a cop finding the rifle. Could've planned for a double-cross out at *Slesinners*. But this? It was no coincidence.

Take it one thing at a time. What about those cops? He looked at the map, saw no roads leading north out of Arkville to anyplace else, but a few spurs that led off into the hollows north of town, any one of which could have been the cops' destination. Something was up. Seeing that couple made it pretty clear that they were on the hunt for Jack. Had the couple ID'd him? Then what, they followed the cops? Maybe the cops wanted them on hand to make an ID.

Baker became more certain. Whatever was happening here was about Jack, not about him. And Jack was in deep shit.

And that girl. She knew his, Baker's, face. Maybe both of them did. He'd checked them out. They lived in Brooklyn. They were looking for houses. Frankly he admired their tenacity, coming up here a week later. Or the cops might've called them back up to look at photos. That was probably it. They'd ID'd Jack from a photo lineup and the cops had asked them to come to Jack's house and make an ID. But they were supposed to wait down here.

So, he wondered. Drop the money and wait to peg Jack on Sunday? The cops might be taking care of that right now. Did that fucker really know his name and license plate? It was true that he'd driven his own car the day he shot those guys. But he hadn't come across anyone.

Cyrus. That wastoid shithead might have taken down his plates in the parking lot of the Denny's, the night he'd gotten his number. After all, there'd been only a couple of cars in the lot, and Cyrus's own car—a K-car that looked skewed like it'd gotten racked, a taxi-sized cluster of those pine air fresheners hanging from the rearview—had been easy enough to pick out. Yeah, he might've passed on that piece of info to a confederate.

But even if they arrested Jack and he gave up the license plate, even if Cyrus had gotten his name from some DMV record and stored it someplace and it came out, they couldn't have an idea that he, Baker, was in town tonight. But Jack could tell them that he was due out at the hotel on Sunday to make the drop. Jack in the woods, Baker could handle. A SWAT team in the woods? Baker knew his limits.

Fuckity-fuck fuck.

He got a coffee at the Stewarts and tried to figure out how to remain invisible once the sunglasses became ridiculous. That hour was rapidly approaching. The shadows of the hills lengthened.

TWENTY-NINE

The table next to them was taken up by four college boys. To Jeffrey, looking past his wife at them, they all looked like Shaggy from Scoobie-Doo. One of them had black discs in his ears and a pierced eyebrow. They ate like Shaggy, too. Skinny boys, sucking down milk shakes and gardenburgers and fries.

They were talking about the Haunted Train ride, he gathered, but their speech was aboriginal, still teenaged. Grunts, deep-voiced sounds with a lot of "aaaauuuu" in them. Laughter. So many inside jokes that they had become their own language, something he couldn't quite follow. Like hearing the cleaning crew at his office speaking Spanish. He'd studied it from eighth grade into sophomore year of college, but couldn't understand a word of the real thing.

"Zombie shit," he heard. Another one said "aauuuu braaau." "Yiiiiip," said another. One sang a snatch of a song. Another one made some beatbox noises.

What he could tell, though, was that they were jazzed.

"Excuse me," he said.

The one closest, who'd had his back to Jeffrey, turned. "How you doing?" he said.

"Good, good. How are you?"

"Good." He wiped his mouth on a napkin. Impressive. He raised his eyebrows, including the one with the little shaved stripe through it, in inquiry.

"Have you done that Haunted Train ride before?" Jeffrey said.

"Oh, yeah," he said. They all turned, began describing their experience with overlapping purple language, expansive gestures and guttural sound effects.

It was awesome, they gathered. Jeffrey raised his eyebrow at Serena.

"Train ride?" he said.

"What about the cops?" she said.

"Maybe we should leave them alone," he said. "Haven't we pissed off Gerow enough?"

"Maybe. Where'd they go, though?"

"Up into the hills, I guess. But I don't want to go up there and meet Gerow in the road. I thought we'd follow them for five minutes and be able to see them pull up someplace and surround a house. I thought we'd be able to park across the road in a field and hide behind the car when the shooting started."

"You had a plan."

"Plans. Schmans. Let's go to Hell."

They left the diner behind the lads, and went to buy tickets.

The shadow of the southern mountains lay across most of the town now, but as they left the diner the sun popped around a corner and shone through a westward notch. Jeffrey put his sunglasses on. Serena shaded her eyes to look down-valley. Her eyes scanned the hills north of town. Nothing.

THIRTY

Baker was fifteen feet away, turned westward, sunglasses on too. He was nearly trembling. She was right back there, so close. So pretty. That adrenaline feeling, the feeling of impersonating a reporter, was back. Different, oddly different, than the focused precision of the shooting, different than the calculated urgency of dealing with Jack. This was raw, for him. He supposed he'd... *imprinted* on her face. That was it. He'd walked into the nest of cops to question the couple and pretended to be Gilbert, and his mojo had been strong, and the core of that had been a conversation with those hazel eyes, her dark hair, the curve of her cheek. She'd looked up at him, she'd put on that little act, the scared little girl act he saw coming a mile off, but he was flattered she'd thought to try. He'd touched her hand in sympathy. He could still feel her skin, the merest brush of soft hairs beneath the pads of his fingers.

And here she was.

And the husband, who was way beneath her league—but who was Baker to judge? It took all kinds, he figured—what was he going to do with them? Nothing here, not with the cops lurking somewhere nearby. Not with the rifle in the trunk, not with the money bag clutched in his hand. He'd put a sandwich in there too so people wouldn't wonder what he was carrying.

When the couple didn't pass him after a minute he turned and saw them across the street heading the same direction as a few college boys on their way to the ticket booth. Okay, that made sense. They could all take a train ride together.

The sun slid behind the westward peaks and wouldn't be back this night.

. . .

Serena looked at her phone. "Bars," she said.

Jeffrey pointed west at a cell phone tower behind the brick town hall. "There you go," he said.

"Ah," she said. "Go buy the tickets," she said, "I'll check these messages."

Rhonda. Gerow. Rhonda. Her aunt Jill.

She called Rhonda and explained where they were and what was happening. Rhonda said "the car is okay?"

"We'll have to wash it, but it's okay."

"I was calling to see if you'd drive it back to the city for me. I need it tomorrow afternoon, but not before. Michael will drive me down in the morning."

"Where are you staying?"

"There's a B&B nearby. Insurance is paying!" She laughed.

"I think we'll be back that way tonight," Serena said. "We're just going to take this train ride thing. We can't find the police. They went up into the hills someplace and we haven't heard anything for the last hour."

Still with the airy yoga voice. "I don't have kids," said Rhonda, "but from what I hear, you're going to want to take your time with your adventure. It's going to change drastically in a few months."

"Rhonda, why are you being so generous?"

"My husband killed himself eleven years ago."

"Oh." Serena stopped walking. The street drew away. She was standing by a public garbage can under a lamp post. Moths were gathering in the chill around the bulb above. Young people rolled by, clad in black fleece and wooly sweaters, girls with knitted hats with flaps, their chilly fingers wrapped in the ends of long sleeves. Boys goofing, shoving. Flasks passing back and forth.

She looked for Jeffrey, couldn't see him.

"I'm so sorry," Serena said.

"I'm used to it," Rhonda said. "But I haven't had your... opportunity. And I think what you're doing now is part of it. But Serena—" she said.

"Yes?"

"Be careful, won't you? And Jeffrey, too."

"We will."

. . .

Baker had followed the husband, as much as he liked looking at Serena. Was there an opportunity here? They'd been together since he'd sighted them...with a train nearby, was there opportunity for mayhem?

He knew that if there were a way for him to put the guy out of commission with zero percent chance of revealing himself, he would do it. He didn't think he needed to kill him or anything, not that. Just...was it possible to scare someone? Give them a bad *vibe*? Make them never want to come back to a place again? If that were possible, he would lay that curse on these two, keep them away from the Marcellus Shale for ever afterward.

Nothing suggested itself, so he let Jeffrey get his tickets and go back to his wife. He knew where they were heading next, and he could be less conspicuous hanging around with the vampire youth waiting for the train to hell.

The whistle blew. The crowd wandered forward and it became a press. Baker saw Jeffrey return to Serena's side as she flipped her phone shut. He hung back, built a buffer of black-clad teens between them. He pulled off his sunglasses, tucked them into his jacket. The cameras were still out, occasional flashes popping here and there in the crowd, but there were fewer, at least.

They all got on the train.

THIRTY-ONE

Charlie Pedrango walked once more to the edge of the overhang off the front of the cabin and looked toward town. The echo of the steam whistle floated up to their perch.

"Brother Jack, you almost ready?" he said.

He had driven in earlier that day and passed a Sheriff's deputy parked at the head of their road. The guy's head had swiveled slowly, tracking Charlie's car, but Charlie had erased all thoughts of money, or guilt, or the weapons under a blanket on the floor of the back seat and continued about his perfectly legal business. He had an idea that cops could smell guilt, so he made it a point never to feel badly about his minor transgressions.

And a little later, Jack's phone had rung. He'd talked for a few minutes, wary, defensive. Hung up, muttered "fuck."

Charlie had ambled in to listen to Jack's end of the call.

"Hey Jack, who was that?"

"That was my cousin. Did you know somebody killed my brother Cyrus?"

"Killed, killed?"

"Yup. Shot."

"The cops think you did it?"

"I guess," Jack said again.

"What you want to do, Jackie?"

Charlie was leaning against the shack's front door, can of beer dangling from one hand. He didn't look particularly tense, but Jack got a sense that Charlie was dangling a little, too.

"Not sure just yet," he said. He was thinking that he'd heard a steam whistle blow, through the phone, while he'd been talking to Glenn. And a few seconds later, he'd heard it, faint, through the front door. He was thinking the jig was up.

Jack sat down on one of the old schoolroom chairs by the kitchenette, hands between his knees, loosely holding his cellphone. He stared at a knot in the floorboard and went back to that day in early September, when Cyrus had called him.

"Yo, Jack, I need you out here, man," he'd said.

"Where?" Jack said. *Why not "fuck you"?* he wondered.

"The fuck, where. My place. Monticello. I'm meeting a guy here and we'll need a ride."

"I don't know where you're living, Cy." So Cyrus told him. And he went, like he always did.

He'd pulled up and Cyrus had this older guy, a soft-looking guy, out of his front door and into his truck before Jack knew what was up, hustling him forward with a jacket over his arm and something shoved into his back. The guy was scared. And Jack had been, too, and Cyrus had the crazy look again. He showed Jack the gun and told him to drive, squeezed in the passenger side and directed him up route 209. Cyrus told the guy they were just going to meet someone and that it was none of Cyrus's business, it was nothing personal, but that's what they were going to do.

Jack forgot Charlie and the cabin and the situation now, fully back in that September afternoon idling his truck out in front of that house on Bone Hollow Road, waiting for his brother and not seeing him, seeing no other cars out there. And finally, after half an hour, stealing back into the woods and finding them. On an impulse he'd grabbed the cell phone clutched in Cyrus's hand. And the gun.

It hadn't been news to him that Cyrus was dead. That asshole.

Charlie snapped his fingers in front of Jack's face.

"'Cause I ran the blockade thinkin' I'd get some money, my man," Charlie said. He came off the door frame, walked over and squatted down before Jack. He put his hand on Jack's knee for balance. He looked up into his face. "If you think you need to talk to the police, I can make the pickup myself. And maybe you could leave my name out of that?"

"I ain't telling anyone your name, Charlie." Jack stood up and paced a tight loop. "You say there was a car down there on the road?" he said.

Charlie slowly rose up from his crouch, smooth and machine-like. "But the one." He took a swig of beer, swirled the can a little after.

Jack wasn't sure he wanted to let slip this other factoid, wasn't sure how Charlie would take it. "My cousin, you know, he's a cop," he said.

"Who's that?"

"Glenn Hatch," he said. "Ulster County Sheriffs. He's a deputy."

The beer in Charlie's hand stopped its gentle swaying. He said "That was him on the phone?"

"Yeah."

"And the Sullivan County guy just happened to be parked down the road? I think you're cooked, Jack. Except..."

"Except what?"

"Except you didn't do it."

"No, but I did torch that house."

"Oh, that's nothing. Even if they could prove that, what does that prove? Can you give them this other guy? He's the one did your brother, right?"

"Yeah, I guess I could."

"Could you wait till Monday on that one? Till we've got the money?"

"Not if that guy down the hill is looking for me."

"You think he was?"

"I dunno." Jack sighed. "My cousin Glenn might know about the cabin, but maybe not. If they're looking for me, someone will be able to tell 'em where I'm at." He'd stopped walking, stood at the kitchenette sink. He turned on the water, leaned down, drank from the tap.

Now Pedrango stalked back and forth outside the front door. The night was gathering, although at this height he could still see the light capping the ridges. The cabin itself was in shadow. Charlie turned and looked up at the slope behind him. There was still light shining through the topmost trees. The shadow of Stone Ridge lay across the road and painted darkness onto Fox Ridge. Beyond that, down closer to the main road, about three miles distant, were the ruins of Schlesinger's.

Charlie Pedrango wanted that fucking money.

He turned back into the cabin. "Hey Jack," he said. "What about we take a couple sleeping bags over to the hotel and make camp there for a couple nights, pick up that money, then give your friend to the police once we've got it?"

"He ain't my friend."

"Well then, if we happen to be there when he shows with the money, you can tell him that. Can you throw some of that Spam in a pack?"

THIRTY-TWO

Hatch and Gerow sat in the car, parked in the gathering dusk. The conversation had gone like this:

"'Tsup." Jack.

"Hello, Jack. It's Glenn Hatch."

"Oh, hey Glenn."

"You know, Jack, I'm working over with the Ulster Sheriff's department."

"Uhh, yeah, I know."

"Right. Well, listen, we've turned up some pretty bad news, and I'm sorry I have to tell you."

"Shit. What is it?"

"Well, turns out your brother Cyrus, well, he died."

"Cyrus died? How'd that happen?"

"Right now it looks like a homicide. Uhh, it looks like he got shot."

"Whoa. Someone shot him?"

"Yes."

"I guess that's not that surprising. He was into some bad shit."

"Yeah, I'd heard some of that. Look, would you say you were close? I know I haven't seen you for a while, so I'm a little out of that loop."

"Not close, no."

"Well, we're trying to solve this thing. I mean, it's weird 'cause he was my cousin, same as you are. So I'm working with the state police, they're looking into it. Do you think I could come over and see you, bring a colleague of mine to ask you some questions? You home now?"

"Well Glenn, now's not so good," Jack said.

"Okay. Can I come by a little later? I'd like to give you my condolences in person, but I'm also working with a team who'll have some questions. We're kind of hot on this thing."

"I'm actually not at home this weekend. I have to do some repairs over at the Woodbourne School, it's gonna take a couple of days."

"We can definitely work with that. Can I come out and see you there? It's, what, an hour from here? We're working out of Accord; Cyrus's body was found out in Krumville. Where was he living, do you know?"

"Last I heard it was Monticello."

"Oh, sure, that's right. So, can we come out there? Or if you can take a couple of hours off this weekend, maybe you could come down to the station in Accord."

"Tell you what, Glenn, can I call you back? I'll check with the lady at the school and I'll have a better idea of my schedule. That work?"

"Jack, this is your brother we're talking about. You sure we can't come talk to you?"

"It's just that I'm not at the job yet, and I haven't talked to them about the schedule."

"Okay, so where are you? I promise, we got these new Dodge Charger cruisers, we can meet up anywhere you like."

"Let me just talk to them and I'll call you back."

"All right, Jack. Call me back."

"This the right number, the one you called me on?"

"Yeah, that'll do it."

"Okay. I'll call you back, Glenn."

"Thanks, Jack."

They'd hung up.

. . .

"I *guess* he's up there," Hatch said.

"Probably," said Gerow. "Not coming down, either. So I guess we're going up."

He got out of the car, then leaned back in through the open door. "Deputy, you can recuse yourself from the operation, if you like. I trust your judgment enough to leave it up to you."

"Thank you, detective."

"But if you stick, I don't want you on the door."

"Roger."

Gerow nodded and stepped forward into the group of officers. "Okay, we believe we might have a suspect up at a cabin about a mile from here. We don't know if he's armed, but there have been two murders in this case using a scoped high-powered rifle from a distance, so we're not going to take chances. We have no reason to believe that the suspect knows we're here."

He handed out assignments. Some would go up along the top of Stone Ridge, the others would array themselves out on Fox Ridge across the road from the cabin, working their way through the woods. No lights. They'd take advantage of the lingering sun high up and the sunset afterglow to pick their way. Two cruisers up the road straight up to the shack. Gerow had a bullhorn and a bulletproof vest.

213

"Turn off your cell phones," he said.

Six men filed into the woods to either side of the road. On the east side they walked through the cemetery and crossed the brook on stepping stones, then angled up through the woods along a deer trail that paralleled the ridge line. Those on the left cut hard up the slope to hit the ridge itself so they could come at the cabin from above.

Gerow came back to Hatch. "I'll want you down here covering the way out," he said.

"Yes, sir."

"We're going to take this very easy."

"Of course." Hatch was impassive. He drew his cruiser across the blacktop with the engine on.

Senior Investigator Gerow considered chewing a toothpick. He didn't have one, and he never did actually chew toothpicks. But it would maybe keep him from craving a cigarette.

Nine times out of ten, an operation like this one would turn out nothing, but you could never be sure. Eighty percent of the other one time, they went as planned, or close to it, no fighting, no chasing. And that last twenty percent of that ten percent, there was that. Guns. He checked his own in its holster.

It took twenty minutes for the radio at Gerow's hip to let out three short bursts, then a second set a few minutes later. They were in position.

"No lights on," said one of the men across the narrow valley through the radio. Binoculars were sweeping the cabin roofline visible through the dusk. Portions of a white car were visible through the leaves. He reported that. Make and model not clear. Might be he was seeing another car, as well, but couldn't be sure in the dusk. If so, it was gray or dark blue.

"Keep your eyes on the front door if you can see it," Gerow said.

Above the cabin the tree cover was harder to see through, but the cops up there could see part of the roof, too. No one moved down there. They could see the white pickup and another car, possibly a station wagon or small SUV. Dark blue. "Two cars," the spotter reported. "No activity, no lights," he said.

Gerow walked back to Hatch. "Glenn, any of your relatives drive a dark blue station wagon or SUV?"

"Not that I know specifically," he said.

Gerow nodded and got into another state cruiser. A trooper came around the front and got in and they started up the road, followed by another sheriff's cruiser. Their engines roared, that power roar of souped-up Authority. The Man was on his way.

It only took a couple of minutes to reach the driveway, a dirt track that made a switchback partway up the slope. There was no mailbox. There were multiple tire ruts, but they weren't collecting evidence, not this trip. Each car sent a little gravel into the mountain laurel as they took the switchback.

The road leveled out before a plank-sided cabin with an overhanging porch roof. There was no flooring beneath the overhang but a square of concrete before the door, which was shut.

Four oaks stood in isolation among sparse grass, leaf litter and needles from nearby hemlocks. A white pickup and a purple station wagon were parked off kilter in front of the building. A paper coffee cup lay half-submerged and weather-bleached in a drift of needles and leaves. No one came out or moved as they arrived.

Gerow had no superstitions for situations like this, no medals to touch, no worry stone to worry. He opened the car door and stood, pulled out the megaphone. "Jack Grant," he said. "This is the police. Come out of there with your hands empty and over your head."

The words bounced straight off the slope in front of him, whistled over his head and bounced off Fox Ridge at his back.

He held the cone to his mouth and depressed the trigger again. "Jack Grant." Echo. Nothing.

He got back in the car and spoke into the radio. "Anyone have anything?"

"Clear on Stone Ridge."

"Fox Ridge, we have—wait a second."

Gerow turned and looked back east across the valley to the slope a half mile or so away. It was nearly dark over there.

Crack.

He lifted the radio as a second gunshot bounced back across the space between the hillsides.

"Fox Ridge, come in."

The cop on the other end was breathing heavy. "Shots fired, suspects are on the move, two men going over the ridge."

"Who fired?"

"Carlson did, missed twice. One suspect raised a weapon."

"Keep them in sight, but if they take cover or stop, do not engage. Just keep them talking. Let's see if we can avoid shooting."

"Received."

He looked back at the cabin. Two cars parked here, Grant and buddy already on the move. Where were they going? They must have been tipped to the cops at the head of the valley. This rusty station wagon must have been one of the cars that the deputy had seen pass by.

He thought a moment more. Something must have spooked him. Maybe Hatch's call.

Gerow pulled out his cellphone, called the state police headquarters, and recited the license plate numbers. He jumped back in the car and held up the radio. "Okay, Fox Ridge, give me your status," he said.

Panting. "They're still moving, making their way east. We're at the top of the hill now, flanking their path. The suspects have continued down the eastern slope, and we're continuing over the top."

"We're going to try to cut them off. Keep me updated."

"Received."

"Hatch, come in."

"This is Hatch."

"Go back down and take the next road north out of town. I'll be right behind you."

It was getting dark for this, Gerow thought as they sped back down the hill. Couple of desperados and a bunch of keyed-up lawmen out there in the dark, bad things were likely. As a patrolman he'd chased suspects through the streets a few times. It rarely came down to a straight chase. There were dodges, and cover, and friendly storefronts. What did they have up here? he wondered. Creek beds. Road bridges. What, caves?

They drove south past the cemetery and into the small grid of residential streets north of the main highway, then cut east on one of the roads that ran parallel. The next road up was something called Hoover Hollow Road. The deputy's map showed it going north a couple of miles and winding around the northern end of Stone Ridge—the hill that Jack Grant was coming down now.

"Hatch, where'd you go?"

"I'm up Hoover Hollow."

They turned and came upon Hatch in seconds, parked by the roadside with his cruiser dark and the engine off. They cut theirs.

Hatch and Gerow met between the cars. "Now it's a pursuit," said Gerow. "Deputy, call for the nearest canine unit, and alert the town cops and sheriff's units to watch the town. Call aviation out of Stewart; we got armed guys in the woods. We'll have to keep between the perps and the town. We're down to minutes here. I don't think they can go far, but call it in. If they get near the populace we'll stop 'em, but I'm tempted to break it off if they're just running. I want no shooting."

Hatch dashed back to his car, drew it across the road and began calling in the new orders. Gerow directed the driver up the road, then stopped him a short distance up. The other car pulled even. They opened all the doors to create a barrier. Gerow and one other cop worked their way up the culverts on either side of the road, guns drawn, eyes scanning the hill to their left. The others stationed themselves by the cars, binoculars trained on the road and the hillsides ahead.

The wooded slope was deep in shadow, backlit by the post-sundown sky. Hemlocks, other evergreens, some oaks and birches stood amid boulders shorn from the shoulders of the sandstone hill.

The hillside came steeply down to the ditch beside the blacktop. There were a couple of driveways along this stretch leading up to cabins or winterized weekend places. Where the policemen walked, there were no house lights visible.

Down the hill away, they heard the steam whistle and stopped to listen as its echoes died.

218

THIRTY-THREE

Serena had burrowed her face into Jeffrey's shoulder, pressed into the crowd on the train. They'd chosen one of the outdoor flatcars, a narrow two-sided bench running up the middle and surrounded by chain link. There were a few families with little kids on board, but mostly college-age and older adult-children. Lots of *Scream* masks and black clothes. Lots of mock-shoving and fake vampire laughs and startled screams as boy-men jumped at girl-women.

The whistle blew a couple more times, calling the stragglers into the station. The mix of those embarking and debarking gave the platform and fairgrounds the bustle of a larger town. Near the band tent, two oil barrels stacked with the wedges of split logs had been lit, and the fire brought the gathering dusk down tighter. Wood smoke wafted over the tracks. The smell made Serena nuzzle further into her husband's wool-clad neck.

Jeffrey hugged her one-armed. His mind ticked over. Was this a romantic getaway? An extension of their house-hunting trip? It was the train trip that was throwing him off, he supposed. They'd been in hot pursuit, on *serious business*. And now they were...what? Fresh from the diner, warmed up, buried in the camaraderie and romance of a mountain town's quaint Halloween tradition.

He was uneasy, sensed that there was some kind of drama playing out just beyond the edge of his vision. Those cops somewhere in the hills outside of town, Gerow kicking in a door someplace and arresting that murderer. But where? And why were he and Serena so close to it?

The train pulled out and headed for the woods. They passed over the main road into town, a short stack of cars lined up at the crossing. The whistle sounded a couple more times. Jeffrey heard Vincent Price laughing through the tinny PA system and the opening strains of "Thriller." He smiled at Serena, who was peeking out from the little nook she had made against his neck and shoulder, looking drowsy.

How does she do it? he wondered. She could compartmentalize in ways he couldn't imagine. Jeffrey surrendered, forced himself to switch out of chase mode, switch to wry amusement at the rustic antics that were unfolding.

. . .

Baker was just inside the door of the passenger car nearest the couple. He could see the gates of Hell approaching down the track, saw a barrel full of flames on either side, highlighting the drapery and the vast fanged mouth but artfully blocked from calling attention to the cherry picker. As they passed beneath the archway, columns of colored fire leapt from the barrels, and a deep voice played out of the night—a better quality PA than the one on the train—"Abandon hope, all ye who enter here."

None of them did, each hoping for something different.

THIRTY-FOUR

Jack had given up hope. He followed Pedrango through the woods, stumbling, trying to figure out how to give up without getting shot. That crazy fucker had pulled a nine millimeter and pointed it at one of the cops up top of the hill.

Figuring the cops might pay a visit if Jack didn't call his cousin back anytime soon, they'd left the house with a couple of bedrolls and a backpack containing food, two sixpacks and one skillet—somehow Jack had gotten the backpack—and made a beeline for the hotel grounds. It wasn't much of a plan, Jack thought, but they were looking for him, he knew how to camp, and maybe getting out of the hot seat would give him a chance to figure out his next move. He could go to Syracuse, of course; he had friends up there who might put him up. Or he could turn himself in and deliver the guy who'd killed his brother, guy named Baker.

All that was fucked now, though. His chances of getting shot had just skyrocketed. Charlie was maybe a little looser than he'd realized, dropping to one knee and pointing that gun. Fucking psycho. In the gloaming he'd aimed for one second and then let up as the cop shot at him. Jack, crawling frantically down the far side of the hill on his belly, had looked back and seen Pedrango's bird-face register a look of satisfaction, as though he'd confirmed that he *could* have taken out the deputy, and was now prepared to move on. The shot had gone past his ear pretty close. He'd rolled to the side and followed Jack while the second shot followed him. Over the top, they'd both stood, Jack dropped the pack, and they'd run hell for leather.

The sight of the gun seemed to have put the cops off a little, but they both figured they had just minutes before a more concerted approach. On the east slope of Fox Ridge, Charlie angled south, toward town, parallel to the road eighty feet or so below them and about a quarter mile off. Lean and fit, he jogged fast, jumping roots and stones easily along a worn deer path. Jack followed, clumsier but still at home in the woods.

Charlie dropped and signaled Jack down. Below, on the road in the gloom, they could see two cruisers working their way slowly up Hoover Hollow. They stopped straight below their position and cops got out.

Pedrango murmured to Jack. "We'll continue south here, and then cut east again, go to the hotel."

"The hotel? Shouldn't we get the hell out of here?"

"Wanna go back and grab your truck?" Pedrango said. "Maybe we can hop the train back to town, borrow a car, figure something out."

"Shit."

They began to pick their way down the slope, listening for pursuit, eyes on the road below. It looked like there were four guys down there, two with the cars and two stalking along the roadside, heading north away from the fugitives.

They'd almost reached the road when Jack spotted another car parked to block the road, off through the trees to the right. He grabbed Pedrango's arm, pointed.

They could see a guy standing beside the driver's door. He stood silent, seeming to scan the slope they'd come down, looking above them. About seventy-five yards away from their hiding spot.

Distant shouts echoed down the valley. The cop's radio crackled. He spoke into it, but they couldn't hear what he said.

"Must have met up with the ones from up top," Jack said. He peered out. The voice drifted across the intervening space. He could see the guy's silhouette, saw his bulk.

Glenn.

"Hey, Charlie, that's my—" but Charlie was sprinting across the street, low, not looking back. Jack sucked in his breath, looking from Charlie's darting form back to the car. He saw Deputy Hatch crouch and pull his pistol in a single motion, saw him aim, saw Charlie's ass disappear on the other side of the road at the same second. Hatch raised the gun and replaced it, picked up the radio again, spoke.

He held the radio to his mouth for a few moments, his head turned toward the spot where Charlie had emerged from the underbrush in the culvert. Jack could feel his sight trailing over the spot, trying to penetrate the gloom.

Glenn hung up the radio and stalked into the woods across the road where Charlie had disappeared.

Jack sat back on his haunches there in the ditch, screened by some scrub oaks and vines.

"Ah, shit," he muttered.

Jack looked left and didn't see anyone. To the right was Glenn's car. The radio was squawking in there. He thought about his cousin going in there after Pedrango. He didn't know Glenn that well, not the last few years at least. They'd been at family gatherings a few times growing up, and the moms shared stories of their exploits. Hell, Jack had plenty of cousins around that he knew better than Glenn.

But now he, Jack, had got Pedrango into this mix; that guy who shot Cyrus had gotten him nervous. Now Charlie had him nervous. More nervous, in fact, because Jack needed twenty-five hundred dollars as bad as the next guy, but when it came to guns and shooting, he could just as easily let that money get moldy under the check-in desk at Schlesinger's, or let some hiker find it, or whatever.

But now there were two guys with guns chasing each other in the woods, and he had sent them both.

He sighed and, ducking low, ran across the road and into the woods after them.

. . .

Gerow and the other cop were trotting back to the cars, which were executing complicated K-turns to point themselves back down the road toward town. Their miniature dragnet hadn't worked—Jack and friend had somehow eluded the guys chasing them above and angled south. At least they'd parked Hatch at the foot of the valley. *One thing I did right*, Gerow thought.

He tried to raise the deputy on the radio, but got nothing. His last words had been "I'm going to pursue," and Gerow guessed he had done just that. *Fucking cousins, that's the issue here,* he thought.

Still, if there was anyone he trusted to do this right, it was Hatch. Good policeman, knew how to listen, thought before he acted. Gerow had heard about him making an arrest without moving from his spot, and without much talking. The guy'd been wanted for beating up his ex-girlfriend's new boyfriend in the driveway of his old apartment house, and Hatch and another deputy had found him at home at his new place grilling sausages on a back deck, bruise on one cheek. According to the story, Hatch had come around the back corner of the house and seen the guy above him, grilling. The guy was about three feet up over his head, the grill a little between them. There were a few empty beer cans on a glass-topped table and a cooler on the deck that presumably held more. Hatch tilted his head over and didn't say anything, hands on his belt.

"Hi, officer," the guy'd said. Smoke drifted up from the sizzling meat. He had a long fork in his hand with a bamboo handle, a beer in the other hand. He poured a little beer onto a sausage, raised steam.

"You wanna come out to my car," Hatch told the man.

There was a long silence. Finally the guy said "can I get these sausages off here?"

"I can wait."

And that was it.

So here's hoping.

. . .

It became a slow chase. Jack listened, but Hatch had apparently turned off his radio, as there was no electronic squawking ahead in the shadows of the woods. The sky still held a glow, but it would only be moments before the first stars popped.

They proceeded. Jack caught sight of Hatch from time to time, stooped over the ground or striding along decisively. He could hear him, although the big man made less noise than he would have expected. Jack himself was treading very carefully. Charlie, he suspected, was up ahead someplace using some crazy Army ninja shit to blend in. Who knew?

If Hatch was following Charlie's actual path, he was headed straight for Schlesinger's. Jack had a pretty good sense of direction, and while he didn't know every hill and hollow, he knew that the mountains rose to the north, on his left, and the long valley where the state highway ran was off to the right. Arkville was that way.

And when he heard the whistle blow, away off through the trees, he realized that the old train ride was that way, too.

Hatch topped a rise and Jack, a hundred yards back, caught sight of his silhouette against some ambient glow coming off the far side. He held a gun pointed down, and broke into a trot, hitting a trail of some kind. Jack advanced, keeping low as he reached the spot, and looked over to see his cousin some way down the trail, jogging now. The trees were thinner here and Glenn had found an ATV trail leading east. Lights were visible far ahead, maybe a mile through the woods, but apparently *in* the woods. The lights of town were still a glow above the trees off to the right, but the red lights ahead flickered here and there through the trees. Then the train whistle sounded again, and Jack could see a steady red light moving along, with flares lighting alongside occasionally, and realized that everything was heading for the old station by the hotel.

Jack glanced up at the stars for a moment. He thought about calling after Glenn. Thought about trying to get to Charlie, talk some sense into him. Where was that crazy fucker, anyway?

. . .

Charlie was jogging along, making a beeline for the grounds of the old hotel. He'd hit the woods on the east side of Hoover Hollow Road and launched directly into a steady trot, figuring he'd been seen but not giving the cop in the road enough time to get the drop on him. That meant he was thirty, forty-five seconds ahead of pursuit from that direction and he only wanted to lengthen his lead enough to lose the guy. He also knew that the cop knew he had a gun. And that ought to give him pause.

The money was still top of mind, as he'd learned to say in the Army, but the pursuit was nagging at him. He had an idea to grab a room at Schlesinger's, stay a night or two. They'd bring dogs, though, wouldn't they? He heard the train whistle off to his right, added it to the mix. He was mapping on the fly, as he'd learned to say in the Army.

THIRTY-FIVE

The train ride was only minimally creepy, depending in large part on startlement, but Serena shrieked along with the half-drunk college girls and boys, laughing as she nuzzled in deeper against Jeffery's jacket, surrendered to the mystery and the gothic horror of it all. Jeffrey was doing the guy thing, debunking each new monster to himself, resisting the urge to point out the mechanisms behind the gags. There were a few pop-out critters that would leap out of the night into the glow of a red spotlight. These were launched by hand from platforms, Jeffrey could see, deer blinds maybe, set alongside the tracks.

There were fires burning a little distance from the tracks, smudge pots, and figures could be seen cavorting around them. Drums sounded in the distance. There was a general smell of smoke in the air, and screams sounded from the woods. Menacing laughter played from hidden speakers. They were in Hell.

Jeffrey began to relax.

. . .

Nearby Baker watched them, hand curled around the paper bag of money in his jacket pocket. His hat was pulled down and he leaned out occasionally to see what lay ahead along the track.

At each end of every car there were stairs that went to nearly ground level. The top step was chained off by thin links secured with a sliding catch. Baker figured he'd just pop off the train at the station, just before it pulled out, make his way to the hotel, break in or find a way in that some other trespasser had left open, drop the money, and make it back for the next train. There were enough performers dancing around in the woods along the track that he wouldn't attract too much notice.

As the train emerged from the thickest woods into the relatively clearer land around the abandoned hulk of Schlesinger's Hotel and Resort, Baker thought for a moment that the building was on fire again. Ah, no. Up the old road he could see that there was a red spotlight shining on the old stone portion of the complex, and two 55-gallon drums held flames that roared upward. Thirty-foot shadows leaped across the face of the building; dancers were passing back and forth in front of the low-slung light. The Duke of Hell's palace.

He thought briefly of the nun he'd bribed in Hawley and gave a chuckle. Was there no place he wouldn't go for this job?

. . .

The platform was in sight, a red-lit island of concrete five feet high with a stout stone building attached on the far side. Stairs from the old gravel parking lot led up through the building into a waiting room, no doors on it anymore. Beyond the platform, the tracks crossed the old hotel drive at ground level, then petered out into woodlands beyond. The embankment disappeared into the darkness.

The train pulled in and a crowd of zombies lurched out of the darkness of the waiting room, pressing made-up faces against the train windows. More screams, laughter, guys punching at the glass where zombie faces left smears of decaying flesh, or talcum powder.

A couple of performers were lined up on the platform at the front of the flatbed car, costumes put away in backpacks, waiting to take the train back to town. Baker made his way over and unhooked the chain and stepped aside to let the lead girl, black braids, black turtleneck, traces of powder around her face, onto the train. Two more followed and in the kerfuffle Baker stepped around them down to the platform, then crossed the platform into the waiting room and took the stairs down without looking back.

The train idled. A dirge played.

And then, more red lights. Flashers. From the south, and the roar of engines. Big engines. Every head on the flatbed car where Jeffrey and Serena sat swiveled thataway as a convoy of State Police SUVs and cruisers careered up the road from the highway and slowed to cross the tracks.

Jeffrey stood. "Come on," he said.

Serena looked at the police cars. There were four or five. There was one that said Canine Unit. One stayed on the south side of the tracks, parked next to the train's engine. Another took up position on the north side, beside the station. The others continued up the road to the apron in front of the hotel's facade and fanned out.

Men leapt from the cars beside the train. Two spoke to the engineer, their necks craned upward. She—*it's a woman*! Serena thought—leaned out the window and nodded at them, raised her cellphone, spoke into it.

The whistle rang out three times. Jeffrey and Serena darted off the train and into the waiting room, through the scrum of zombies as the engine escalated gutturally. Serena felt sleepy, as though she'd been dreaming for the entire afternoon and was now waking again to her real life. The rules were unclear for a moment. Pursuit was real, but she forgot what they were chasing.

In the meantime, the lights of the police cars would do. They dashed across the parking lot and paralleled the road up to the hotel, watching the cops through the trees.

There was a chain-link gate, but it was open for the show. A single sheriff's cruiser was parked beside it, pointed downhill toward the station. They hadn't seen it come up with the others and Serena concluded that it must have been stationed there to keep an eye on the performers. There was no one there; the other cars had passed straight through and were parked in a cluster of flashing lights at the hotel entrance.

The train pulled out of the station, back toward town.

There were a couple dozen performers in the woods. Some filtered out of the trees. A few zombies and demonic cavorters were gathering in a loose ring a distance from the police cars. They were young, mostly, high school or college kids up from New Paltz. There were a lot of piercings, and some of the white face, thick eyeliner, black lipstick, looked very much at home. This must be a theater program. Or a Renaissance festival in the off-season.

Cops got out of the cars wearing flak jackets and vests, carrying serious weaponry. One had a German shepherd on a leash. Radio squawks, piercing beeps sounded.

Jeffrey and Serena had come through the gate and closed the remaining distance, joining the crowd at its edge.

Then Serena saw him.

The fake reporter. The guy. He was *there.* Across the ring, staring intently at the cops, edging slowly backward. Wearing a

Yankees cap, but definitely him. The puffy face, the very slightly bug eyes. He didn't look like the sketch, now that she thought about it.

He wasn't looking at her. She turned, casually, slowly, getting the light off of her face, and pulled at Jeffrey until he turned too.

"Him," she said. Inclined her head back. "Don't look."

He looked, but only for a moment, and understood. He turned back around, looked at the trees before them.

Their shadows flickered against the wall of trees at the edge of the driveway. The firelight and the flashers from the parked cruiser brought the trunks and leaves into bright relief, simultaneously making a new darkness of the woods beyond. The orange fire and the red flashers drained the trees of their color, sapped the oranges and reds from the leaves, left them white against the blackness of the woods.

"We can get him," Serena said.

"You mean tell the cops he's there? You have Gerow's number?"

"I can't call him. He'd shoot me."

"So how can we get him?"

She glanced back at the crowd around the fire and straight to the imposter's face. This time, his eyes, glittering in the orange flicker, were pointed straight at her. They met hers. His eyebrows went up, slightly. He gave a little grin.

She felt that touch on her wrist again and shivered.

Then the guy was gone.

"Fuck," she said. "He saw me."

"We can tell these cops we saw him."

A policeman was talking to the crowd. It was a Sullivan County sheriff's deputy, probably the one who'd been stationed at the hotel during the show. Someone had handed him a megaphone.

"Folks, I'm going to need everyone out of the woods here. We'll be meeting up right here, and we've called the bus that dropped you off to come back a little early. We have to break down the show for tonight."

"Why?" called one of the zombies.

"A fugitive was reported to be in the area, and we want to ensure everyone's safety while we check it out."

That got a murmur going.

The other policemen and women looked ready for action. The dog was sitting calmly, looking up with that dog-smile at the cop holding the leash, who was listening to another cop, who was gesturing at the woods. They had some serious guns.

"Well?" said Jeffrey.

Serena stepped back until the firelight was off her face again and the light from the flashers was blocked by more members of the gathering crowd. Where had that fucking creep gone? She looked around, but couldn't see the Yankees hat.

Her heart was pounding. What the hell had he been doing out here, anyway? Working the show? Waiting for them? Were the cops after *him*? That seemed unlikely. Although she didn't know the details of their investigation; perhaps they knew his name already, maybe they found something that had led to him, and they knew that he lived here. Maybe they'd been staking out his house... no, his condo... and were ready to make an arrest. He could be the very fugitive they were chasing. She'd be doing them a favor. But dammit, if Gerow caught them here, *they'd* be the fugitives.

Jeffrey joined her. "I'm not digging this whole wrong side of the law thing," he said. "Let's tell that guy—" he pointed at the deputy, who was talking on his cell phone and asking questions of two show workers who had clipboards and walkie talkies "— that we just saw a guy who might be wanted, and let the chips whatever whatever."

She sighed. It probably couldn't hurt, except for when they went to jail for interfering with a police investigation.

"This isn't very romantic," she said.

"Sure it is," he told her. "It's very romantic."

Serena stepped forward. "Excuse me, officer," she said. He broke off from his cell phone conversation and looked at them. He had bushy eyebrows and jowls, wore a nylon jacket with a faux fur collar and various brass bars and patches on it, in addition to his badge.

"Yup," he said.

"I'm not sure if this has anything to do with—" she gestured at the crowd and the cars "—this. But my husband and I just saw a guy who's wanted by the police. He was standing right over there about a minute ago." She pointed.

"What's he wanted for?"

Jeffrey spoke. "Part of an investigation in Accord. Detective Gerow is working on it?" He made it a question, looking for a reaction to the name.

Nah. "Into what?"

"Murder and arson," Jeffrey said.

He looked them up and down, assessing. Into the phone, he said "call you back," and snapped it shut.

"Where was this person?"

. . .

Baker followed the receding lights of the last train car. The ground sloped away on either side of him, and once used to the darkness it was easy enough to follow the tracks. He didn't expect any other traffic along here. The rails led straight back to town. And that's where he needed to be. Among people, blending, and then to his car, and going west.

His heart was beating a lot harder than it should have been from the exertion. *A fucking SWAT team. Shit.* The cash drop thing, the hotel, that had gone out of control, and this was him cutting his losses. Getting the fuck out of Dodge. Heading for the hills. There just didn't seem to be a percentage in this. Just as he'd made up his mind to steal away back toward town, to ditch the whole thing, he'd even spotted Serena and Jeffrey in the crowd around the police cars. What the fuck? They'd snuck off the train—had they been following him?

He paused, looked back along the tracks. Nothing.

He fingered the paper bag in his pocket, felt the reassuring chunkiness of packets of small bills. He still had his stash, which was a lever, and with the right lever he could move whatever shit there was, could move it right out of his way. He turned and continued to place his feet on the wooden ties, darker patches amid the bluish crushed stone that lay between them.

The popping of gunshots in the woods off to his right made him hit the deck, lying down flat on the tracks, hoping the rails rising a few inches on either side would shield him.

There were two more shots, far enough off to convince him they weren't for him. He got to his knees, crouching forward. Some shouts off that way, faint. Keeping low, Baker rose and scurried into the night. He followed the tiny, red, winking eyes of the train ahead as they led him out of hell.

THIRTY-SIX

At Schlesinger's every head turned. The deputy spun around and began barking orders. Within seconds of the shots, every cop broke into action, drawing weapons, grabbing bulky vests from the back seats of their cars, forming up into a tight line.

Two stayed behind and started ushering the onlookers in the direction of the train station, away from the sound of the shots. They moved willingly. A few other kids ran out of the woods, zombies fleeing the sounds of death, and joined the crowd. Their energy transferred itself to the moving mass of people, and like a flock of starlings the crowd shivered and flowed along the road, faster now. Near the other police car that had paused where the road to Schlesinger's crossed the stunted end of the train tracks, the majority of the group stopped and turned.

At the back of the sprawling crowd were Mr. and Mrs. Gale. As they passed through the open chain-link gate halfway to the station, Serena stopped.

"Wait, Jeffrey," she said.

He turned and stepped close to her. Looked off into the woods at her back. The police who had shooed the crowd hadn't followed; none of these kids from the college drama department wanted to get shot, despite their innate car-wreck curiosity. They had run, and the cops had turned their attention back to

236

preserving disorder, or whatever it was they were doing there on the cracked asphalt apron of the hotel.

Jeffrey saw several policemen move into the woods, the K-9 unit and its man among them.

"Yeah?" Jeffrey said.

"What should we do?" Serena said.

"Run," he said. "Probably."

He held her to him. She was shaking. Jeffrey felt exposed out here, standing beside the road in the darkness, fall air quickly cooling.

She was humming. He gave it a second, got it. *California Dreaming.* Just the opening lines. "All the leaves are brown (leaves are brown) / and the sky is gray (and the sky is gray)..." She laughed into his neck. "It's been in my head since we got here."

He ran his hands over her back and shoulders, pulled her in closer, trying to melt her off the spot and away. She wouldn't move.

"What's happening back there?" she said.

He looked again over her shoulder. Whatever was happening, it was happening in the woods. Empty police cars arced beams of red and white light across the old hotel, its limestone facade and concrete additions looking like a selectively lit architectural survey.

"Nothing," he said.

She said "Gilbert."

Jeffrey leaned back and looked at her.

"What's that?"

"Gilbert," she said. "The reporter. The real one." She was excited, patting her pockets.

"And?"

"I'm calling him," she said, and pulled out her cell. She punched his name up in the contacts. "He'll be able to find out what's going on," she said, and held the phone to her ear.

"Hi, Mister Gilbert," she said, and Jeffrey guided her by the elbow, back toward the crowd, away from the woods where shooting and death were on the prowl. His eyes scanned the darkness around them for the other guy, the imposter, the one they'd seen not five minutes earlier.

"I just saw that guy again," she was saying. "The one who pretended to be you. And there have been shots, in the woods. I'm in a town called, I think, Arkville. They have this train ride?" She paused.

"Serena Gale, that's right." she said. "Listen, you probably want to get here as soon as you can, or send someone, or whatever you do. There's a ton of cops up here. We followed them from Accord; Detective Gerow was yelling at me—"

"My husband and me."

"We borrowed a car from the owner of the house that burned down last week."

"I know. She's very accommodating."

They reached the bundle of onlookers. A curious mob again, now that they had crossed an arbitrary physical division—the thin, paved-over line of the rails—that gave them a sense of boundary, of safety behind an impenetrable wall.

"There's a diner here in town," Serena said. "We can meet you there. But the real action is out at this old resort at the end of the train tracks."

She hung up and kissed Jeffrey, unclenching, breathing out an impossibly long-held breath, a sob at the end. He took her arm.

THIRTY-SEVEN

Pedrango's thought had been to get to the hotel and hole up, or somehow get aboard the train and double back to town, or just mingle with the drama club kids and play dumb. That was all moot, because he couldn't shake the big cop who'd followed him into the woods. The guy wasn't that fast, but he was steady. The zombiefest was still too far off for Pedrango to build up enough lead to make his move for the train, or hide in the hotel, or hit the highway and thumb his way east, or anything. And up ahead, over by Schlesinger's, he could now see red and white flashers. He was cut off, it looked like.

But the hand holding the gun was remembering the kick of it, a reminder of that sense of *force* fucking *majeur* Charlie had had on the two occasions when he'd fired on Iraqis—although then he'd been scared shitless and shooting an M-16. People took you seriously when you fired at them. Charlie Pedrango was the kind of guy who liked to be taken seriously.

Of course, killing a policeman was a little outré even for Charlie. Getting caught was bad, too. So he'd taken a position behind a tall pine just off the trail and laid for Glenn Hatch, figuring to threaten him and get him to lay off the chase.

Pedrango was surprised when instead of the cop, Jack Grant had appeared around the last bend in the trail where Charlie had his gun pointed.

Jack stopped. Neither Glenn, whom he thought he'd been following, nor Charlie, were visible. Jack listened hard, heard nothing.

Charlie could see, dimly, bits of filtered police flashers lighting Jack's face once in a while, more gray and pink at this distance, through the trees.

Then Jack spun around as Hatch stepped from the trees at his back, having pulled the same move as Charlie. The deputy leveled his pistol.

"Do you have a gun, Jack?" he said.

"No," Jack told him.

Glenn pointed his own straight up.

And Pedrango stepped out from behind his tree, gun out, saying "Now listen," figuring he was just going to *explain,* but Glenn brought his gun down and pointed it while Jack spun around to face Charlie and stepped between them, holding his hands up to Charlie, saying "wait a second, Charlie," and Charlie was startled and he pulled the trigger two times.

Charlie's bullets hit Jack in the neck and the belly.

Glenn squatted as Jack crumpled and when his cousin's toppling form had cleared the line of fire, the deputy shot Charlie twice, Charlie diving sideways trying to get in a shot where Hatch had been standing a second before. Charlie took the bullets in the left calf and in the middle of his chest and he hit the ground dead.

The deputy was at Jack's side in that instant but gouts of blood were erupting from his cousin's neck and his eyes were wide and he squirmed a moment and lay still. The flow didn't stop for a long time.

Hatch looked down at Jack. He said nothing, not even when Gerow and the others caught up, with their guns drawn. Not even forty-five minutes later when Oscar Gilbert moved through the woods into the clearing, slipping under the tape being strung up.

THIRTY-EIGHT

Winter came. Word got out that it was the Reverend Peterson who'd been found dead out there in Roosa Lake in New York, and his congregation took it in and some of them took it hard. Some in particular felt they owed that minister a debt of a certain sort, and they were hard men in their way, tempered by his work and by their work, and by the company of the aging coal miners and their stolid wives—bakers, knitters, sewers of clothes. They'd become soft men since prison, maybe, or they'd become better men.

So Doug Wills, Clarence Prince, and Lagrange Johnson met under a bulb at Clarence's trailer to talk about what had happened, and about the work they'd been doing for the reverend. Not the raking and pruning, that was important, but the other work, the running work. Lagrange had out a six pack of cola in little plastic bottles and three mismatched but clean glasses and they each took ice from the freezer when they needed it, and the foil-and-crumb carcasses of takeout hoagies were on the table, too.

"Who did it, you think?" Doug said.

Clarence spoke the names from memory; they didn't like to write stuff down. "Could have been Century. Maybe WestGen. Canfield."

The prohibition on talking about their work was very strong, but their leader was dead and the three of them—Doug and

Clarence more than Lagrange—were a little off-balance. The rules had been relaxed, at least for this night.

Doug and Lagrange agreed. They hadn't done work against any other gas drillers.

"What about a property owner?" Lagrange said. "Someone pissed off about royalties."

"Could be," Clarence said. "But all of this still leaves the question of how anyone found out about us."

"Us, us?" Lagrange said, and gestured at the three of them.

"Well, the Reverend. The anti-fracking stuff. Tips. All that."

"People knew," said Doug. "Secret of two, a secret is true... how does that go?"

"It goes," said Clarence, "three can keep a secret"— and he looked at his companions, the closest thing he had to friends, and that was not as close as it might have been before he went inside, "if two of them are dead."

Doug laughed, but Lagrange let it wash over and pass away before he spoke. "That still leaves open the question of who," he said.

"It does," Clarence said.

Doug spoke. "What about this guy they found him with? Cyrus Grant. Both shot. What was that about?"

"It was a setup," Lagrange said. "Had to've been. Someone got them out there and offed 'em."

"Yeah, but who was that guy? Paper made him sound like a redneck."

"I don't know. Some badass. Maybe was his job to get the Reverend out there and maybe he was just making a few dollars for it. Maybe he was supposed to do it, and didn't."

Clarence again. "What about that house burning down? Man, this thing is crazy."

"That it is," said Lagrange.

"Crazy is the word," said Doug. He poured some more soda. "So?" he said. "What do we do?"

THIRTY-NINE

March 2009

She woke with her hand on her belly and Jeffrey breathing beside her. It was round now, her belly, but not unwieldy yet. The sunlight came through the back windows, down through the weedy trees in the courtyard of their building. It was the one slice of daylight they'd get and sometimes it was gone before she woke, but today it was there, the light coming earlier and staying longer with winter gone.

Closing. The word held mystery, promise, danger. Today they were closing. And in a month they were moving. Shuffling off Brooklyn, shedding it like a skin, molting it like down, shearing it off like—

"What time is it?" said Jeffery, expecting an answer with the peculiar telepathy of the married, although she had not moved and his eyes were shut.

"Six-fifty," said Serena. She rolled over and kissed him to the left of his lips. His hand found her belly and he stroked her, eyes still shut.

"We will crush the opposition," he said without moving his lips much.

"How's that?"

"At the closing table. We will take no prisoners." He stretched, groaned. It was a Thursday, but they had taken the day off, again.

"But Jeffery," she said. "They've been so kind."

"Okay, you're right. We'll take them prisoner." He rolled and looked at her.

"That would be nice," she said. "Rhonda, certainly. Not sure about Michael."

"There would be a good ransom."

She kissed him. "True," she said.

The closing was to take place in a lawyer's office in Kingston, not far from the hospital. Rhonda liked to drive, she'd told them, and she wanted to take them. Both parties were using the same lawyer. There was no mortgage on the place, but the Gales were taking out a loan. They could keep the apartment and make payments on the house for about four months, they'd figured. Serena was pretty sure she'd be able to work in Kingston, or from Kingston—right now she'd talked about the house as a weekend place to her boss.

And in June, in three months, the baby.

She brushed her teeth.

"Have we figured out the gap yet?" she said.

Jeffery was showering behind a curtain that had a sort of renaissancey floral motif in an aged-looking bronze sort of color, something *classy*, they'd felt, but that had been a couple of years before. Now, having seen the inside of ten or twelve houses up thataway, it looked false and dated, very of the oughts. They'd seen wide plank floors they couldn't afford, and they'd seen particle board chic and allover pine paneling—including ceilings in one memorable instance (Captain's Courageous, they'd named that one)—and none of it had been THE house, but THE house was mostly burned down.

Which had dropped the price some.

Michael Harrison had balked at rebuilding, favoring taking the insurance and selling the land—to the Gales if they wanted it, and he'd throw in the original plans if they wanted them—but Rhonda was apparently a lot like their mother the psychologist and Michael eventually gave up.

It wasn't a rebuild, technically, she'd explained. It was a restoration. The foundation was good. The chimney was still fine. The whole back of the place was intact. They could put it back together...and Rhonda had acted as general contractor. She'd patted Serena on the arm over a pot of manure-smoke lapsong suchong, said "don't fret, Serena," and told them to make an offer.

From late February to March, the house had re-emerged. It wasn't done yet, wouldn't be till summer, but they had some space they could claim in there, and they'd scheduled the close.

"The gap?" he asked, leaning out of the shower, reaching for his towel across the toilet, arm dripping as it did every day. *New bathroom will not do that,* he thought. *We'll invent a towel dispenser.*

"The employment gap. The money gap," she said.

"Ah. No," he told her.

He'd been thinking of it, of course. It loomed there, the gap, and they'd talked about it that way. Between moving and surviving. They could work, she could work, maybe, up in Kingston; he could do freelance work, even write for his current employer, maybe. But it was all maybes, and they knew they were running for the hills in a way that perhaps wasn't prudent, but fuck prudence, there'd be time enough for prudence after the baby.

"Fuck prudence," he said.

Serena spit into the sink and turned the tap back on. "Who's Prudence?"

"No, I mean wisdom. Fuck wisdom."

"Oh. All right," she said. She cupped some water to her mouth, rinsed, spit it out. "Howso, though?"

"House. Baby. Gap," he said.

"Baby Gap?" she said, but she was with him now. The schtick.

"Yeah," he said. "Once we've closed the baby gap, we can think about employment gaps."

"They're closing the Baby Gap?" she said. "Where are we gonna get clothes for the—" but by then he was kissing her, towel around his waist, fresh mint against his tongue.

"Let's go close the housing gap," he said.

A short time later they left the apartment, Serena reflexively looking to the spot where a cop used to wait—although it had been months since the police had bothered, all silent on that front—and turned right toward the subway.

There were two men sitting on the stoop one house over, smoking cigarettes. They were neatly dressed in button-down shirts and khakis, one with a brown blazer, the other in a denim jacket. One dark-skinned with short dreadlocks, the other pale and with a crew cut. Crew cut was smoking and ground it out as they passed.

" 'Scuse us," the other one said. The Gales stopped, turned. The men stayed on the stoop.

The white guy spoke. "I'm Doug, and this is Lagrange," he said. "I'm sorry to bother you, but are you Mr. and Mrs. Gale?"

Jeffrey moved very slightly to stand partly in front of his wife, who took a half step back.

"What do you want?" he said.

"Wanted to help catch the guy who killed those people upstate." He frowned and shook his head, as though at the memory of a tragedy. "Wasn't quite..."

"Wasn't quite fair," said Lagrange.

"Fair," said Doug. "That's it. Not quite fair, really, this guy getting off."

"We think we can find him," said Lagrange.

Serena stepped forward again. She had her cellphone out. "Listen," she said. "Why don't we call the police and ask them if they want your help?"

A woman walked by with twins in a stroller. Jeffrey touched Serena's arm and indicated that perhaps they'd want to go alongside her. But the street was peopled—it was Thursday morning and the neighborhood was on its way to work. Doug and Lagrange remained on the stoop.

Serena looked at Jeffrey. She shook her head slightly and stayed.

"We could do that," said Lagrange.

"But, really, we thought maybe there were other ways to handle this," said Doug.

Jeffrey said, "I don't. I think the police are the way to handle this. Unless by 'this' you mean something besides the murder and arson we know about."

"No, that's the this we mean," said Lagrange.

"Well, who the hell are you?"

"Ah," said Doug. "We're friends of the deceased. The Reverend Peterson."

"Oh," Serena said. "I'm sorry."

"Yeah," said Lagrange. "Yeah, he was a decent man. And we'd very much like to get the guy who killed him."

" 'Get' him?" Serena asked.

"It's just..." said Doug. "It's just that we think whoever it is might be smarter than the police."

"More imaginative," Lagrange said.

"What do you mean?" said Serena.

Lagrange waved his hand a little, vaguely. "You know, this person maybe does things a little different than your average person. His—his motives aren't clear."

"You mean he's crazy?"

"No," said Doug. "Or maybe only a little. He knows what he's doing."

"What's he doing?" Serena said.

Doug said, "we think we know. But before we'd tell you, you have to agree to help."

"Help what?" said Jeffrey. "Without the police, I'm not sure what we're talking about. You want to kill the guy?"

Lagrange actually looked startled. "No! No, no, no, no, nah," he said, holding his hands out and down, tamping down earth.

"We want to...implicate him," said Doug.

Serena said, "You know who it is?"

"No," said Lagrange. "But we know the kind of person he is. Probably we know more or less what he thought he was doing."

"We think," Doug said.

"So how do you want to implicate him?" she said. Then she looked at her cellphone and saw the time. "Shit," she said.

"Yeah, sorry," said Doug. "You're on your way someplace?"

Jeffrey laughed. He gave Serena a vaudeville elbow to the ribs. "Wants to know..." he said.

"...if we're going someplace," she finished. "He says." She sighed.

"Why again no cops?"

"We want to be sure," said Doug.

"Nothing dangerous," said Jeffrey.

"Everything's dangerous," said Doug. "You think it was dangerous, that time you went to look at houses upstate? Look how that turned out."

"Yeah."

"But no bullets," said Lagrange. "Probably. And that's another reason to avoid the police. They *always* bring bullets."

Serena said, "give me a number to call you. We have to go."

Doug gave her a number. She added it to her cell. "Where are you going, anyway?" asked Doug.

"Upstate," Serena told him. "We're buying that house today. C'mon, honey."

And she and her husband walked off, he with a wave.

The two men stared after them. Lagrange raised his eyebrows and turned to Doug.

"Fancy that," he said.

. . .

"Haha limber up your signing hand," the bank's lawyer said, and they all laughed, Serena and Jeffrey a little manically and Rhonda a little bit at them for being manic. The lawyer laughed because he was going to make $1200 the easy way.

So they signed and signed and got the house, or the foundation and the back half and a lot of framing and some Tyvek sheathing and plywood.

The signing didn't end, exactly, it petered out, papers sliding across the table between the lawyer and the title insurance lady and Rhonda and Jeffrey and Serena. They wrote a check, they saw a pre-printed six-figure check slide across the table (Serena ran her finger over it as it went by and she laughed). Then they signed a few more checks and the papers went from one tall pile to three different piles and these were gathered and they were shaking hands and walking outside.

"Lunch?" said Rhonda. She had tears in the corners of her eyes and didn't acknowledge them at all.

"I want to see our house," Serena said. "Can we drive out there? And then we're buying you lunch."

They drove out to Bone Hollow and there it was, one pine tree still bearing yellow crime scene tape around the trunk, tape that Serena had now seen four or five times and still hadn't decided to take down. The workers left it there anyway, and it looked like part of the whole construction deal. But she knew it, reflected on it every time she saw it—the shooting, the burning—the kick to the head. And then the building. From heat and violence, something was growing and it was hers.

She looked again. There was a white rectangle tucked under the yellow tape. The word CAUTION ran across it on the tape. An envelope.

And in the envelope, a picture of the house under construction. And beneath that, a picture of the front of their apartment building in Brooklyn.

She grabbed her cellphone.

FORTY

Baker lifted his coffee cup, looking again at the November newspaper clippings, as he did from time to time. They were getting older now. And the new police sketch. And the quotes from that anonymous Brooklyn couple. They weren't anonymous to him. They were known to him.

TWO KILLED IN ARKVILLE POLICE ACTION
by Oscar Gilbert

The headline he could live with. Jack Grant was dead, that was okay, and the guy who'd killed him, well, he was dead too. Charles Emery Pedrango. Jack had been sought in connection with the discovery of two dead men near Accord in the fall, one of them his brother. So many gaps left so many possibilities for supposition. Maybe Charles Emery had also shot the Reverend Peterson and Jack's brother Cyrus. Maybe Charles Emery and Jack had worked together and killed the Reverend Peterson and Cyrus Grant, and maybe it had been over drugs or women or old grudges.

Baker was home, in the Rittenhouse Square apartment, not the country place, and he was drinking coffee and listening to the radio and reading newspapers under thin early spring light and a bright white kitchen fluorescent. He picked up his cup, looked at the aging news some more. He smiled.

253

This was how it worked—you made something happen, you forced action, you broke situations up, you extracted something valuable.

Deputy Glenn Hatch had been on administrative leave, but was found to have acted in accordance with training and with the law during the incident. In a bizarre twist that made even Baker wonder about Fate and layers of conspiracy, Jack Grant, one of the deceased, was revealed to be the deputy's cousin. The original shooting was still under investigation. State Police Senior Investigator William Gerow was leading the case.

That was all fine. That was terrific. Baker tried to think like a cop, like that Gerow, while admitting that he didn't really know how they thought. Sometimes so smart, often so dumb. Or apparently dumb. They specialized in questions, streetwise scientists, asking asking asking, and then accusing and accusing till they heard what they wanted. They had a good success rate, but with sometimes staggering dumbness, big missed opportunities, so many questions unanswered. Hampered, maybe, by rules, by rote, by not being surprised.

But these guys were getting surprised, Baker reflected. Baker bet that Deputy Hatch guy had been quite surprised. He smiled again.

Thinking like Oscar Gilbert, that fuck, was even harder. What did he know? That article had been written by someone on the scene. How'd he gotten there? Who knew? The cops would never have made that call. Which led to the part that bothered him.

The part that bothered him was the subhead, further down. "Possible Accomplice Sought." That was him. Eyewitnesses had seen a third man at the scene whom police wanted to question in connection with the case. Eyewitnesses. Fresh-faced eyewitnesses, sparkly eyewitnesses. Serena and Jeffrey Gale, he knew now. But especially Serena Gale. Yes. Most especially she.

POSSIBLE ACCOMPLICE SOUGHT

Police and eyewitnesses described a third man at the scene who may have had some connection to the gunman or to the other victim. Investigators are seeking a white male aged 35–45, between 5 feet 6 and 6 feet tall, of medium build. He was seen wearing dark trousers, with a Yankees cap and jacket.

Again, so many holes in their knowledge. So much room for happy resolutions to the scenarios that unraveled before him. But so many cracks. They'd seen him and he wished they hadn't.

But he had almost been able to see... her... across that circle of onlookers, and he just needed to step forward a foot, to see the white lights of the cars shining on her face, and her eyes had turned, and he'd felt the double thrill of seeing her *notice* him, and feeling an unaccustomed *risk.*

Since then he'd caught himself imagining her watching him a couple of times, going about his rounds, driving, solving problems. He knew it was a warning sign, knew it signaled a loss of objectivity and focus. But, he told himself, he was such an unlikely candidate for any of this stuff. The lines to him were so tenuous, such gossamer filaments of time and place. He was golden. And besides, they'd given him a Yankees cap in the police sketch. It looked nothing like him.

Plus he had layers of protection; he blended. He never lingered, he paid cash, he avoided tolls, and he drove the speed limit. He didn't make nobody no trouble.

Although he would make trouble for Serena Gale, if she wanted. He looked again at the article. That had been the second time she'd spoken about him to police. Sure, he had to admit that both times it was because of risks he'd taken. And that first time he'd *had* to. He'd needed to get into that hospital and find out what they knew. But in Arkville, it was pure stupidity. He had only been able to see the side of her face, and the desire to step forward into the light so he could see her whole face, his need to compare her face to the memory of it that he couldn't shake, had been too strong. He'd wanted her to see him, too. He knew that. Mocked himself for it, but he couldn't deny it.

Looking at her was a little like taking a drink of water. Even now, looking at the newspaper, remembering how dangerous that all was, he wanted to look at her again.

He'd tried, but hadn't found any pictures of her online. But he'd found something else, searching on the Bone Hollow Road address, found a county record of a title search, and had found that the house was under contract. He'd called the realtor and heard her say "a couple from Brooklyn," and he'd hung up stunned.

They were buying the fucking house? Were they twisted?

After the newspaper article, he'd tried to treat this project like he would any impediment to drilling. Nuns get paid, assemblymen get bribed (*salaried, more like,* he'd thought), rights-of-way get purchased privately before public auction, homeowners get threatened with lawsuits. This would be similar. Snoops get threatened.

So he'd taken a shot of their Brooklyn building off Google street view, driven out by Accord in a rental as a side trip on some other business and paused long enough to snap a shot of the house under construction. Then it was easy to print that from a thumb drive off a library computer in Newburgh, down by an interstate he could take back to Pennsylvania, and tuck that into the envelope. Then, two weeks later, on another trip through Ulster County, early morning, it was easy to tuck that envelope into a remnant of the police tape.

He'd played it many times and didn't think it exposed him any further. If it scared them off, great. If it didn't—well, it didn't give them anything new to go on.

As he'd driven away from the house that morning after dropping the envelope, he replayed his last glimpse of Mrs. Gale again. The lights flashing in the woods. She'd looked a little stunned, but that lively intelligence had been there, and when she turned, when her eyes flicked his way and he'd felt that double thrill of danger and of visibility, her eyes had widened and her lips had parted in a gasp and that was embedded pretty firmly in his memory. Driving up Bone Hollow Road away from the house after placing the photo, he presented himself with a question: how much of this heavy-handed threat thing was just a wish to send her a little note?

Not much, he thought.

You sure? he asked.

A few miles later he'd pulled over. And went both ways on the question of whether to leave it there, and finally said out loud "fuck it," and drove back to Pennsylvania. Sometimes when there was a seam, you had to force it open to make it pay.

Now, back in Philadelphia, reading the articles a final time, finishing his coffee, he marked the fourth week since he'd dropped the envelope. His fourth week seeing and hearing nothing related to the project.

Well, he'd seen one thing. The house closing had gone through. He'd seen it under "recent sales" in the realtor's ads just a week prior. Lowball price.

This, the tail-end of the Peterson job, seemed to be winding down. The Gales were uneasy now, assuming they'd gotten his note, and were maybe less enthusiastic about pissing him off. They had a house to think about, now. He gave it sixty percent that he wouldn't be hearing from them again.

And that would wrap up Accord for him. The shale was thirty and more miles west of Bone Hollow Road, and he never got much more than fifteen miles from there in his day job.

And it had been a job well done. Peterson had been a nagging pain in the ass; he had specifically, it seemed, been responsible for informing a couple of town council members in the western Catskills about the problems in Dimock. When WestGen's PR folks had persuaded another town council to issue a letter of support for fracking and circulated it to town boards in the area and beyond, asking them to ratify it (a hit or miss tactic, he'd thought, and of little use, but the PR team had its ideas), Peterson had been the source, Baker thought, of another letter that refuted the points in WestGen's letter. Three town boards had actually adopted a resolution *opposing* fracking.

It's not like the guy would've overpowered the company's lobbying arm, or the actual lobby in Washington, or anything. But Baker was both general and foot soldier fighting a fucking insurgency. He was the guy paying the nuns to get drilled and fracked. He was the guy who had to grease the wheels, on the ground, day in, day out, well below the Washington radar, at the individual homeowner level. And Peterson, he'd been operating down there, too. On the QT. In the dark.

And that's where he was now, forever. And Baker figured he could close out the Accord thing. Let 'em seek another person of interest. He was not one of those. And the Gales had other things to think about, now.

FORTY-ONE

Doug hung up, turned to Lagrange.

"That was Serena," he said. "Mrs. Gale."

"The homeowner, you mean?" said Lagrange. He was sitting behind Reverend Peterson's old desk above the storefront church, looking through a sheaf of papers. It was a copy of a complaint filed by two ranchers against Fairfield Extraction in Texas. Their cattle had been sickened by benzene-tainted water that had welled up into a couple of drainage ditches.

"That's the one."

"What'd she say?"

"She said she'd be happy to help. Asked again if we shouldn't talk to the police first."

"That's never worked out too well for me, somehow."

"Me neither."

Clarence wasn't with them. They'd read a legal notice in the local paper about extraction licenses granted to WestGen by an abbey near Beach Lake, and he'd driven out that way. He wanted to see if anyone knew who the decision maker was on that one. Lots of times there'd be a community activist or an editor or someone who wrote a letter to the editor or gave a talk at a coffee shop, and those people—those isolated individuals, powered by the internet but acting alone or in very small groups when it came to their particular problem—they often could point you

259

to what had gone wrong, where the leverage had been applied. Which specific town board member had a brother on the payroll, or who stood to make some serious coin when it came time for a company to lay down a facility or erect some tanks.

Doug had been reading through a stack of local papers from the area. He'd buy them at greasy spoons and gas stations, use them to follow who was pushing what. Some towns had plenty to say. "FRACK NO" signs on every other lawn, "ENERGY INDEPENDENCE" on the rest. Minds made up.

Of course, the ones calling for independence had lots of acreage, and stood to get roads paved onto their property, and royalties, and whatnot. There was undeniably profit to be made out here, and if it weren't for the relative proximity to New York City and its water supplies and its tourists, this wouldn't even have been a fight.

But there they were, New York, with its vampiric hold on the region, and the good thing was that the eight million people at the other end of that long straw wanted their water clean. Too late for Dimock or Clearbrook, but if they could just get to one of those tipping points people spoke about, they could make it unreasonable to mount these incredibly expensive projects.

"How you want to play it?" said Lagrange. They'd discussed it, the three of them, and had agreed on a need for flexibility. But that didn't stop them, in twos, or all together, chewing it over now and then, or going off alone and playing the scenarios.

Doug dropped the paper. It was a little like drugs, he figured, only he was the DEA for a change. When you had a drug market, someone was going to supply it. And if the DEA or the cops tamped down on one meth lab or one corner dealer, there was a little shakeup and the operation either moved or another one took it over. But when you continually harassed the supply chain, arrested people higher up the processing and distribution networks, you could have an effect as the business knowledge dissipated further down.

He himself had been part of one of those harassment campaigns, just on the downward end of it. He had been the guy behind the slit in the door of a crackhouse in Pittsburgh, pushing out nickel bags in exchange for limp five dollar bills, and the fear and exhilaration would stay with him for a long time, he supposed.

They arrested him on his way in to the house one night, three guys in flak jackets stepped out of an alley right into his path and another one came up behind him, and he couldn't believe he hadn't known they were coming, there were supposed to be warnings, he had *people*, he thought. Only he didn't. He had crackheads, and they had been moving further and further from acting like people as they got consumed by need.

. . .

The three ex-cons' parole officers—they were all off parole at this point—would have been surprised at their improvement. These guys were rehabilitated. It had happened practically by accident, of course. No place else to go had brought them out of prison in the middle of Pennsylvania looking for work. Community service assignments had brought them into contact with Peterson. Compulsory AA and NA had brought them together. And, well, as far as rehabilitation goes, he'd been a model.

Peterson had once asked the three of them to visit with him over the church, early on, after Doug had joined a raking crew. Lagrange and Clarence knew Doug, knew each other, hadn't known one another inside, but both knew who Doug was from in there. The reverend started his pitch not with exhortation, but with confession.

"I've never been in prison, guys," he'd said. "But I've done things I'm not proud about."

He told them about losing it over a woman at an old job and the trouble that came from that. He told about skimming from his job as a pharmaceutical sales rep, selling painkillers on the side, small doses, never getting caught. He told them about some of those small moments, here and there, where he'd treated someone else like shit, said something that now made him cringe, been hateful.

"I bet you could go a lot deeper than me," he said. "And someday you might want to. Might want to unburden yourself to something higher—I know they tell you about a higher power in AA and NA—or to someone you trust. Me, I've done it a bunch of different ways, and I feel cleaner every time."

"But I didn't invite you here to supplement your AA education, or the counseling you had in prison," he said. "I came to tell you what I did, and what I do now."

"Right now, instead of any of that destructive shit, I try to do something right. This place we're sitting right now, and the people we help out, are under threat."

He laid out the case against hydrofracking, a word none of them had ever heard before, and something Peterson didn't speak about in public. It took about ten minutes, talking through the science, a couple of diagrams on a white board, a couple of press clippings from Texas, and from Dimock and Clearbrook, closer to home. He told them about the money that flowed from drilling companies to politicians through lobbyists and other less obvious ways. How they wrote legislation, bought scientists, paid marketing agencies for radio public service announcements and PR agencies for spin control. Their expertise with courts and lawyers and threatening letters and sales pitches and their particular ability to put wedges between groups of "stakeholders" (another new one for them) and convince them they had different interests. Their greed. Their disregard.

And then he brought it back around. "I see this greed, here, and this disregard for the people who live here, a lot like the same impulses that led me to do the things I told you about," he said.

"But it's not all a done deal. There are people trying to stop them from getting dug in, trying to keep it fair at the very least, put some protections in place."

And then he told them about the interest groups and uncorrupted politicians, and documentary film makers, and others who fought that battle in public.

"They're working very hard to keep these chemicals out of the ground, and out of the water" he said. "But even there, there's another campaign," he told them. "Bribes. Threats. Cheats. Fixes." He told them about the flip side of the public battle. And what he'd started to do to balance out that side of things, how he'd been working to counteract some of that.

He got nearer his point.

"I told you about all that stuff, about my—you can call 'em my sins if you want—because I suspect you've found those same kind of impulses inside you, and sometimes you've fought them, and sometimes you've lost. Am I right?"

They nodded.

"That's a hard battle to fight, inside yourself. And I figured out a way to fight it outside. I find that the more I fight that battle outside of me, the less I have to fight it on the inside."

"And best of all," he said. "When I fight this battle on the outside—when I get some information into the hands of a farmer that warns him about the dangers of fracking and gives him the number of a lawyer he can talk to if he hears from a gas company, or when I get someone in to take some pictures of safety violations at a WestGen operation, and those get in a local paper—I win even when I lose." He took a sip of water from a glass on his desk.

"Maybe they put in a new well, you know? I've lost, you'd say, right?"

Clarence said "Okay." The reverend nodded at him, smiling.

"But have I? I did what I could. I resisted. I fought the greed, the disregard, I resisted, and I fought it through to a conclusion. And when I was unsuccessful, what had I done? I had done good. When you lose that battle inside, against your own greedy and selfish impulses, you lash out. You take drugs. You hit somebody. You steal. But when you lose the outside battle, you're still clean. You didn't hurt anyone—not yourself or anybody else.

"And when you win? Well, you've accomplished something. But that's almost beside the point."

He stood up. "I have one last secret. I may be a preacher, but I'm not too strong on God. I think if he exists, it's because we make him exist. God's just the resistance to those same greedy, selfish, destructive impulses. Those are the devil, and the devil is always ready to move in if people don't create God."

They were still seated, in front of him, Doug and Clarence on the couch and Lagrange in a wooden armchair. Peterson came around the desk and sat on its edge.

"I want your help, not just 'cause there's good work to be done out there, but because I think it'd be good for you. Even though we might not always win. Are you with me?"

They were.

And now it was a couple-three years later, and the battles had been waged, like Spy vs. Spy from the old Mad magazines, Doug thought, and their best spy had been outed somehow and the other spy had swung a wrecking ball or whatever and smashed him and he was gone.

There'd been a big funeral for the Reverend, back in the early winter, once the police had released his body. The whole flock, and a lot of the rest of the town, had come out. The Lutheran minister had presided, and a line of people came up to speak, and no one mentioned his other work. Clarence and Doug had each taken a turn, and both of their eulogies harkened back to that conversation. Clarence even found a little poetry in him, and his voice went up a bit at the end until he might have been leading a little revival meeting of his own. He took the Devil-as-greed-and-selfishness line, and he pledged to keep fighting that fight on the outside, and to keep pushing back against that Devil wherever he found him. Without, of course, mention of fracking.

He wrapped up with a ringing warning, and it struck a chord, until the assemblage was laughing with it, chanting it. "Run," they said in unison. "Devil, run."

. . .

Lagrange spoke, and it brought Doug back. "Like judo," he said.

"How's that?" Doug said.

"You asked how I want to play it. I say, like judo. You know, you use your opponent's energy against him."

"Draw him in, like."

"Yeah, and make him do something dumb," said Lagrange. "You remember what Reverend Peterson used to say?"

"Yeah. 'Apply pressure, and things leak.' But," Doug said, "what if he's too smart?" They'd been over that possibility, too. "You think he'll go for the Gales?"

"Yeah, that's what I think. Mrs. Gale said they got a threat note. She also wanted to know how we found out about them."

"She didn't go to the cops with that?"

"I guess not."

Doug got off the couch. "We do *need* the cops, though, right? For the end game here?"

"The other option?"

"Being we figure out who killed Jim, and we..." Lagrange said. He held his hands palm up, out to the sides, raised his eyes to heaven. Then he answered his own question. "We need the cops, is what I'm saying."

"Agreed."

They'd been questioned by the Pennsylvania state police and by some police from New York, plus a few follow up visits by the Pennsylvania police. But what's funny is that all three of them, as far as each one knew, had been clean since they got out. And certainly had had nothing to do with the reverend's demise. Something they'd all learned in prison was that you couldn't necessarily trust other people—but you couldn't not trust other people. That's the risk that keeps on paying back dividends.

The door downstairs opened and shut and Clarence's sneakered footsteps came up the stairs. He was back from the abbey. He had a story to tell.

FORTY-TWO

The nuns had gotten sorta greedy, he told them. They started out friendly, but it didn't last. They did give him a name, a guy named Baker from WestGen. This Baker had given them a file of studies he claimed proved the safety of the process, and in particular of WestGen's own sterling history.

The key to these things, Doug and Clarence and Lagrange knew, was that no one reads beyond the Executive Summary. That's the only important piece of any business document; that and the last page. So those studies could say pretty much what they wanted as long as the PR department had a go at the Exec Summary.

In any case, the other most important page in Mister Baker's presentation had been smaller and had a dollar sign on it. That had been the one that radically changed the nuns' viewpoint on fracking. They seemed to be wholly in favor of getting fracked now. And the board that ran their order, well, they'd been okay with it, too. Times were hard, and money was tight.

The long and short of it—Clarence had called upon the Lord. He laid out some cards, told the sister about the Reverend, told her they were pretty sure someone from one of the gas companies, or a landowner with a gripe, might have been behind it. Told her about their little church.

"She didn't seem to understand about the church," he said. "Kept asking about our diocese and stuff."

But she'd seemed sincerely sorry. She'd suggested he tell the police about his suspicions.

She'd been polite, and he'd left.

But that Baker. That was a new name.

FORTY-THREE

The reporter was on his back under his car trying to thread the plug on his oil pan back into the hole and cursing more or less conversationally. His phone buzzed a split second before playing the irritating, jazzy default ring. As usual he wondered how that was the common denominator in terms of taste. These companies were smart and big enough to have a reason to put certain sounds onto those phones, weren't they? And was this really the statistical center of the ring tone world? This was how a big telecommunications player wanted to announce itself, with a sort of almost-Seinfeld theme song? Maybe it had been fresh in the early nineties, he mused, and rolled out from under his car, leaving the plug on an old Orange County map he'd placed beneath the pan to catch drips.

He missed the call, but the number was there, a city area code and...yeah, that was it, the Gales. He called back immediately.

"Serena, hi, it's Oscar Gilbert," he said.

"Hello Mister Gilbert. I hate to say it, but I think I have another story for you."

"What's it about?"

"It's about how we can maybe identify the man who posed as you in the hospital last year. The man who most likely killed those other two men out by Bone Hollow Road. The one we spotted at that train ride thing."

269

"You *identified* him? To whom?"

"To no one yet, but we can, to you."

"You have a photo? Or his name? Who is he? And why aren't you on the phone with Detective Gerow?"

"Detective...who?" she said.

Gilbert laughed a little. "You know I work with men like Detective Gerow a lot, right?" he said. "In fact, I work with that man himself from time to time. He tells me things. I write them down, or check them out. If he were to stop telling me things..."

She could picture him on the other end of the phone, at a house someplace maybe, or an apartment in whatever town where it was they did that newspaper. He was at a stool at a breakfast bar, like one of those morning-show style countertops with sunlight spilling over it. Although it was evening. So he had a plate of cookies there and some milk, but his cell was on his belt.

Because he was a reporter.

"So you're saying," she said, "you have to go to the cops before you're allowed to learn anything?"

Gilbert still lay on his back in his garage, looking up at cobwebs that surrounded a moth-enshrouded double-bar fluorescent nailed to the ceiling joists and trying to see where this was going. The dolly on which he lay had some strips of carpet glued to it, for comfort.

"Well now," he said, but his voice was mild. "You haven't read my *oeuvre*. I've outed crooked cops before. The honest ones who stay, they appreciate it."

"He has an *oeuvre*," she said to someone else on her end, voice fading out and coming back as she turned her head to say it.

Faintly he heard a male voice, the husband. "An *oeuvre,* she says."

These two, he thought as he lay there looking up, belonged in the Catskills after all.

"So what next, Ms. Gale?" he said. "You want to meet? Or do you have something to tell me?"

"I told you. We think we know who he is, more or less. We're going to tell the police."

"But you're telling me that first. When exactly are you going to tell the police?"

"Ah, well," she said. "We were thinking about that. Wouldn't it be cool if there was an article in the paper first that said we were going to tell the police, so the police would get all excited?"

He thought rapidly. He'd worked a lot of crime stories before. There were all sorts of desperate people in the world, and a share of them lived in the region his paper served. Murders. Drugs. Corruption. Thievery. He'd had to work with the police from time to time. He left out details of an investigation on request, as long as he and his editor agreed that there was little public interest in revealing them. He emphasized poignant story details to motivate public outrage, to generate tips and leads in his own investigative pieces.

But this didn't make sense, really. As far as he knew, the Gales had no reason to leave Gerow out of it. If they truly could ID the guy, why not let him know?

"I still don't see why we're not talking to Detective Gerow," he said.

"There are...other parties. They don't want to be bothered unless they're sure they have the guy's name right. But then? Hoo boy."

"Hoo boy?"

"Yes, Mister Gilbert. Hoo. Boy. They will then want to be bothered, and they will want the murderer bothered. Bothered into the pokey. The big house, or whatever."

"Or executed?" he said.

Serena Gale, she of the quick riposte, actually paused. She'd forgotten that. Sure, New York had the death penalty, but it seemed to her like that old canister of rat poison she'd found in the utility closet in the laundry room of their building. It was a metal can with an old-looking skull and crossbones and an image of a dead rat, X-ed out eyes, belly up. A faded paper ribbon was affixed over the top of the can, to be broken on first use. There it was, lethal, redolent of age and a somehow more serious era, subterranean, unused.

"Well, that's one reason to only call the cops if they're sure," she said. "Be a shame to execute someone who didn't do it."

"So what's his name?"

"I didn't say we knew that," she said. "I said we could identify him. He works for a gas drilling company."

Gilbert sat up fast on the dolly, shifting his weight forward to the edge that projected out beyond the wheels. The end dipped, the dolly flipped up, and the other end smacked him in the back of the head. He dropped the phone.

"Fuck!" he said.

He heard her laugh through the earpiece, from his place on the floor. "Yeah, I was surprised, too."

"No, that's not it," he said, picking up the phone and rubbing his head. "I mean, yeah, that's surprising, but I hit my head."

"At a breakfast bar?" He heard her turn her head to say "Hit his head." Heard the husband say "Ouch." He thought maybe they were driving.

"What? I'm not at a—" he said. "Look. A drilling company? In Accord?"

"That, I think, is misdirection."

"Yeah, okay." He was standing now, walking into the lower level of the bi-level he and his wife shared outside Middletown. He crooked his neck to hold the phone and grabbed a rag off the shelf over the washing machine as he passed by. The phone, a modern index-card-sized slab instead of the curved piece of furniture he grew up on, slid down into the crevice until the mouthpiece was nowhere near his mouth and the earpiece was nowhere near his ear. From experience, he knew you could still talk.

He wiped his hands on the rag while he did so. "Tell me why you think that," he said.

"Well," she said, "that minister guy? Mister Peterson. He was sort of an anti-drilling activist. What do they call it, again?"

"Fracking?"

"Yes, that's what they said. Hydro-fracking. He was against it."

"So are lots of people."

"Not like him, from what I gather. He was a *guerilla*." She gave it a Spanish pronunciation so there'd be no silly misunderstandings.

"I assume you have more than that?"

She and Jeffrey were cruising one last time in Rhonda's German sports car. They were driving to their house. They had camping equipment in the back, because they were going to sleep there. Her belly was round. She felt kicks sometimes. It was a weekend, and she wanted to sleep in their house.

After finding the photo, she'd called Clarence and made the skeleton of a plan. She'd worked the phone. Asked Rhonda if they could borrow the car, promising to buy a used one next week. Told Jeffrey to drive them to Saugerties to buy camping equipment. Called Oscar Gilbert on their way back. To sleep. At their house.

After all, it was partially roofed, and there was a little brick firepit in the back. They'd camped before, in their fleeces and their sleeping bags. The high-pitched sound of zippers startling in the stillness of woods. Here would be different, of course, here in their house.

They'd debated whether to go out to Messerbergh, meet up with the Cons, as they'd taken to calling Doug, LaGrange, and Clarence. That made some sense if the one name they had was right. Donald Baker, not listed in WestGen's 10K filings nor on their website, but it had a certain resonance coming from the nun's lips to Clarence's ear. So they could have gone out to Messerbergh, to near the company's home turf, to make themselves a burr in the side of Mister Baker, showing up in the same place as the last burr.

There was a problem there, though. To *really* implicate him they had to *draw him out.* To Accord.

Gilbert was waiting to hear what else they had.

"He had refused a bribe from a drilling company in the past."

"A bribe for what?"

"To stop his guerilla war against them."

"How do you mean?"

"Well, I'll tell you. We've met some people who used to work with the Reverend in that capacity," she said. "It was clear that, behind the headlines and the public statements and the lawsuits, there was something else going on."

"Isn't there always?"

"You'd know better than me. I just know that these people figured someone else was working to get drilling approved in towns all over Pennsylvania, and later in New York, the same way they were trying to fight fracking operations."

"How do they fight drilling? Sabotage?" He was doodling at a pad, actually sitting at his breakfast bar now, not writing yet, waiting for a point of fact or assertion in her story upon which to hang a note.

"They way they tell it, they were counteracting sabotage. Finding out about bribes. Handing reports and press clippings to town boards. Taking photos of polluted waste pools. Getting company air quality data that wasn't released to the public, and sharing it. Obtaining sealed court orders. Strictly," she said, "on the QT."

Oscar Gilbert started to write. "Any chance I could get some of that information?" he asked.

FORTY-FOUR

The construction crew had knocked off for the day and the house was a Tyvek-sheathed skeleton of its old self. There was sawdust everywhere. There were two pallets of oak floorboards in the middle of the front yard. A blue tarp, weighted with cinder blocks, covered them.

The living room floor was sheets of plywood, except for one stretch that hadn't been laid down yet, where a four-foot-deep crawlspace was revealed under the house, floored with blue three-quarter-inch stone, walled with cinderblocks that made the foundation. Jeff shone a flashlight down in there, and it looked dry. He didn't see any spiders or skunks or families of bears. Cool air flowed up.

Serena unrolled a couple of camping mats, sleeping bags. One of those little plastic battery-powered lamps from a gnome's living room. They had eaten in Accord, at a café they'd come to like, and they had used the bathroom there and brushed their teeth. There was little to do at the house other than sleep, and talk, and look up at the ceiling joists and feel the kicking baby through Serena's taut skin.

The car was parked behind the house, on the grass, between them and the head of the little trail down to the pond. There was a bag of groceries in its trunk, stuff that didn't need a fridge. Pop tarts, bottled water, the cured meats of the camper.

It grew dark. Stillness entered the clearing, and crept into the house. It was too early in the season for the legions of screaming insects that Serena remembered from camp. Too early for crashing thunderstorms, or tourist cars or rowdy bonfires. After all, Serena and Jeffrey weren't in season. They were year-round, now. Oh, sure, they still had the apartment, but only for another couple of months. Her resume was on desks in Kingston. His management thought they could work a telecommuting arrangement, but he'd have to be in the city, or northern Jersey, two or three times a month for meetings.

They tried on the silence, reading by the light of the little lamp. The sounds of their bodies moving on the nylon surfaces, the dry slide of a turning page, a cleared throat. Their fingers trailed over one another's hands from time to time, anchoring.

After a time, Serena stood, and walked a few feet away from their pool of battery-light, judging the degree of shadow. She wore jeans with an elastic waistband and a maternity top with that kind of Jane Austen waist he hated, but which looked right at this point in a woman's pregnancy.

Serena chose her light, and when it was half golden, half shadow, she stopped and looked back at her husband over one shoulder, the hair gathered to that side. He lay down his book, folded his arms beneath his head and watched her. She smiled, giving it the full Sphinx, then turned her back, cocked one hip, and raised the shirt, the light painting the muscles of her lower back. A last glance back to him—*do I have your full attention?*—as she pulled it up and off. A black bra, which she reached back in that Houdini gesture to unhook. Turned back to face him, the lace of the thing covering her newly larger breasts, her belly simultaneously beautiful, cute, and gravid with implications. She was lit, from this angle, gently, but like a planet nonetheless, with a day side and a night side. She now had a phase, like the moon. Waxing gibbous, he figured. Serena held the bra against her chest with two hands and let the straps slide down her arms, pinning it while she pulled first one arm, then other, free.

Turning her back again, she drew the bra away from her chest and dropped it behind her, then slowly swiveled her hips, bending forward a little with another glance over her shoulder. She had gained some pregnancy weight, sure, but not much, and not really from back here. They'd both read up on and heard a lot about how a woman carries, and if you can't tell from the back then it's a boy, and whatever, they didn't care. At the moment, he didn't care at all.

The elastic was impossible to sexify, so she just stood up straight and pushed the waistband of the jeans down over her hips to reveal a black thong. Serena stepped delicately on the jeans cuff on one side, drew out her foot, then did the same on the other, then turned to face him. Her hands caressed her belly, top and bottom, then passed over her breasts. She bit her lip at him, some hair over one side of her face in the golden light of the little lamp. Let her fingertips trail over herself and gave a perfectly understated, theatrical little gasp, all of it with a straight face.

It was the loudest sound they'd heard in an hour or so.

She came to bed on the camping mats, the whisper of her body sliding against the sleeping bags and their breathing and the minute smacks and adjustments of their lovemaking, sounds that emphasized the quiet and melted into the hemlock branches and out over the dark water under the stars.

. . .

When the morning came it started directly over the house, with the star-shaped gap in the branches changing from black to gray to pearl to blue pearl to blue to *blue*. It was pearl when Jeffrey stepped out into the back and pissed in the ferns back behind the firepit, away from the trailhead. There were animal tracks in the dew across the car's hood. He carried a plastic water bottle.

Shadows were still deep on the path down to the pond. No one had taken down the police tape, wrapped around trees months before. There was a strip at the trailhead that had been knocked down by branches falling during a winter storm. He cleared them and wrapped the tape into a loose bundle, then put a couple of limbs on it to keep it in place.

It wasn't night, precisely, there under the trees, ferns to either side, the bones of the earth jutting through thin topsoil here and there. Twilight seemed to live under these trees. Jeffrey walked down slowly, his first time down this path since the day they'd found the bodies. It was very familiar to him, despite that. He even imagined that he remembered individual trees. His feet made no sound on the pine duff. The path seemed worn by thousands of feet, needles a natural mulch and the smooth curve of its surface testament to generations of deer and skunks going down to drink.

There was a lighter patch ahead where the open sky gave onto the pond and he reached it in moments. The pond was higher. Snowmelt had brought its bank back up to the very foot of the path, and Jeffrey understood why you wouldn't necessarily put a terrace down here; you'd never know where it stood in relation to the water. Still, though, a little fire ring and a clear space, that might be nice on a fall night.

His eyes scanned the shoreline, mentally placing the floating figures in their places. A branch had fallen out in the middle and floated, twigs pointing upward with green needles still hanging from the ends.

He took a sip and in that wet place it felt strange. He looked up through the pale opening to where he could see the top of the hill. The shooter had been there. Jeffrey went that way, a thin continuation of the trail just at the verge of the water.

It wasn't far, but pools rose between the roots of trees. There was a viscous mud here, needle-covered and solid-looking. He stuck to roots and rocks, themselves slippery with dew and moss, and periodically a shoe—a pair of brown hiking sneakers that closed with an elastic cord secured by a spring-loaded plastic crimp—slid suddenly down into darkness and emerged wet and heavy.

Where the ground began to slope upward, on the far side of the pond, was a tangle of berry bushes, hairy red thorns snagging against his fleece. What path there had been dove under their archwork, the highways of rabbits, while a trace seemed to take a shot around to the side. He followed it, arms raised, trying to butt his way through the thorns with his hips, snagging as he went.

In the end, he got through the thorns, over a last muddy rill that came into the pond from one side, and into oaks that grew in the rocky soil partway up the hill's flank. The black fleece was studded with thin red thorns, burrs clung to his belly and hips, and his hands bore the thin red signatures of the grasping plants. He was sweaty and irritated.

As he started up, two deer bolted out of the edge of the thicket to his left with a crash, then shot leftward diagonally up the hill to a shoulder where they stopped. Jackrabbit ears flared out as they craned their heads around, rumps toward him. He stopped, too, and they all looked at one another. Then he glanced back toward the top of the hill, and when he looked back they had gone over the slope. He found another deer trail that led more directly upward and took it.

This went into some pines and up over sandy soil with smaller rocks poking through, eroded lines of sedimentary stone. Bottle caps and broken glass shone through the pine needles here and there. The going was easy enough, and the sun came up at his back. He was going to love having this hill behind his house, he thought. He was going to come up here and lay down some flat stones on the top and carry one of those canvas folding chairs up here sometimes and sit in the woods and read.

He came to the top. There was a ragged fire ring and burnt-ended logs that had been fed into the disorganized middle. A scorched pizza box lay amid the ashes, with a fair supply of broken bottles. A couple of larger logs were rolled up as seats, butt-worn. A different path led out the far side and down, and looking over he could see that it cut a slightly curving trail down the hillside to the double-lined road below, not very far. There was a pullout floored with sand.

He turned back and looked the way he had come. There was the pond, just the sandy edge at the foot of the path. A hundred yards. He walked forward, angled for the best view of the beachlet. Hunkered down. Imagined the person who'd been here before him, done these same things, laid for his enemies.

Jeffrey went prone, propped on his elbows, looking down the hill, imagining sighting on two people standing there, maybe talking. Maybe one held at gunpoint by the other, maybe just wrestled there in a headlock, who knew? The one guy a rangy tattooed hard case, the other a soft-bellied preacher and failed businessman. Engineered into place down there by someone with a Plan and a Gun.

Whodunit? He tried the one name he'd heard. Don Baker. Was he of average height? Average build? Yankees fan? Average age? Would he have the guts to pretend to be a reporter and question a potential witness to one of his crimes? They'd looked for him online, found nothing—not on the social-media business websites, the social-media friendly websites, the websites of any fracking companies, newspapers, nothing. Did they find some Donald Bakers? Yes. Lots and lots of them. A couple in Pennsylvania, even. But not near Messer—

"We can check this," he said out loud, suddenly. They had the police sketch of the fake Oscar Gilbert, and the nuns had the name. This would be a piece of fucking cake! The Cons could visit the nuns again and just ask, real simple-like, *is this Mister Baker?* They didn't have to do this crazy trap thing.

He stood and strode back down the hill, around the time that the *Caller-Dispatch* was getting taken into houses up and down and across Ulster, Greene, Duchess and Sullivan counties.

Its website, of course, had been updated when the paper edition had gone to press, and Don Baker's saved search alert function had already pinged his phone and let him know that there was an item on the Peterson killing, and what it said made him angry and curious and only a little nervous.

FORTY-FIVE

What ten years before would have been the city room was now the *Caller-Dispatch*'s whole editorial operations space, desks arranged in a grid, no cubicles but a few dividers that gave a little space to tack phone numbers. It was just after eight on that Sunday when Oscar Gilbert walked in, greeting a security guard and juggling his ID badge into place against a flat plastic panel that unlocked the door. He had a leather satchel over his shoulder bulging with papers, writing implements, and odd technological detritus whose time had passed or was passing. He had his keys and coffee in one hand and a paper deli bag in the other, weighed down by a cardboard cup of plain oatmeal and a banana.

Gerow was standing in Gilbert's cubicle, holding a cell phone to his ear and watching the reporter approach with an unreadable gaze.

Although Gilbert wasn't a huge fan of oatmeal—it was basically a prescription medicine, as far as he and his doctor were concerned—he had been sort of unconsciously imagining eating it, and this mundane fantasy now vanished. He stopped where he was, still a few feet away from his desk.

"Good morning, Bill," he said. He forced himself to step forward, sling his bag to the floor beside his chair, put down his things. He turned to face the policeman.

"Just tell me," Gerow said, putting the phone into the pocket of his gray suit jacket, "that what they have is actually nothing."

"They have a name," said Gilbert. "They just weren't sure it was the guy."

"And you didn't call me."

"I knew you'd see it and that we would have this conversation."

"We should have had it before you printed this bullshit." He didn't slap a newspaper onto the desk. He just waved around the room, as though the story was infused into the air they breathed.

"I told them I wouldn't talk to you until it printed. Now it's printed. We're talking."

"Where are they? More important, where is *she*?"

"As I understand it, they're at their house."

"Their house up here? I thought it wasn't finished."

"That's right. Said they were camping."

Gerow looked at the garbage can for a second, wanting to kick it. He shook it off, settled instead for running a hand through his hair.

"Okay," he said. "We're talking. Tell me what they told you."

They'd told him pretty much what he'd printed in the article. Some associates of the minister had come forward and thought they might have a line on a guy who had talked to someone else about fracking rights. That was the only part he hadn't printed. It would have been crazy to put that in, the way things were with fracking. If this panned out, it was multi-story special report national news Pulitzer stuff, and he wasn't going to let Gerow's anger over this bit get in the way of that possibility. Nor was he dumb enough to start pissing off gas drilling companies and all of Pennsylvania and probably half the upstate legislative delegation by printing it here.

So he'd invented a reason for them to hesitate in talking to the police.

POSSIBLE CLUES IN MINISTER SLAYING

Witnesses to events in the unfolding investigation into a double murder tell the *Caller-Dispatch* that they may have identified a prime suspect. The bodies of James Peterson, a Pennsylvania minister, and Cyrus Grant, last of Monticello, were found near Roosa Lake in the Town of Accord last fall. Police have been seeking an unnamed white man in his early 40s (see sketches, below left) in connection with the shooting deaths. The man has remained elusive and has so far been unidentified.

The brazen suspect was sighted twice after the discovery of the two bodies, once posing as a reporter from this newspaper, apparently in order to question witnesses to an arson at an Accord house near which the slain men were found. Police later revealed that the man had been seen again near the site of a fatal October police shootout with two other men, one of them the brother of Cyrus Grant. That man, Jack Grant, was the prime suspect in the arson. Investigations in Pennsylvania, Ulster County, and elsewhere are ongoing. The murder suspect has not surfaced since.

But now two witnesses, who spoke to the *Caller-Dispatch* on condition of anonymity, say that a name may have been attached to the face, or is about to be, based on a chance interview with two of the murdered minister's associates in northeastern Pennsylvania. The witnesses were unwilling to share the name with this reporter for fear of misidentification, and indicated that they had retained a lawyer before sharing their new information with police. Left unclear was the reason for their hiring a lawyer, nor the intended timing of their revelation to authorities.

. . .

. . .

"They said to tell you they don't have a phone in the new place, either," said Gilbert guardedly, looking at Gerow.

The detective ran his hand through his hair again. "That woman," he said, and he grinned a little in preparing his next words, "has never had a proper respect for the police."

"I blame the parents," Gilbert said.

Gerow was standing. The reporter had sat down and put his breakfast out but hadn't touched it during their conversation. The tall cop paced for a minute, asked a couple more questions, then went out to the lobby and hung on his cell for a minute. He returned.

"I don't need to tell you—" he said. Paused. "ask you—to give me a call if they should tell you the name. Right?"

"That's right. I'm not a vigilante."

Gerow left. Gilbert ate his oatmeal and read his email.

. . .

They made themselves hard to find that day, staying clear of Accord and the house, keeping out of Kingston, which is where they thought Gerow was. They toodled around the rolling farmland and hill country. Their cell rang a few times, but always the 845 area code, always the name "Gerow." Talking to Detective Gerow wouldn't do, Serena thought. Because if he told us to do something and we didn't do it, he could probably charge us with something.

"What was it they charged you with in college, that time?" she asked Jeffrey.

They were looking at antiques in a barn.

286

"Interfering with administrative procedures," he said.

He'd been sitting drunk in a stairwell when cops thundered down it chasing someone who'd thrown a bottle out of the dorm. One of the cops had stepped on Jeffrey's foot, going past him. Jeffrey had slurred "watch your hooves."

That had ended in handcuffs.

"Good ol' college," he said.

"Well, anyway," and she lifted a pewter candlestick, "I don't want to get charged with that. Tarred, as it were, with the same brush."

The baby did a slow roll, some angular bit of him/her pushing against Serena's belly in a gentle wave from one side to the other. She took her husband's hand and guided it there, let him feel.

"June tenth," she said.

He checked his watch as he always did when someone mentioned a date. April 11. Plenty of time.

For lunch they drove to an old mill that had been converted into a restaurant and distillery. There was bourbon there, precious bottles as little as though bees had made the stuff and it was rare and artisinal and magic. They couldn't afford any once they'd eaten, but Jeffrey got a small one on the house since Serena was driving, and as their waiter said, *a propos* of their impending date, "you're going to remember this night, and this shot, for a long time, even if you don't think so now."

Jeffrey's cell rang, a 610 number, as they got into the car. Pennsylvania.

It was Clarence. "Lagrange and Doug went out to that convent this morning. It's about a two hour drive from here. I should be hearing something soon, or nothing, or seeing them coming back."

"And then what?"

"Well, if it's the guy from the sketch, we could tell the cops."

"If not?"

"The article, that might work. You said he was right on top of you the night they burned down that house, right?"

"Yes, that's right."

"How's Serena?" Clarence said.

Jeffrey paused. They trusted these guys. But they were, no doubt, rougher than most of Jeffrey's acquaintance. They'd been in prison, all of them, and Jeffrey was hazy on the details.

"Okay," he said, and moved Clarence along. "Where are you?"

"Nearby," Clarence said.

They made plans to meet that night at the Country Inn.

FORTY-SIX

It was mid-afternoon and Gerow was sitting in one of the unmarked cars, pulled into the next driveway up Bone Hollow Road, on the Upper side, with the trooper Meg Sherman sans Smokey hat, when they saw a small red Toyota pickup drive past and slow as it approached the driveway of the new house. A dark-skinned guy driving, a guy with lighter skin, blowing cigarette smoke out his window, in the passenger seat.

Gerow murmured to the cop beside him. "We know those guys."

"We do?"

"The...work-release guys or whatever they were. The minister's friends."

A distance down the road now, the pickup turned into the Gales' new driveway, backed and turned, pointing outward, and stopped its engine. The driver's side door opened, Lagrange got out and stretched. A little more blue smoke drifted from the passenger window. Gerow and Sherman could hear voices carrying through the woods in casual tones, but couldn't hear words.

The detective's mind was racing as he dialed the cell, called for everyone to come.

. . .

There had been a round of forehead-smacking when Jeffrey called with his simple plan. They didn't *know* it was this Baker guy who had pulled the trigger, but this was a name they'd never caught before, and they had heard most of them. And they had this sketch. Maybe someone could connect or disconnect the name and the face?

Sister Margaret hadn't wanted to talk at first, and then Lagrange had produced the sketch from the previous fall's article, when a mysterious fellow had arrived at the hospital in Kingston to quiz two Brooklynites who'd found a couple of bodies and then been attacked. And he showed her the other sketch from the night of the shooting at Schlesinger's.

The sister was, of course, shocked, and looking at the face, at its over-brutalized brow ridge and slightly exaggerated jowls, she'd stared for a bit, then drew out the folder Baker had left.

"He gave us this," she said. "He was with WestGen."

There was no business card among the testimonials, the clippings, the pictures of playgrounds and sun-lapped meadows with tasteful barn-red well heads poking out of them. But there was a number for WestGen's operations center with instructions to call it to move the process forward. They had a little old Xerox there, and Doug had Xeroxed those pages, many of which they'd seen before.

Back in the car the men had looked at one another. That was something they rarely did; prison didn't teach it. In fact, prison taught you the opposite. The people around you were largely bodies, and you developed radar. Looking at faces was for threats or for goodbyes. Here they looked at one another, and each could see a little bit of triumph in the other's eyes.

Lagrange said "Okay now. We have to be pretty careful with this."

"Yes," said Doug. He lit a cigarette. "But pretty quick too. I don't think that nice lady was going to wait too long before she called the police. Won't be too long after that she talks to someone on the case."

"Yeah. Let's get back with Clarence. I want to tell them all in person."

"Agreed. Then what?"

"We decide together. I think this is enough, we don't need to draw the guy out, trap him, try to trip him up. When it's time, we can tell all about what the Reverend was doing behind the scenes. That's motive. Maybe this guy Baker has the gun, assuming he actually pulled the trigger. They got bullets out of, you know, out the bodies, right?"

Doug thought. "Sure, more evidence."

They were driving east now, crossing the Delaware in the pickup they used for yard work. Though their phone was a cash-up-front prepaid, they had learned to speak of this *sub rosa* stuff rarely, if ever, by electronic means.

After all, they both knew, that's how Baker did it.

Sister Ann did in fact call the police in Messerbergh, and they said they'd call back, and they did so, very quickly, and it was a homicide detective with the state police. She had rehearsed a story, but was only about a sentence into it before she felt herself being driven along a route. The detective asked questions, stopped her when he'd gotten enough of an answer, moved to the next one. Sister Margaret could almost see the layers of her story peeling back, one by one. It was a fascinating method, not one she'd seen before, she whose role was often that of present listener.

Many of the questions involved her visitors. Some few involved the man in the sketch, the fellow from WestGen. The detective thanked her and said they'd send someone out to take a formal statement a little later in the day, if that was okay.

It was. She walked to the refectory and poured herself a cup of coffee. They only had skim milk, but that was all right. That check had cleared, that was for sure, whatever else was going on.

. . .

Doug and Lagrange did talk to Clarence once and held off his questions except for giving him a simple "yes." Which of course didn't quiet him but they got him to agree to wait and said they'd meet at the Country Inn later on.

They came east on 84 and north up the valley of the Neversink through the old farms, and the horse country, and the beat old places with the barns that were either restored or waiting for it, a rare few making the final journey into collapse. The white ridge lay to their right, and at one point they passed under a kettle of hang gliders hoisting themselves on the early spring upwell of northwesterly breeze.

"Crazy people," Lagrange said, craning forward to peer up through the windshield as he navigated the curves.

"That they are." The Catskills grew in the windshield up ahead, slowly, slowly, became impossibly tall.

They neared Krumville but didn't want to sit at the bar of the Country Inn for two hours, and they didn't know anyplace else. They hadn't seen that morning's paper. Even if they had, they wouldn't have thought there'd be a problem with a visit to the house. The Gales weren't there. There was no reason for anyone else to be there at this point. The trap was baited, but it was only hours old. The kids knew the local cops, and the murder investigators, and the local press, and the house wasn't even finished. They were all supposed to meet at the Country Inn later. That was Doug and Lagrange's thinking as they found Upper Bone Hollow Road and went down it.

Gerow's people actually did send a SORT team, out of Newburgh. They came over the hill back behind the house, through Jeffrey's thicket. They crept along the game trails and deployed in the trees at the back, Gerow keeping their dispatcher apprised of the position of the two at the front.

Those two at the front were just sitting there. They weren't hiding. Both had come out of the car a couple of times. They'd admired the house wrap on the new construction, but hadn't gone inside.

"Trooper, does that look like an ambush to you?" he asked Meg.

"That's your department, Detective."

"I'm asking."

"Well then, not really." While they'd waited, Meg had called in for someone to read her the interviews and the files on these guys; the undercover car didn't have a printer or a computer hookup. Doug was the smoker. Lagrange was the other one.

"I wonder where Clarence is," Gerow said.

Lagrange now sideways in the cab, legs out the door, resting on the seat, while the two men talked. Gerow could see them handing papers back and forth.

What he didn't see were weapons. But then he didn't have an eye into that truck. Cars drove by on occasion, but the two men in the driveway didn't seem alarmed, didn't try to hide.

Gerow was still on point. He had state police units at either end of the road. The tactical unit was almost in place. But he wanted this to be calm.

"Trooper, we're going to take this real, real easy. But we're both going to go."

"Yes sir."

"There's four dead already in this thing," he said.

"I know that, sir."

He checked that she was wearing a vest. "We've been here an hour and there are only two of them," he said.

"Affirmative."

"We've seen no weapons."

"That's right. If you're asking if I'm ready, that's a roger."

"My gut told me to take the direct route a while ago. I'm just letting my brain catch up." He checked in with the SORT commander a final time. They had the subjects in sight. Gerow opened his door gently.

They'd arranged that he and Sherman would be on the north side of the truck and would come no closer than forty feet from the subjects, drawing their attention, hoping for talk, allowing the tactical team to approach obliquely and keep their colleagues out of the line of potential fire.

Meg opened her own door and put on her Stetson. They were screened fairly well from the men as they approached, a few scrubby pines at the very edge of the road, some underbrush with last fall's leaves hanging on.

She drew her gun, held it in low ready, walking a little off to the right and slightly behind Gerow. He kept his holstered. Doug was out of the truck, leaning on the back bed, smoking. Lagrange was sitting with his legs out of the driver's side door, reading.

Doug happened to be looking that way as they approached. He saw them step out from the side of the road and saw her

Smokey hat and gun at the same time that Gerow called out "is that you Doug? Lagrange?"

Neither man hesitated for even a second. Their hands rose steadily and high. Doug, hands up, dropped his cigarette and ground it out as he took two steps away from the truck. Lagrange stood very slowly and walked a couple of steps forward as well, arms all the way up, papers fluttering to the ground around his feet.

The four SORT guys came around the house low, leapfrogging coverage positions, two with MP5s and the others with Glocks, and stopped about ten feet away, spread out, every barrel trained on something soft in the two men.

Gerow spoke. "Turn around, please, and bring your hands down behind your back low."

He and Sherman stepped forward, cuffed the men, then frisked them. Nothing. Gerow looked into the truck. A folder. Some loose papers. Glossy brochures. Xeroxed articles. The WestGen logo.

He raised an eyebrow and looked back at Doug and Lagrange.

"You have the right to remain silent. Anything you say or do can and will be held against you in a court of law. You have the right to speak to an attorney. If you cannot afford an attorney, one will be appointed for you. Do you understand these rights as I have explained them?"

"Yes, officer," said Lagrange. He was patient, calm, relaxed.

"Yessir," Doug told him.

The SORT guys relaxed. The had come all this way, but that was all right.

Four other cars pulled in. Sheriff's cars, another state trooper, a State Police car. Men and women piled out, radios and cell phones going.

Gerow looked at the convicts, who were just standing, waiting to be asked something, offering nothing.

He held up the sheaf of papers. "Should we talk about this?" he said.

FORTY-SEVEN

There was only one message from Bill Gerow ("Call me, or trouble"). One from her mother (Call me, want to hear about your camping adventure"). One from Angela LaPorta.

"She's at the office," Serena said to Jeffrey. They were heading for the Country Inn, driving down from Woodstock and the mountains. "Said she has a welcome packet and a little something for us."

"It's a plant," Jeffrey said.

Serena considered other options for a moment, looking out the open window of Rhonda's car at the pines and the bare-limbed deciduous trees. Patches of snow glimmered here and there, last year's leaves black amid the melted patches. Low, slanted light touched down in spots, cutting obliquely under a near solid cloud cover. This wasn't the crisp autumn, nor the warmth and cicadas of 1993.

She dismissed framed print, food, calendar. "Okay," she said. "It's a plant. What kind?"

Jeffrey thought about Angela. She'd have on a turtleneck and jeans today, with chunky gold earrings and a thick chain. A suede jacket would be draped over the back of her chair. She carried a heavy ring of keys with a lot of fobs.

"Arbor vitae," he said.

"Arbor vitae," Serena said. "What's that, a water plant?"

"No, it's like an evergreen."

She leaned her head on the doorframe, let the air blow against her hairline. She was suddenly bored of being pregnant. "You might as well be right."

Angela answered the phone at her office and said she was going to head out soon, but she'd love it if they came over to pick it up, if they were on the road already. It was just five minutes from the Country Inn, and they figured they still had an hour before they had to meet the Cons.

They didn't make it. They passed by Bone Hollow road, both ends, without taking a side trip to the house, unaware that Gerow was bundling Doug and Lagrange into two troopers' cars a little way down there.

Accord was sleepy. Too early in the season for lots of tourists, too much mud and slush still out there under the trees and on the hiking trails. The real estate season, what little anyone expected, hadn't heated up much.

Plus, it was Sunday afternoon getting on closing time.

They pulled up outside the CountryHome office. Angela's enlarged, Photoshopped face smiled out at them across the sidewalk, behind the token picket fence and little strip of lawn. Green fingertips of tulips or daffodils were thinking about making an appearance. Some crocuses were already a couple of inches high, closed buds at their tips.

They got out and Jeffrey pointed to two dark green, tapered, six-foot shrubs on the right side of the CountryHome lawn, growing out of a little patch of dark mulch almost up against the building next door.

"Arbor vitae," he said, and opened the door, ushering his wife within.

298

Angela called from the back, through a door that led to the former home's kitchen and out back to a hall to the back parking area.

"Hi kids. Come on back."

Serena led the way through the photos of dream houses on display, back through the history of their search for The House, which had been no search at all, really. The place had called to them, and this dalliance with the realtor had been to check their first impression. Back through time they walked, and into the kitchen.

Where they came face to face with Don Baker and the barrel of a black handgun. Angela was tied to a chair, tears lining her cheeks.

The weird thing, Serena thought much later, or at least one weird thing, was how Baker's eyes had gone straight to her belly and only then flicked up to her face. She couldn't read his expression. He probably had something wrong where his brain and his face were connected, probably helped him get away with all this shit.

This was Jeffrey's first good look at Baker without a hat, without a disguise. He was surprised to realize that the guy was a little dweeb. Sweaty, pale-faced, off the rack suit that actually bagged up a little at the ankles. Baker was squinting at them like he had an astigmatism, clutching that gun. Jeffrey didn't remember this all, later. He had other things to think about later. But he knew one thing. This guy was a lot less than he'd seemed.

"No," Jeffrey said. "That's fucking enough." He was here, goddamn it. He stepped in front of Serena. What was the worst this guy could do?

Baker said "don't," and shot him.

It was a flat, incredibly loud sound in the small room, but there was no echo, and there was no interval between it and Jeffrey's collapsing. His right leg kicked out backward and his hands made a feint toward his knee, but he was already toppling over, a whooshing involuntary gasp and massive indrawn breath his only sounds. His head hit the floor next to Angela's feet, but not hard, and his face changed to a fishbelly white, and his eyes showed white while blood started to flow from his knee.

Serena screamed his name, but couldn't dive to his side, ungainly with the baby. She sobbed and performed a very rapid but awkward sideways wobble to get each leg into position, then bent from the knees to a squat and then leaned forward on one knee and grabbed his face. He was breathing as though in the third stage of labor, those quick breaths, a sort of *kshee kshee kshee.*

His knee! She looked, and his jeans had a tear in them and everything there was black with blood. Dark liquid was welling up from the hole Baker had made, spilling onto the wide, over-varnished pine planks of the kitchen.

The anatomy charts in hospitals and medical offices where she'd worked had taught her something, and she knew that the femoral artery still carried a lot of volume at the knee, but that was about it. She didn't know where to apply pressure, she didn't have any clean white cloths, she was flailing, pushing her hands down onto his wound and blood was still coming from between her fingers and onto the floor, making smears.

The pudgy man watched, leaning against the counter behind Angela, gun held out and down away from him. For Christ's sake, it was only a .22, probably hadn't even broken the guy's kneecap. But something funny happened to Baker, seeing Serena floundering around on the floor there saying her husband's name over and over, trying to stop the blood from his leg. What happened was that his stomach turned a little bit. At the blood. The skin on his face went a little cold.

She looked up at him for a split second—she had obviously forgotten why they were there, thought maybe someone there would help her, but all she saw was his graying face and Angela LaPorta's terrified slack mouth. Angela's foot, the one nearest Jeffrey's head, had pulled back against her restraints in an unconscious shrinking away.

Baker sagged a little. He was back on the hill, sighting on the redneck, Cyrus Grant. Grant had the minister by the collar, had just arrived at the bank of the pond and had just started to swivel his head around looking for Baker when the slug entered his forehead and snapped him back. Oh! *That* had been something. Peterson had seen it happen, tracked back up to the hill, maybe saw a glint of light from the barrel, but he dove for the water and got hit there, landing with a splash. And *that,* that had been something too.

That had perhaps been the high point, Baker thought now.

This ugly scene in the office kitchen wasn't like that, with the leaves and the sunlight and the man doing the thing that needed doing. This was tawdry, and stupid, and full of risk, and for fuck's sake, he hadn't even meant to shoot the husband, not right away. The sun-dappled simplicity of those woods struck him again—and then he was back again in CountryHome Realty, feeling a faux-stone countertop beneath his sweaty hand, and the woods went away forever.

And now what. Look at her. Face working, snot coming out of her nose, hair stuck to her forehead. *That belly.* He felt a stir of reflux, burped a little at the liquid rising up the well of his esophagus. He lifted the gun and pointed it at Serena.

Then he lowered it for a second. He felt faint.

Through tears Serena saw the gun droop, where she knelt on the floor, six feet away, and she took in a whooping breath, another half-sob that she cut off savagely in her chest. And that savagery suddenly rushed through her. She felt it like a shock run down her body.

And she somehow...uncoiled. Something *surged* up through her. Her lips pulled back in a snarl and she came up off one knee, took two long strides, squatted just a bit, and threw her entire weight—baby and all—into a perfectly formed fist, straight up into the point of that weak chin. He started to try to raise the gun, panic in his eyes, but no.

Her uppercut connected, hard, and the shock ran down her arm while his head snapped back. She saw a little spray of blood fly up off his bottom lip. He grunted. The gun flew from his hand, landed by Angela's foot, and Baker fell back against the counter.

Serena stood before him, arm drawn back, chest heaving, the sob coming back up, but her face wore only rage. She waited till his eyes refocused on her, his gun hand groping the air, the other steadying himself. And words came out of her.

"I'll fucking kill you," she said. She stepped between him and the gun, which he hadn't even looked at.

Baker had no idea what had happened. His vision was tunneling. His ears rang. He'd bitten his lip. He shrank away from her, edging along the counter. And at its end, he stumbled a bit, saw the blood on the floor, and swerved to avoid it.

He just wanted to get to his car, around back, but he'd have had to walk through Jeffrey's blood to go that way. No. He stumbled down the hallway, making for the front of the building.

He shambled onto the sidewalk, blood starting to drip down his chin, and turned right to walk up the little walkway at the side of the old house toward his car. Then he heard something and turned left and saw it—a charcoal gray armored truck with the one big white word on the side—SORT, not SWAT, but he got the message—its engine a roar as it took the corner at the end of Accord's main street.

Don Baker started running.

FORTY-EIGHT

One thing Clarence noticed about the Country Inn, and this didn't surprise him exactly, was that they didn't seem to get a lot of brothers in there.

Everyone was late, and he was on his second cola. He knew he had thirty-seven dollars in his pocket—Clarence didn't trust plastic—and was thinking about some of the sandwiches on offer. The fries looked good, sort of old school looking things like diner fries but cooked more.

No one had been answering on any of the cell lines, not the Gales, not Doug and Lagrange, and that was it for phone numbers. He had those in his head, and had been using the pay phone at the back by the bathrooms to try those.

And then around six, in one came. The guy had glasses and thinning hair, a little white on the temples, chocolate skin. He was wearing a brown sport jacket over jeans with a white shirt open at the neck, button-down collar. He had a leather bag with him, like a messenger bag or a briefcase. He put that down next to a stool two over from Clarence and ordered a beer. It was an Old Capital, whatever that was, but they had it on tap.

Clarence looked ahead at the bar back, past the row of taps, to the smallish liquor display. This was a beer place. There was a billboard-sized wall of beer names to his right, each one on a plaque that could be slid out of little brass slots and replaced. He looked at those, again, debating whether to leave and go over by the Gales' house or head back to Messerbergh. Something must've gone wrong.

"Hate to have that job," said a voice beside him. He turned slowly. The guy was leaning partway across the intervening stool, hand out. The ex-con looked at his hand, then up into the face. The guy indicated the big board with his eyes, smiling pleasantly. "Having to change out those beer signs?"

Clarence reached out and shook.

"I'm Oscar Gilbert," the fellow said. "Wanted to let you know, your friends are safe, but they've hooked up with some policemen. The guy you're after? He's caught."

Gilbert was a man full of questions, Clarence soon learned. But that was all right.

. . .

If there was one thing the driver of the SORT van recognized, it was the panicked look and sudden sprint of the guilty. The smear of blood on the guy's face had been a curious addition, as his moon face saw the truck and the guy took off. The driver was a young guy, crew cut, muscled. He gunned the motor to see Baker running for a car at the back of the building, and said to the guy next to him "what the hell?" They reached the alleyway and pulled in diagonally. He hit the flasher. Men piled out of the van, checking loads all over again, pointing their guns up in the air, scrambling in a cover formation one after another, into the alley and around the back. The driver got on the two-way again, calling for backup, then followed.

Baker heard the doors open. He gave up the search for his keys, abandoned his car, and ran out the back of the parking lot and into a belt of trees with a little stony brook running along. He made for the creekbed, which was free of brambles, and started flailing his way up along it from stone to stone, splashing through shallows and skirting pools.

It was when Baker ran past the corner of a cinder block garage about a quarter mile along, red-faced, puffing, shirt untucked, blood and snot coming down his chin, looking back wildly, the thinning hair on top of his round head all askew, that two tons of Glenn Hatch landed on him.

Baker went down hard and wet. There was suddenly cold mud and gravel up in his face. As the deputy's full weight struck and bore him the rest of the way down, his chin struck a larger stone and he felt his teeth connect through part of his lower lip. He yelped.

Hatch wrestled him up a bit to keep his face out of the flowing creek. He straddled the small of Baker's back, pulling his arms up and across, cuffing him.

"I've known this creekbed my whole life," Glenn said. "And you've got the right to remain silent." He paused, breathing heavily, and searched for one more word.

"Asshole."

Epilogue

After Baker's guilty plea, the company's apology was delivered that September as a full-page ad in the *Caller-Dispatch* and the *Wall Street Journal*. And there was a very short news conference in which Victor Generro, WestGen's CEO, read from a statement that Jeffrey had negotiated a chance to read beforehand. It had been one of those non-apology apologies, but once Jeffrey was done with it and the lawyers had gone over some of the finer points, it had Generro saying he was sorry for Baker's actions.

That got played a lot, on the television.

No one had tried to make Generro or anyone else at WestGen swing for it. They couldn't draw a line, not through email, not through phone calls, not through memos or anything else. Gerow believed that Generro knew nothing about it. He didn't care, though. There was enough shady stuff in WestGen's past to keep Pennsylvania's attorney general busy, and it looked like the feds were starting to take an interest too. The Gales had a civil case pending.

Drilling permits in New York were on hold. And Hollywood was sniffing around. The company could really, really have used someone like Don Baker right now. But Baker was gone away for a while.

Serena was there. Jeffrey was with her. The previous owner of the house in Bone Hollow, Mrs. Harrison, her name had been

Dorothy. Though the Gales *claimed* they hated to do it, they had both immediately agreed to do it... so little Dorothy Gale dangled from one of those Swedish contraptions on Jeffrey's chest. They were in the front row, the little family, and some of the cameras trained on them, too.

After, the mob of press people walking out of the nondescript office park that served as WestGen headquarters had brought the Gales up almost back to back with Generro, who was working his way toward his car. He faced a mobile bank of lights, cameras, microphones, and coiffed faces glowing with makeup that receded before him reluctantly. Fracking was news now, dammit.

Serena heard him talking to the press. He'd read his piece. That was his obligation. But the business he was in, it was a dirty business with little visibility on a national stage, and he didn't have to look too contrite. There were short memories for this kind of thing. They'd been paying their way in Pennsylvania. Someone had fucked up. Someone in jail, it needed mentioning. WestGen would probably pull through.

So what he said to the camera—to the pissant yelling at him the way they did "What does this mean for the future of fracking?"—was "gas drilling in the Marcellus Shale is a viable path to long-term, sustainable growth for this region, and for energy security for the United States of America. WestGen intends to be at the forefront of profitable, clean development of this valuable national resource."

It didn't play that well, that Jeffrey limped up behind him, baby Dorothy wide-eyed at the bright lights, and then Serena stepping in from the side. She looked at the cameras, eyes averted from Generro's face, from him rolling his eyes in irritation, which showed up later in quite a few broadcasts. Cameras flashed.

Her face was calm, and would look good on TV. "He means they're going to keep trying to screw people out of their land and clean water," she said. "But it's okay. Let him try." She pulled Jeffery up against her. "We're going to keep having babies."

And after that, they went home.

The End

ACKNOWLEDGMENTS
& AUTHOR'S NOTE

I am deeply grateful to many people for their help in creating Bone Hollow. My thanks especially to my wife and first reader Claudia Depkin, to New York State Police Sergeant Gail Sherman (remaining technical or procedural mistakes are mine, not hers), and to Eric Berlin, Doug French, Mike King, Mark Lerner, Bill Lovejoy, Antonia Malchik, Morgan Noel, Mark E. Phillips, Amy Plum, Kelly Robinson-Finn, Michael Strong, Emily Waterfield-Buttner, Lucia Watson, Bill Webber, David Whitmer, Michele Winchester-Vega, and to the memory of Mike Pecora, upon whose memorial bench portions of this novel were composed. Additional caffeinated gratitude to Mikey Jackson, Aurelia Winborn and the staff of 2 Alices Coffee Lounge.

While the events of this story are fictional, the observed effects and additional potential dangers of hydrofracking are not. Similarly, although the actions of a character involved in that industry are completely manufactured, representatives of that industry have described opposition to hydrofracking as "an insurgency," and have recommended that energy companies adopt military special operations tactics to confront it.

HUDSON HEARTLAND BOOKS

An imprint of Sloan Publishing, Hudson Heartland Books brings you the stories, real and imagined, of this realm between the rivers. In the coming years, we will introduce themed libraries, from mysteries like Bone Hollow, to fairy tales, to new editions of historic works written and set here.

The production of our books is sourced from within the region to the extent possible. Visit hudsonheartland.com to learn more.